Tales Of The
Blue Panda

Tree of Life Publishing

A CIP catalogue record for this book is available from the British Library.

ISBN: 978-1-905806-93-5

Tree of Life Publishing
Devon, UK

Tales Of The

Blue Panda

Maggy Whitehouse

For Ariadne, who never got to ride with the physical Jon in his blue Panda.

With grateful thanks and acknowledgment to Douglas Adams, C. S. Lewis and Lee Hazlewood without whose talent and imagination both my life and this book would have been even more impossibly, unbelievably implausible.

Chapter One

DAWN CAME AT last; a soft sheen of gentleness creeping through the trees.

I hadn't known for sure that there would be any dawn at all in this deep, silent place between worlds. I'd hoped and longed for one and, in the end, I had begged for one in the star-starved darkness of a seemingly endless night.

But before the dawn was the limitless liminal time. They told me later that it has to seem eternal to out-run the demons of thought. Obvious in hindsight; terrifying in the moment.

I had woken into this darkness from no-thing-ness. I had no idea who I was or where I had come from; all I knew was that I was conscious—and conscious of *being* conscious. I believed that I had eyes because there was blackness in front of them; I believed I had ears although there was nothing to hear until I moved and then the only sound was my own.

I could touch, I could taste and I could perceive the slight fragrance of grass. At least, I thought I could because I was lying on what felt like grass and each sense informs the others from memory. I turned over and sank what I knew was my face into what I believed to be greenness. Yes, it had a scent.

Apart from my senses there was nothing familiar. I had no name, no history, no memory or even certainty of *others*. I knew 'others' as a concept and the second demon was the fear of calling out for them in case there *were* others but they were not friends.

The first demon was the darkness itself. I knew that light existed (or I thought I did) and that it came from the sun. At first, I presumed the darkness meant that I was shut in somewhere but the feel of grass put paid to that. And the air was clear. I was definitely outside. Somewhere.

The third demon was fear that there *were* no others. It was almost amusing to watch those two terrors fight.

I had amusement then. That was good.

I sat up. I knew that was what you did. Tentatively, I put out a hand. Not tentative enough because its first contact was the bark of a tree which hurt. So, there was pain here. And trees. I remembered both. I sucked my slightly-scraped hand and reached out more carefully with the other, drawing it along another rough trunk. I knew I had two hands and two arms and I knew I had a body. So, I hugged this body for reassurance and then felt around it to see how familiar it was.

Very familiar. And rather tubby and totally naked, both of which were more than embarrassing. So, I'm ashamed to say that the fourth demon was just that: shame.

Fortunately, I'm wired in such a way that I was interested in the fact that I had just judged myself as being naked *and* wrong... and that the feeling of being wrong was a concept with which I was very familiar. I watched as my mind worked out *exactly* how fat I was—acceptably fat or unacceptably? And whose judgement was that? And whether I could find something with which to cover myself for when I was found?

For when I was found.

All at once, the desire to be found surged up; a yearning so deep that it made me gasp. The knowledge of the touch and smile of possible connection sparked some deep re-wiring as if a part that was very broken had suddenly been repaired.

And following it came more fear. Fear of *not* being found; fear of being lost forever, fear of being found by the wrong thing and of being eaten alive.

Assuming I was alive...

'Don't be ridiculous. Of course you're alive,' said a thought. 'You have a body and you are thinking.'

'And you've already hurt the body and you don't know what to think,' said another thought.

It was the strangest thing. I could hear, feel and experience these thoughts but beyond them was a knowledge that seemed far more important. A knowledge that spoke from deep within.

'This is the dark night of the soul' it said. 'It is to be endured. It ends with peace.'

I was to use those words over and over again in the darkness. 'It ends with peace; it ends with peace; it ends with peace.'

It certainly began with war. The war of uncertainty, fear and shame. It escalated through hatred, grief, cruelty and terror into demons that broke through and out of me, tearing, roaring, entreating, poisoning, scratching, tickling, enticing, threatening and then—finally—discounting.

'You are nothing,' they whispered. 'Nothing, nobody, worthless, pointless, futile, damaged goods, hopeless, helpless. *Nothing.*'

And they were right. So, I began to laugh. To be told that you are nothing and nobody in total darkness in a strange land/ dimension/whatever is so utterly ridiculous that it cracked me up. I began to laugh and laugh and laugh. You can call it hysterics if you like but it worked. The demons withdrew, as if offended, and ranged themselves around me, watching for a crack through which they could attack again.

To keep myself laughing I gave them names, imagined them in pink tutus and wearing bad orange wigs. Then, the strangest thing happened—I started to love them. I was appreciative of their role in my laughter and they were, at least, company of sorts.

Of course, as soon as I loved them they were pointless, so they vanished and I was alone again.

I thought I might sleep but it seemed that there was no sleep available in that dark country so I had a careful feel around me to see what was there and was lucky not to fall into a pond not two feet away. Tentatively, I touched the water but I didn't taste it as it didn't seem sensible to drink water that I couldn't see. That made me laugh too. I wasn't thirsty, nor hungry, thank goodness; neither even occurred to me. I was in the dark about a lot of things.

So, what *did* I know? That I was a woman; I was a human; I was breathing.

I stood up and banged my head on another part of the tree. That *really* hurt. So, I swore and sat down again.

The demons came back, enticed by pain. I imagined them in

spotted pink tutus and wellington boots with flowers on them. It didn't work for quite so long but it bought me a little time.

'It ends with peace; it ends with peace; it ends with peace,' I told myself and tried to believe it.

And then, in the heart of this eternity, a light appeared in the darkness. Not the light of dawn but of something bright approaching from a distance. It came from what I assumed would be the sky, dappling through trees and pushing a warm breeze ahead of it.

Now I got to choose between excitement and fear. Oddly, they both feel pretty much the same. Turns out that it's how we interpret the butterflies in our stomachs that matters.

An angel landed on the other side of the pool. It was golden, about nine feet tall with six wings, incredibly beautiful and it radiated a soft, steady light. Awe inspiring, terrifying, mesmerising.

I hid behind the tree; its rough, riddled bark offering stark comfort. I knew that hiding from this magnificence was pointless. But it was an angel, right? Angels were good things so I should be safe. I just didn't feel safe.

'Show yourself,' it said (but it wasn't speech).

I crossed one arm over my bare breasts and held the other over my pubes as I came out. But then, some strange, inner prompting like the 'it ends with peace' one made me stand up, straight-backed with arms by my sides.

We looked at each other, this angel and I. I could almost taste the glory and glamour of its being but I couldn't see its eyes; there were eyes but they were somehow unclear.

'Let me see you,' I said. I think it smiled but nothing else changed.

Some remnant of memory came back: someone, once, had told me that humans are children of the Creator and angels the servants of the Creator so, in theory, they should obey us.

'Show yourself,' I said.

It did. I saw its eyes and they were as cold and dead as a shark's. So then I knew.

I laughed. Really, that's all you can do when you find yourself standing in the Garden of Eden with Lucifer standing in front of you. Probably not a good idea, in retrospect, laughing, given the comparative levels of power between us.

'Eat,' he said. For the first time, I noticed that the tree next to me was groaning with fruit: ripe, succulent, purple figs. Suddenly I was starving; craving the glorious, juicy sensation of fig in my mouth, on my tongue, of biting deep into succulence with nectar running down my chin.

'This is ridiculous,' said my mind. 'You're hallucinating. This is not the Garden of Eden.'

Turns out that angels can read human minds. 'You ate of the Tree of Knowledge of Good and Evil every day of your life on Earth,' it said. 'Everything was judged. Eating of the real tree will heal you. Now eat.'

So, I was dead then.

'Yes.'

Oddly I didn't mind. Probably because I couldn't remember my life; whether I had been married, had children; what age I was—anything that could inspire grief.

'Eat,' said Lucifer. He meant it and he was irresistible.

Neither Judaism nor Christianity were in my culture; I knew that. But I had lived in a nominally Christian country and I knew the story well enough. Did Eve have this kind of glamour pushing her to disobey? The yearning and craving for that fruit was undeniable. I was starving and thirsty and I simply had to eat. It never occurred to me that dead people probably don't eat and even though I tried hard—really I did—not to succumb, it was impossible.

I reached up, took a fig and bit into it. It was disgusting, tasting like rancid dust in my mouth. I spat it out.

The angel vanished, leaving me in the pitch black, alone.

I howled in a great baying of loneliness and fear and betrayal and sat, with my arms over my head in shame.

I don't know how long I sat beneath that tree of knowledge but on Earth it would have been many hours. Longer than a night. And for every moment of it, I was afraid. Afraid of judgement; afraid of the demons and their king; afraid of the future; afraid of whatever God might turn out to be.

It took me a while to realise that there were no more demons. Well, why would there be? I was worthless...

It was silent and dark and nothing stirred apart from me. In the end, something within me began to repeat that phrase again, like a mantra. 'It ends with peace. It ends with peace. It ends with peace.'

And eventually, after I had visited madness and returned, came the dawn.

It began with the slightest flush of pearly pink, so soft it was almost indiscernible, but slowly and steadily it grew. You'd think I would be happy but I was scared stiff. What would happen now?

As the suns rose (two of them!) I saw I was in woodland. Between the trees were perhaps half a dozen pools of water. I would have looked closer but with the dawn came its goddess and she drew all attention. The trees, the grass, the water all attended. She was both golden and silvery and she was old, which surprised me.

Her eyes were clear and beautiful.

'Did you eat, child?' she said. No greeting or condemnation; just a simple question asked with love.

'I did eat,' I said. 'I spat most of it out but I did swallow some. I'm sorry.'

She smiled. And when the goddess smiles the whole universe lights up.

'Why did you eat?' she asked, gently.

'Because I wasn't strong enough not to,' I answered.

'You do not blame, child,' said the goddess. Her smile became even more beautiful. 'Well done.'

She held out her arms and I melted into them. It was like bathing in liquid light.

'Now,' she said. 'Let us talk,' and I knew I was safe. Totally, utterly, peacefully safe. You can have no idea how good that felt.

We sat by one of the pools. Some memory began to stir as I looked at them in the light of those two risen suns.

'Yes,' the goddess said. 'C. S. Lewis. *The Magician's Nephew*. The world between worlds. He was a wise man. You read the stories when you were a child. We always try to use familiar images and you loved Narnia.'

12

I did. But that meant…

'Yes,' she said again. 'Each pool leads to a different universe. One of them leads back to your own. You have the choice; you can stay here or go back. But if you go back…'

'Yes?'

'If you go back you will always live between worlds. Like Persephone ate the pomegranate seeds and had to return to Hades for the winter.'

'Do I have to decide now?'

'No. The decision cannot be made until the decision is ready to be made. You will make it in the perfect time. Now, let me show you paradise…'

And she did.

Chapter Two

IT'S NOT A good idea to wake up in a mortuary. It's likely that there will be an awful lot of screaming.

In my experience, it's not necessarily the mortuary staff who do the yelling; they're probably used to the occasional stiff suddenly sitting up and demanding a cup of tea. No, it's the pseudo-corpse itself. One thing you can guarantee once you've safely been declared dead is that any pain killers they might have given you earlier will have run their course and any stitching will be purely cosmetic.

In my case, the screaming was also caused by claustrophobia. Being shut in a tray in a fridge in a body bag doesn't rank on my list of favourite experiences to repeat any time soon.

But there I was, not dead, with a body that couldn't tell me which bit was hurting the most, yelling my head off and adding insult to injury by bruising my arms as I tried to break out of the bag.

Some months later, when I got some much-needed counselling, I overheard the therapist talking to her superior.

'She has irrational fears of being trapped in a drawer, of being attacked by a shark and of being abandoned.'

'Has she ever been trapped in a drawer, attacked by a shark or been abandoned?'

'Yes. All three.'

'Then they're not irrational fears, are they?'

I got a referral.

On the day itself—and thankfully it *was* daytime—there were staff in the mortuary who heard my yelling and banging and opened the drawer. And it could have been worse: I would have hated to have woken up during a post mortem. Or at any time that they were replacing my blood with formaldehyde.

Underneath the pain and the confusion, there was also an indescribably weird feeling of machinery attempting to start up when it's old and rusty. My blood had spent some time obeying gravity but now it had to pull itself together and work out how best to start flowing again.

My heart was pounding pistons on a steam engine and my whole body felt like a puffing and blowing, ageing walrus heaving itself out of a hole in the ice.

Then it *really* got confusing. I was on a trolley, being wheeled up and down corridors, with people sticking needles and drips in me and asking if I knew my name and who was the prime minister. The first bit was easy: 'Bella Ransom,' though they didn't seem impressed. The second bit I was inordinately proud of: 'Tony Blair.'

That went down like a lead balloon.

'She thinks the prime minister is Tony Blair… she thinks her name's 'handsome.' Did she have a CAT scan when she came in?'

'No, she'd been pronounced dead.'

'Ah. Better get one now then… definitely something going on in the brain.'

You think?

What was going on in the brain was a mélange of thoughts, memories, screaming and regret.

You see, after the first, scary part, the whole being dead thing had been really rather nice. Obviously, we don't get told that or we'd all start jumping off bridges or allowing ourselves to be eaten by sharks. But it is.

When the panicking people gave me an anaesthetic so they could start sorting out whatever it was that had killed me, I thought for a joyful moment that I might be going back.

No such luck.

Next time I woke up I was Bella Ransom, aged six, lying in a children's ward. My dad was sitting in one of those high-backed chairs, asleep. I had no idea why I was in hospital but a quick check proved that I still had both arms and legs so it couldn't be too bad.

'Daddy,' I said quietly. He opened his eyes and smiled at me.

'Possum,' he said lovingly; the nickname that only he ever used.

'Is Mummy here?'

He shook his head, and took my hand.

'Darling Possum,' he said. 'We're having some trouble re-establishing reality. We'll get it sorted soon, I promise. Try not to worry.'

'Okay.' I didn't know what he was talking about but it didn't matter. I was so sleepy.

For a while—maybe days?—I kept moving in and out of sleep and different realities. At one point, I was twenty-one-year-old Bella Ransom, just graduated from Uni, travelling in Australia with my friends, Josie and Ben. Tony Blair *was* prime minister and I lived in Bristol. I'd been attacked by a shark. Another quick check established that all limbs were present and almost correct though my right thigh which had taken the brunt of the attack was heavily bandaged and hurt like hell.

Another time, I was Bel Nazam, aged 29, in yet another hospital. It was night and the humming and bleeping sounds were different. A kind nurse told me that the timeline was still out of kilter and offered me a cup of tea. I said, 'yes please' and promptly fell asleep again.

Then, it was Jon who was sitting in that high-backed chair that skulks by every hospital, bed. He was dozing.

'Hey,' I said, quietly, feeling relief flood through me. I knew that I was seventeen. I must have mistaken Jon for Dad and it had all been a dream, what with the dying and all. I wondered why I was in hospital now but I was obviously more or less in one piece so I could relax.

Jon opened his eyes, smiled and took my hand. He raised it to his lips and then leant forward.

'Bel,' he said. 'It's going to be a bit rocky for a bit longer but hold on. It's nearly sorted.'

I just smiled and nodded and drifted off again.

I woke up again, alone in another hospital, still tied up with tubes, I could still remember being dead and I still thought the prime minister was Tony Blair. They told me I was Bel Nazam and I knew that Jon and my parents were dead, so long ago that grief was only a soft sorrow, but I couldn't remember where I lived, who, if anyone, I was with or even what I did for a living.

'It will all come back,' said the registrar brusquely. She seemed to know what she was talking about but that was no comfort right now.

There wasn't a lot of comfort anywhere. This time, I was in Eilat in Israel. I'd been attacked by a shark (what, again? Or was it the first time? Truly, I didn't know) while snorkelling in the Red Sea but it wasn't a shark bite that had killed me because this had been a rather unimpressively small shark—it was smashing my head on a rock while trying to avoid it that did the damage. Apparently, I had drowned which is why I was still alive. Bodies do strange self-preservative things when they drown. Even so, to be attacked by a shark once is unfortunate; to be attacked by one twice looks like carelessness...

It appeared that I was on holiday on my own. Nobody had come to enquire after me. This did not encourage me to believe that this particular incarnation of Bella Ransom-Whatever was living a particularly fulfilling life. Luckily, others in the water had dragged me out before said shark could get another bite at its lunch. Sometimes, people doubted the existence of all these sharks in later years but all I ever had to do then was show them the bite-shaped scar on my leg. Or was that the Australian one?

Shit.

Okay, what *do* I know? I was *compos mentis* enough to look around me and discover that I had a beach bag containing a wallet, a towel and some very stale food that I had obviously nicked from breakfast in a hotel. Not a lot of money, a driver's licence with my unfamiliar name on it but no mobile phone and no clue as to where I was staying.

No hospital that is used to regular inundations of stupid tourists who have fallen off unsuitable horses, drunk themselves silly or had the temerity to interfere with any local wildlife with teeth is going to be one of the kinds of locations where you're going to get any extra level of nurturing. I think they'd have discharged me when I came round from surgery if I'd been able to walk. But I was interested in the fact that I knew that. A young Bella wouldn't have done.

It was all rather overwhelming, not to mention confusing, so I went back to sleep.

When I woke up, I was still in Eilat. Progress then.

The ward sister was staring at me crossly, tapping beautiful white teeth with a Parker pen.

'You can get up and go,' she said in accented English. 'There's nothing wrong with your head but a bump and your leg is barely scratched. We have other patients who need your bed.'

'But... but I... you just operated...'

'We were going to operate,' she corrected me. 'We thought there was pressure on the brain. But the CAT scan showed there was nothing wrong. You can go.'

I sat up. And I *could* sit up. No tubes attached.

'But I was dead.'

'You're not dead.'

'Don't you want to keep me in for observation. I was *dead!*'

'No,' she said. She was being very emphatic. 'You weren't dead. You were unconscious.'

No, I bloody wasn't. Whatever the hell was going on, the dead bit was the only constant I had.

'I've lost my memory,' I said. 'I don't know who I am or where I'm staying. I don't know where to go.'

'You're staying at the Almog Hotel,' she said. 'You can get a taxi.'

'The what hotel?'

'Almog. A... L... M... O... G.'

But how do you know that?'

'Pshaw,' she said, or something similar and stalked away.

I felt a lump in my throat but I bloody well wasn't going to cry. Whether I was nine, nineteen, twenty-nine or (horrifyingly) much older, I'd always been stubborn about that. I'd cry on my own but not in public. No one but those I loved got to see me cry.

'Get a grip,' I said to myself, wrapping my arms around my body to hug myself.

I rocked back and forward for a minute and then took a deep, deep breath.

Okay, Bella, get practical. Take a good look at your body. What kind of shape is it in, in this particular moment's reality?

Relatively good. I gave a sigh of relief. I could feel that there was a part of my head that was shaven with a large plaster attached but I appeared to have hair and, from what I could see, it was about shoulder length and dark. Tentatively, I raised the sheet and saw two, fully-present legs. One thigh had a huge, ugly, old, jagged white scar that looked very much as if it might have been a shark bite and two straight scars where the repair scaffolding had gone in and was strapped up just below the knee.

Hadn't I just been bitten? Again? I guess that was the wound, if so. A gentle poke elicited the answer. Ow.

I pondered who might be prime minister and realised it must be David Cameron. So, I was about thirty-five then. I could handle that. Though why I might be in Eilat was quite beyond me.

Carefully I went through my bag again. The picture on my driving licence looked like a forty-year-old woman.

Oh crap.

I was sore and confused but mobile and the sooner I got out of here, the better. There was a swimming costume, sundress, sun hat, towel and sandals in the bag and I probably did have enough cash to take a taxi to the hotel. Then I could find my room and discover who the hell I really was, what I was doing here and when I was due to go home… not to mention where that might be, who might be there or whatever it was that I did for a living. I *thought* I was an archaeologist specialising in ancient languages. I knew I *had* been an archaeologist and I *liked* being an archaeologist and I couldn't see why I'd have changed that. Perhaps I was on a dig out here? That would make sense. But why hadn't someone enquired for me? How…? What…?

I got out of bed, shakily, and managed to walk to the bathroom. I gulped when I saw myself in the big mirror there. This was definitely a much older Bel than I expected which meant that more than a dozen years of my life were missing. Even worse, I'd got a lot fatter. A wave of loss and deep loneliness came over me. It wasn't as though I hadn't travelled alone in my youth—I'd done a lot of travelling. But right now, someone to love me and hold me and tell me it would all be okay would really, really have helped. I couldn't even remember who the hell had given me the surname of Nazam which was as perplexing as it was annoying. Certainly, he wasn't around right now. That is, if he even was a 'he.' I simply didn't know.

I walked out of the bathroom and directly into Jon. He caught my upper arms and looked deep into my eyes.

'We've stabilised the timeline,' he said. 'We had to divert you here to sort out your injuries; we shouldn't have, technically, but we're going to need you in the land of the living. Get some rest and I'll be back when I can.'

And he was gone.

I sat down heavily on the hospital bed. I'd gone mad. There was no other explanation. While I tried to sort my head out, I looked through my wallet.

Hidden behind some debit cards, I found a folded-up *Post-It* note:

You are Bella Ransom.
You are currently 43 years old and single.
You live at the Old Rectory, Tayford, Devon.
You work in between worlds in soul retrieval.
You are protected.
Jon will come to fetch you in the blue Panda.
You went night riding with Josie in Rador when you were 16. The pony was dun with two white socks. There were five stones, not four.
Bel x

No one but Josie and I ever knew about the night riding or the hidden fifth standing stone in the meadow.

I am Bella Ransom and it would appear that I retrieve souls.

Chapter Three

I WOKE UP in hospital.

Again.

A different hospital.

For fuck's sake.

I was covered in tubes, everything hurt and from the sound of the voices around me, it was a British hospital.

I opened my eyes and then shut them fast because there was a vicar sitting by my bed. That wasn't a good sign. I don't generally mind vicars but there's always that embarrassment factor when push comes to shove and you have to admit you're an agnostic. But if there's a vicar by your bedside, does that mean you're going to die?

Again?

On the off chance that there is a God I addressed him/her/it in the imperative, instructing him/her/it to get his/her/it's fricking act together. It can be a he from now on; I'm not complicating life further with political correctness. Except of course that I said 'fricking' because there was a vicar by my bed. I know, I know, but I'm not quite myself.

Okay. On the hopeful basis that this is me, Bel Ransom, fully awake this time, what do I know?

I can still feel arms and legs (but can't you still feel them if you don't have them?). I can see and hear. I know I don't like being called Bel Nazam any more. I know that there is no Jon and I know that I'm a linguist and archaeologist. I think I'm twenty-nine because I'm dreading the big 3-0—but surely I was older last time I woke up?

Bugger.

Start again.

Bloody hell, I'm hungry.

I sighed and someone, probably the vicar, took my hand.

'Bel? Can you hear me?' It was a man's voice, squeaky and unattractive. I nodded slightly, keeping my eyes closed.

'Bel, it's Robbie. You've had an accident. A car crash. You're going to be all right.'

Well that was different. No shark? Almost automatically, I reached down with my right arm to touch my thigh. Yes, scar tissue. That had still happened, at some time in this dimension, but not lately. I felt further down. Yes, another scar, smaller and mouth-shaped. Not new.

'You've got a head injury. They say you may be quite confused for a while. Do you know who I am?'

This time I did open my eyes, surprised that I apparently knew a vicar.

'No,' I said.

Oh my, Robbie had been behind the door when looks were handed out. He had thinning, mousey hair with the beginning of a comb-over, a colossal nose with matching ears and what appeared to be acne which is bad enough at fifteen and Robbie was probably forty. But he was beaming at me with what was, unmistakably, affection.

Shit. Am I dating a balding vicar?

'Hi Robbie,' I managed.

He squeezed my hand, his eyes lighting up. And when Robbie's eyes lit up, his whole face was transformed.

'You do know me!' he said.

'No, no, I don't. I'm sorry. I hardly know who I am, let alone who you are. And I seem to be changing hospitals and times by the minute.'

'My dear friend, Bella,' he said, indicating that he hadn't understood a word but was not going to say so. Definitely a vicar and, thank God, not my boyfriend. 'I'm going to tell the nurse you're awake.'

He didn't so much stand up as unravel himself and stalked away across the ward like a black-clad stick insect. While he was gone, I checked all my relevant bits, found everything that the current me believed that a functioning human female should have and heaved a sigh of relief. Mind you, I might wake up somewhere else again tomorrow.

From then on, there was a lot of hustle and bustle and questions. Robbie was chased away in case he inadvertently saw a women's bits and accidentally exploded and nobody else who knew me turned up so, once I'd been prodded and poked and talked over, and reassured that my memory would (probably) return, I was left in relative peace. Somebody brought me the cup of tea I'd been waiting for, for at least a week. It was still hot. If Robbie had still been there, I would have asked him to recommend them for a sainthood.

Somebody else brought me a sandwich and I ate it. It was egg mayo in case I was a vegetarian. For all I knew, I might be. Tough shit if I were vegan, I guess.

It was a pretty rubbish sandwich and I couldn't help wishing I were dead.

I'm not sure I can explain being dead properly and I'm not certain that I want to. After the goddess and I stepped into one of the pools, there was a tunnel of light and I was met by people/ spirits that I knew and loved—but ask me now who they were now and I have no idea. And then there was a place where you could taste the light, smell the colour and touch the sound. I was shown how to integrate this Earth life into my soul and how to transmute the pain into something like fertiliser for another life. I lived inside my own golden-silvery-purple soul of light and other souls sang to welcome me—and it was a song of such beauty that even the shadow of the memory of it makes me glow. There was no religion and they demonstrated the whole God thing and the cosmic hierarchy so beautifully that it *all* made perfect sense. It wasn't anything you can explain; only experience. And when I asked why all of this was on offer to me, who had been at very best an average sort of human being who'd done her fair share of mad, bad and dangerous things, they said it was available for everybody.

I didn't want to come back and I knew that I had to. It both was a choice and it wasn't.

If all that turns out to have been a hallucination, then I'm keeping it as a magical secret forever because I need that memory kept pure. I can remember times when I was a child when I told people about the fairies I *thought* I'd seen (see—I'm saying I thought I'd seen when, before I told them, I *knew* I'd seen) and I was mocked and laughed at and disparaged and the fairies went away—anyway, you get the gist.

The next day, I woke up in the same ward, with the same body.

And the next.

Progress at last.

I managed to sit up and had several tubes disconnected. It was a major victory to walk as far as the bathroom, holding tightly to the portable stand that was carrying my drip. I looked through my (different) handbag for every clue I might find as to the life I was living. There was a driver's licence with my name (no mention of Nazam), cards, some cash, a scattering of tissues but nothing else of interest. No mobile phone so I couldn't even find myself on the Internet. I searched through my wallet for the note I'd written myself but it wasn't there.

I had no visitors and no one came to claim me. I had occupational therapists and counsellors and all kinds of medical people instead. They told me that memory loss from a head wound was spasmodic which was why I could remember that the Internet existed but not who I was or where I came from. I even had the police, who told me that my silver Renault Clio had been hit side-on at traffic lights in Worcester. The other driver was dead. Both cars were write-offs. They wanted to know what I knew about the accident or what I'd been doing. I had no idea.

Robbie didn't come back. He telephoned instead. He was terribly sorry he hadn't been to see me but it was summer and he'd had to fill in at weddings and there were two funerals, too. He was very sorry that I hadn't remembered anything yet and he was very sorry that, unexpectedly, the archdeacon was transferring him to another parish, starting the following day because of some kind of emergency. So, he would be moving away. But a new assistant vicar would be arriving almost immediately, just so I knew. He was very sorry about all of it.

He really *was* sorry. Sorry and upset and confused. I managed to say the right sort of things and forbore to point out that I couldn't have given a toss about any new vicar because I wasn't planning on going to church anytime soon.

I asked him why I'd had no visitors. He said that there were plenty of people who would like to visit but the hospital had told him that if I didn't know who they were, it would be too distressing for them. And probably for me.

I was starting to feel just a little bit paranoid.

And bored. Mind-bogglingly bored.

Jon arrived at about midnight on the third night. Tall and rangy and tawny just like he used to be before he got sick.

Seeing him made my heart jump with joy and fear simultaneously (it's *Jon!* And 'Oh fuck, my brain's still screwed.')

'Are you ready?' he said. 'We're on assignment.'

'Jon, I can't remember anything,' I said. 'My memory's gone. I don't know what you're talking about. So, I'm not ready, no. And I can't just get up and walk out. And… and… Well, you're dead.'

'We'll see,' he said, pulling the hospital blanket off me and handing me a neatly-folded pile of clothes and a pair of trainers. 'Get this lot on. There's a vending machine just outside the ward so I'll get you some chocolate while you're dressing. Oh, and I'll drop you off at home after.'

It seemed to me that time had stopped. The ward was suddenly totally silent—no more annoying bleeps—and no one moved in the slightest. But then, I've got a head injury. What do I know?

I did know that even if I didn't remember what or where my home might be, I really, really wanted to be there.

The clothes felt vaguely familiar: tee shirt, sweat shirt and jeans all in dark blue. Totally unremarkable. My feet fitted into the trainers as if they knew them well. I picked up my bag and walked, fully clothed, out of the ward and no one even noticed. There were three nurses at the nursing station and not one of them looked up as I went past.

'There you go,' said Jon, arriving out of nowhere with a

Cadbury's Twirl and a baseball cap. 'Put this on, it'll cover the bandage.'

We walked through the silent, still hospital to the front door. An old and battered blue Fiat Panda was parked directly outside. Thoughtfully, I ate the chocolate as I climbed into the passenger seat.

'Buckle up,' said Jon, starting the engine.

We started off quite normally. Jon drove out of the hotel grounds and onto the main road which, too, was astonishingly quiet and bereft of traffic. As soon as I had finished the chocolate, he smiled at me, patted my hand the way he always used to do and then the car flew. Of course it did.

Obviously, I'm quite mad. But I don't care. It was marvellous. We both did a few 'whoo-hoos' circled above the city and then shot upwards and through the atmosphere and out into the solar system past the Moon, Mars, Jupiter and Saturn. I was so busy gazing, I didn't ask any questions. My mind was perfectly at peace; I could even recognise where we were in space. It didn't need to make sense because nothing did. When we reached the Kuyper Belt we went through what looked like a worm-hole (as if I knew what a worm-hole looked like) and then we were back in the country of the dead.

This time, it looked astonishingly like a cleaner, brighter version of the country of the living. Where we landed (was that the right word?) was somewhere like a long drive to a country estate.

'Shhh,' said Jon when I tried to speak. 'You're seeing what's necessary. I can't explain it to you. It will all become clear.'

I was tempted to mutter, 'I bloody hope so,' but I found I couldn't feel cross. Or lost. Or even perplexed. It was okay; it just was.

We pulled up outside a big, cream-coloured Georgian-style house with a porch covered with blowsy-pink climbing roses. On earth, in England, the month was April. It didn't matter.

'Go on in. I'll wait for you,' said Jon. So I did.

I knew the hallway from somewhere. Wide and tall. Dark wood, panelled with a deep, ancient fireplace to the left surrounded by comfy armchairs. The fire was lit and two souls were sitting beside it. I say 'souls' because they were human but gold-silvery as well. Their names were Callista and Sam and I knew them both. These were my family.

I knew too, why I was here and what we had to do. So, there was no need for anything other than an affectionate greeting (I'm not a natural hugger and they knew that) and we walked through the hall and up to the mezzanine where the reception room would be.

I'm still a bit of a beginner at this so, right now, my only job was to be an incarnate human during the process of reunification; someone with both soul and persona linked together in one body. That alone is often sufficient to help a lost soul realign itself. It's like recognition: 'Oh yes, I was like that. That makes sense' and soul and persona will merge and move on. Please don't ask me how I knew that; I just did.

So, I sat, quietly, in a chair on the blue carpet, looking with confused familiarity at the book-lined walls while Sam went down through the well in the middle of the floor to fetch the persona and Callista went up through the well in the ceiling to fetch the soul.

She arrived back first with a silvery child; the most delicate, tiny little girl as beautiful as she was sad. Instantly, I knew what had happened to her and how she had died and, even here, I felt a shiver of fear. No wonder her body had broken away. How could a human persona that had faced so much terror possibly believe in safety and union?

I knew, too, that she was one of the fortunate ones. Her soul had flown up and kept going as her persona screamed and pulled back. Some vestige of hope had survived the call of the demonic emotions and kept flying, giving the persona no choice but to come too or break away. It had broken away and you could see the unhealed wound, still bleeding purple, down the little soul's back.

'This is Holly,' said Callista and I held out my arms. 'Holly, meet Bella.'

'Hello Holly,' I said, gently.

She climbed onto my lap and curled up peacefully. I was surprised, expecting suspicion, but Callista smiled. 'Holly has been here before,' she said. 'She knows she is safe with us.'

I didn't understand then but I was happy to hold what felt like a six-year-old in my arms, rocking her slightly as though she were a baby.

Then the rumbling began. It echoed up through the well, growing louder and harsher. Instinctively, I wanted to run away. Callista put a hand on my shoulder.

'Relax,' she said.

What looked like smoke began to curl out of the well; there was a moaning and a roar and Sam exploded into the room, encased in darkness. He was roaring himself; the noise was colossal. Holly hid her face in my chest and whimpered a little but otherwise was calm.

Which was more than I was.

The darkness raced around the room, a great, exploding echo of terror and fury. It was hatred and horror and hopelessness and it wanted to destroy.

How do I describe this? Sam *herded* it. He had a team of little lights acting like sheep dogs which responded to his voice and they rounded up the darkness and cornered it on the opposite side of the room. It roared and rumbled and—the nearest analogy— tossed its head and stamped its feet like a lassoed bull.

'Now,' said Callista, indicating that I should stand, still holding Holly in my arms. Her head was still tucked into my chest and she was trembling slightly.

'It's all right. I'm here,' I said, softly. They were probably the most useless words in the world but they had to be said. She clutched at my sweatshirt with one hand.

Slowly, I walked over to the rumbling darkness carrying the tiny soul. Callista walked beside me and Sam and his lights kept the blackness at bay.

When we were within a couple of feet, Holly lifted her head and looked directly at the darkness. It was silent. Then she and Callista began to sing.

I can't describe the beauty and the longing in that song. It was music to make you weep and to hope, sung in a language of celestial resonance. Callista's voice was succulent with melody and Holly's, at first, faint and trembling.

28

But she sang. She sang and sang, her voice strengthening with every word and, as she sang, colours streamed from her towards the darkness. It spat at her and harrumphed and seemed to circle inside of itself and spat again.

The song continued with Sam now joining in with a solemn and powerful bass tone.

I knew I had to move closer for Holly was now leaning towards the darkness and holding out her hands to it. Streams of light flowed from her; they seemed to be coming through and from me as well. Eventually, she spoke.

'Come home,' she said.

A weak and angry voice came from the darkness.

'I will not forgive,' it said.

'Come home,' said Holly.

The darkness hesitated. I could feel its uncertainty.

'I will not forgive,' it said again.

And then, Holly was too heavy for me to carry. She was growing and brightening. Her feet reached the floor and I was forced to let her stand on her own.

'You don't have to forgive,' she said, standing up to full height. 'You can come as you are. I have forgiven and that is sufficient. I need you to come home. Please come home.'

I felt a haze around me, almost as though I was standing in a cloud. Both Callista and Sam were still singing but incredibly softly. Holly walked forward. The darkness flinched.

'It's okay,' she said. 'We are meant to be together. I need you. Please come.'

There was a sudden crack and a flash of what looked like lightning and then Holly was inside the darkness and the two became a flow of colours: scarlet, silver, purple, blue. The song rose again in crescendo and then there was silence.

Before me stood a full-grown woman with one arm shrivelled by burning and one eye blind. But her face was beautiful and her expression serene.

'Tell me,' she said to me. 'Tell me what I am.'

I blanked. What the hell was I meant to say?

'Tell her she's human,' breathed Callista.

'You're human,' I said.

Was that it?

For a moment, Holly stood still. Her blind eye twitched.

Then there was a roar, a cacophony, a screaming and the darkness re-emerged, huge and threatening.

'NO!' it raged and sucked itself out in a great column of smoke.

Sam jumped forward, lights streaming from his open hands but there was nothing he could do. The darkness skedaddled back to the well and dived. It echoed and rumbled and then the whole room was quiet.

Holly shrank. In just a few seconds she was a tiny child again and the light around her wept in purple.

I picked her up and she clung to me tightly.

'Bugger,' said Sam. 'Let's have a drink.'

Chapter Four

SO, WE WENT for a drink.

As you do.

Apparently, heaven has bars and you can ask for whatever you want. For free. And you can get drunk. Only happy drunk, obviously, which was ironic as I wasn't feeling happy at all.

'It was so close!' said Callista, over a mauve, sticky cocktail with an umbrella in it. 'Much, much closer.'

'Yes, yes,' said Sam, who had a pint of scrumpy. 'It's really good.'

It hadn't felt good to me. It had felt like disaster.

I had been left feeling shocked and confused, cradling the little soul in my arms. But, then she sighed deeply and her shape changed. She seemed to gather herself up into a long, tall line and transformed into a soft pewter-silver, still with that purple wound. Gently, she removed herself from my arms and stood before me in a line of light.

'Thank you,' she said in a thin, shiny voice. 'Perhaps the next time.'

Then she flew upwards, into the well in the ceiling and was gone.

I had a lot of questions. I also had a glass of *Crémant de Bourgogne* which didn't seem to empty no matter how much I drank from it.

'Why are you drinking that rather than proper champagne? There's Pol Roger or Bollinger here already and we could summon up any other brand you like,' said Callista.

'True,' said the barman. I'd been ignoring him because he was a column of yellow light and I wasn't quite up to dealing with that concept yet.

'It's not really a cause for celebration,' I said.

'Pshaw!' said Callista. 'Every movement towards healing is a cause for celebration. We expect it to take a few goes when it has been a tragic life and a difficult death like Holly's. It can take fifty efforts like that but it works in the end. The problem is that it *does* take time and we're stuck with the backlog not to mention more and more souls being poisoned on earth.'

'Poisoned?'

'Yes, fuelled with anger and hatred and the need to be right. In the old days, when it was just religion, they had at least been taught they *had* souls so once they were up here and had got over the shock, the majority of them were willing to work with the darker aspects of themselves.'

'Okay. But I'm so confused. I know you and I, somehow, know I've been here before but I don't remember much. I'm sorry. All I do know for sure is that this isn't the place I visited when I died. So is this heaven?'

'No,' said Callista. 'You *were* in heaven. *This* is paradise.'

'...?' Sometimes expressions speak louder than words.

She laughed. 'Paradise is like going on holiday. It's a rest area; a place where people sort themselves out and relax a little. Sometimes they need recovery time in the equivalent of hospitals—some terrible illnesses have to be dissolved for example—but mostly it's a place of meeting and greeting; you know, you find your family and spend some time together, you find your pets; you make up with your exes...'

'I don't think many people would think that last bit was paradise.'

'If they're not connected with their souls, they don't. If they are, they do. That's the whole of the Work,' said Callista. I noted that 'Work' was definitely capitalised.

'That's why we do what we do here—and as soon as folk get here if possible. There are thousands of us meeting and greeting people and bringing through the best possible souls to be their first contact. Hopefully, you'll remember and, if not, you'll see all that another day. We need to get you back now. There's only so long you can spend here without losing Earth consciousness.'

They both walked me back to the great entrance hall where Jon was waiting. He seemed to be reading an aviation magazine but I didn't have the energy to enquire about mass media in paradise. Callista, Sam and I shook hands. I realised that the longer I spent with them, the less celestial they appeared. Now they seemed just human, like me. That was a bit sobering.

'One last question,' I said, as Jon opened the front door for me, like the gentleman he was.

'Jon can answer that,' said Callista, waving.

'Try me,' said Jon as I walked down the steps to the blue Panda.

'Why me? Why am I doing this work?'

'Because throughout most of the years you can't remember, you've been asking to be of service to the World. And because you have died and come back. That means you can be fully physically human in paradise. And in hell, for that matter. And because you are fully human, souls and personas can both recognise you and can use you as a linking mechanism.'

'There is a hell then?'

'Oh, there's hell, all right,' he said. 'A completely terrifying human-created hell of hopelessness and fear.

'Clearing that is the greatest form of service there is.'

The car speeded up down the drive and then took off into the night sky.

'Hell is subjective,' said Jon. 'Callista and Sam can't conceive of hell so they can't experience it. Those who can, do.'

'There was hell in the world-between-worlds I was in when I died.'

'There was? Well a world-between-worlds sounds like a sorting place. Face your demons and move on into the higher levels. You get to choose when and how you leave hell. Was it like that?'

'Sort of.' I didn't want to say any more because we were through the worm hole and the solar system was so breathtakingly beautiful that I wanted to let go of all the complexities and just bask in its splendour.'

'Are you okay?' said Jon after a few minutes.

'Yes, I think so.'

'You've lost your memory and you're being driven through the solar system in a 1999 Fiat Panda by someone who's been dead for two decades and you're okay? That's impressive.'

'I don't really have a choice,' I said. 'I don't think this is one of those situations where screaming helps.'

Jon chuckled. 'Let's do a detour on the way back,' he said. 'I've got time points. How about we have an ice cream and watch the birth of our sun?'

It sounded like a plan, so we did.

I had a raspberry ripple and he had a choc-ice, just like we used to do when I was a kid; and they tasted just as good. We picked them up from a flying ice-cream van. As you do.

Then we sat in the floating blue Panda in the annals of time and watched as gases and the dark matter formed our sun. We gasped as it flared into light and we nearly swooned at the beauty of the formation of the planets. It was the best twenty million years I've ever spent.

And then Jon took me home. We didn't go back to the hospital but flew down to the south west of England.

'Hang on,' I thought I lived in Worcester now?'

'No, you had your accident in Worcester. You live in Devon.'

'No wonder no one came to visit then.'

But Robbie had...

Jon took my hand. 'Don't worry about it,' he said. 'It will all sort itself out in time. A good night's sleep in your own bed will make a lot of difference. I'll get you back at about 10pm so you can have a nice bath and get to bed before midnight. Now don't spend hours trying to read up on your life. That's tomorrow's job. Promise me?'

I promised. Reluctantly.

We landed on a narrow country road with high banks on either side with trees growing out of them. I knew it and that alone was such a lovely feeling. And Jon stopped the car at the end of a small village, outside a lovely old stone house, with a latchet gate and a short path through a surprisingly neat cottage garden to the front door. Behind it, a Norman church stood still, silent and elegant in the light of a waxing gibbous moon.

I realised I didn't have any keys. They were still, presumably, in the smashed-up car.

'Under the second flower pot on the left,' said Jon kindly. He leant over to kiss me. 'See you again soon. Remember: bath and *bed*.'

'Okay.' I felt exhausted but also excited; I was going to discover my home. Already it felt like rediscovery; some part of me knew this lovely place and yet another part couldn't understand how on earth I had ended up somewhere so beautiful.

But as Jon drove off, my heart still sank. I was alone in an unknown reality. I knew no one and I didn't even know myself. But… but… but I had just had the most amazing adventure *and* I was pretty darn sure I'd spent plenty of my youth travelling this world alone. If I had what it took back then, I must still have it somewhere now. Even so…

'Don't think. Just get into the house, find your bedroom and have a bath,' I told myself, looking under the flower pot and finding the key.

My hand went automatically to the hall light and I picked up the mail. The kitchen was to the left; a lovely, big farmhouse kitchen with a well-used rectangular wooden table. And there was warmth from an Aga… and a very hot kettle on the cooler section at the top which had obviously long boiled dry but fortunately hadn't exploded.

Sensibly, I picked it up with the oven gloves that hung on the rail in front and put it on the draining board. There was an electric kettle by the sink and teabags in a cupboard above. The milk in the fridge was, amazingly, just about okay so there could be tea. This was good.

While it brewed, I explored a little. Not a big house but more than big enough for one; three bedrooms, two living rooms, one with a big dining table covered in papers and a closed laptop. Heroically, I put the mail down on the table without looking through it and didn't touch anything on the table. There was a cloakroom downstairs and a small conservatory with plants that needed watering. An old green watering can with water in it sat on the windowsill, so that part was easy.

My bedroom was dusty. Untidy and cluttered. That fitted. There was a Teasmade by the badly-made double bed and a half-full tin of biscuits. I didn't look in the wardrobe; I suddenly felt exhausted so diverted to the bathroom to start the water running for a bath. Instinctively, I knew how to set the taps so it would run in the perfect time for me to make the tea and come back up.

It was a good bath. Deep. I piled my hair into the waiting bath cap, wincing slightly at a twinge from the strapped-up wound, and lay in steaming hot water with a mug of tea in hand (the mug read 'Whatever the problem, tea is the answer' which fitted just fine for the moment). Three ginger nuts from the tin in the bedroom had inexplicably found their way to the bathroom too. They were so soft I didn't even need to dunk them. Automatically, I turned the hot tap back on with one foot, to top up the water, and pondered the patchwork of memories I retained.

I half-remembered living here, in that I knew where the switches were and how to run the bath. I half-remembered Jon— that he was dead and had been for a long time. I half-remembered being on an archaeological trip to Israel where I was attacked by a shark in the Red Sea and banged my head on a rock. For fuck's sake, what kind of woman got attacked by a shark twice in her life? I *fully* remembered the Australian attack and, for a ridiculous and yet not ridiculous moment, felt scared being in any sort of water at all including a bath.

I shuddered for a moment, remembering the cold, dead eyes of both sharks. I took a long look at my scarred leg, remembering operations, metal plates and physiotherapy and years of walking with a stick. I could see quite clearly that there *had* been more than one bite; the first one had nearly severed the leg; the second was only a nibble.

I remembered my childhood and my parents' deaths. I remembered Jon's death, years later. I remembered university and my friends. I remembered travelling and working all up to the age of thirty or so. But very little after that. I couldn't remember anyone who might have given me the name Nazam.

What I *could* clearly remember was *all* my given names: Phaedra Amabel Velvet, FFS.

My parents named me after their favourite song, *Some Velvet Morning* by Nancy Sinatra and Lee Hazlewood, which is fine, but very few people have ever heard of it. And, if anyone actually checks the name Phaedra, I appear to be named after a Cretan princess who fell in love with her stepson and, when he rejected her, accused him of rape. She ended up topping herself and going into legend as the ultimate victim and bitch.

Good call, Mum and Dad.

To compound the calamity, they didn't make my second name *Annabel* but the French version, *Amabel*. In English, that name means Blithe or Bright and Lovable. At school it meant 'let's stick her head down the lavatory.'

And no one, NO ONE, could ever spell it. Faydra Annabel was about the best I got from anyone. Velvet, at least, is impossible to shorten and it was so far down the list of outrageous names that unless they had read Enid Bagnold's *National Velvet*, no one even registered that one.

Fay I utterly loathed; Amy, ditto, and even Bel has its issues with the number of Ls when it comes to spelling. Bella is only allowed to those I genuinely love and that doesn't seem to be a lot of people.

I have spent most of my life (I am sure that includes the forgotten part) being furious about spelling. It's got to the stage when I can *hear* how someone's name is spelled when they pronounce it. I can hear *Catherine* over Katherine every time, *Anne* over Ann, *Jayne* over Jane and *Claire* over Clare. I beat myself senseless if I ever spell anyone else's name wrong and offer abject apologies. I relentlessly correct people who get my name wrong in emails and on social media (ooh, I know about social media so that's a fragment of later memory I've managed to retain).

There was a brief pause while I battled the temptation to look myself up on Facebook. There was a laptop in the dining room... *No!* Tomorrow will do.

Big brownie points there, Bel. But back to the name, Phaedra. Technically, it should be Phædra but even I gave up on that one.

Because of the myth I've never even dared look at anyone even twelve months younger than me and I put up with a hell of a lot from far too many men in my youth because I was never going to shout 'rape!'

Which was stupid. Full stop. Especially stupid when very, very few people researched who the original Phaedra was *including my parents* and I wouldn't use the name past the age of ten anyway.

I once went to see a fortune teller with my school friend Sarah. We went to the local fun fair down the road during our summer holidays. The woman knew my name even though I didn't tell her and told me it was karmic; that I'd been a liar and an evil woman in a previous life and that I was lucky I'd got the name this time to remind me to behave better.

I don't think I emerged from my house again for about a week.

Sarah, on the other hand, got the tall dark stranger and a life in Italy. And she did marry an Italian though he was barely five foot nine.

I woke up in the bath about half an hour later. That was the first time, ever, that I'd fallen asleep in water and luckily I hadn't been eaten by a shark.

Bed then. And sleep.

In a book that would happen, wouldn't it? Our heroine would sleep like a log until woken by birdsong. It's never her bladder, which would be the case in real life. And don't get me started on how everyone in books and the movies has sex without ever needing a pee first ... or afterwards, for that matter.

But I don't sleep that well at the best of times and even though I was grateful to be back in a real bed in a real home, I couldn't get my mind to stop frantically searching itself for information.

I dozed… and woke… and pottered to the bathroom. And ate another slightly softer-than-it-should-be biscuit. And remembered that I liked my biscuits that way. I considered more tea. And dozed… and woke… and pottered to the bathroom.

At four am I gave up, went downstairs, made another mug of tea and opened the laptop.

Probably a hundred emails came in. I ignored them (which turned out to be *such* a good call).

Instead, I opened Chrome and clicked on the Facebook bookmark.

I read my profile with increasing confusion.

Jesus H. Fucking Christ. How did that happen?

The note I wrote was right. I was forty three. *Forty three!*

But worse than that. Worse even than that, I was a vicar.

Chapter Five

I PROBABLY NEED to apologise here. I've loaded you a lot of weird information in a very short time. Perhaps a pause and a bit more of what back story I actually can remember might help? Stuff about sharks and all that. Who knows, it might turn out to be relevant.

I'd like to start with Jon.

Jon was my older brother. In a way, he was my father too. And my mother. He was my mentor and my guide and companion.

My parents had two children. Jon, the planned-for one and me, the mistake with the ridiculous names. I'm pretty sure I was a mistake because my mother was twenty-one when she gave birth to Jon and forty-five when she gave birth to me. I know that I was a happy mistake, by the way. My parents made sure to let me know that I was loved and welcome.

However, we didn't get a lot of time to talk about it because both my parents were killed in a car accident when I was seven. Jon was driving and, although the inquest totally exonerated him, I don't think he ever forgave himself. The car was hit side-on by another car driven by a drunk driver running a red light, so how it could possibly have been Jon's fault is hard to imagine. I think it was mostly survivor guilt because how Jon and I weren't killed in that crash is a total miracle. His car was slammed sideways, off the road and down into a culvert. Both our parents died instantly and Jon was in hospital for more than a month with broken ribs and extensive bruising. I was almost completely unharmed.

'They' put me in a foster home for the interim because my father was an only child and my mother's family lived in India so there were no convenient Uncles or Aunts to take care of me. I vaguely remember being confused at why I was being comforted by two kind strangers, being given Lego to play with and then waking screaming from terrifying nightmares to find the two kind strangers trying to comfort me again.

Jon showed up at their door after five weeks and claimed me back. He would brook no opposition and, as I ran to his open arms, what could they say? He was my closest living relative and he wanted to take me home.

Jon sold our parents' house and moved me into his own place, one of those lovely three-floored terraced houses with a long thin garden at the back where we grew flowers and vegetables. He had never married so there was no one to argue about my adoption or, if there had been, they weren't given the opportunity. As time passed, I had a couple of 'Uncles' who, I only later realised, were Jon's lovers. Uncle Harry moved in for a while and I adored him. We were both sad when he left.

In retrospect, I'm amazed that we got away with it all. Jon was a professor in ancient languages at Bristol University and I went to a local school. He managed to arrange for a school friend's mother to drop me off at home on weekdays and I became a latch-key child at the age of eight. That was our secret. We invented a Mrs. Mahoney, our own Mrs. Doubtfire, a fictional housekeeper, who would be waiting for me whenever I got in and Jon was out. We even had a cassette player by the front door with a tape of Jon pretending to be an elderly Scottish woman. I would press the 'play' key when I opened the door so there was a welcoming, 'Hello Bella! How was your day?' greeting for anyone who cared to listen.

I was an odd, independent child with a bony forehead, straight, black hair that slid out of every form of tie or Kirby grip and a complete lack of interest in dolls or the colour pink. I loved languages instead. I learnt Latin, Sanskrit, ancient Greek and Hebrew almost at the same time as I expanded my English vocabulary because Jon and I had ancient language suppers where English was forbidden. Jon always treated me like an adult; a fellow adult nerd but an adult all the same. I've never been officially tested for Asperger's but the online assessments I've filled in would explain a lot.

Once I had come to terms with suddenly having no parents, I was quite happy. I had echoes of my mother, particularly, from her cookbooks—Madhur Jaffrey was a favourite—and her clothes which Jon had kept for me, should I want them later. I couldn't wait to be able to wear her silk saris and jewelled slippers and I would gaze in total delight at the contents of her jewellery box, full of that strangely-bright Indian gold and semi-precious stones. In the genetic collision that was our parents' marriage, I was grateful that I had inherited my mother's sleek, black hair to go with my milk-coffee skin; Jon took more after our red-headed father and what hair he did have (which was not a lot) was tawny. He simply looked tanned while I was definitely coffee-coloured. Strangely, we both had blue eyes which, in Jon's face, were merely striking; in mine, they were startling. I always wished I'd had my mother's Indian beauty and almond-shaped, almost black eyes, but my Scottish Dad's line was obviously, somehow, genetically-dominant and I had his Celtic eyes and his Roman nose, too.

Jon was certainly the archetype of the absent-minded professor and if the online tests had existed back then, I'm sure he'd have scored highly for Asperger's, too. He never really wanted to go out much or socialise. In fact, I've no idea how he managed to achieve the few relationships he did have. Living with such a happy hermit I, too, developed very few social skills and didn't have a lot of friends. I didn't mind. I loved Jon and, when I'd got tired of being educated, I played with my toy farm and zoo and I built pyramids and ancient temples with building blocks. I might not have had dolls but I could write in hieroglyphs by the time I was twelve.

For Easter and Summer holidays we went to magical places like Israel, Jordan, Egypt, Sudan, Ethiopia, Iraq, Iran and Syria, visiting ancient sites, eating fabulous foods and wandering around archaeological digs. I saw my first skeleton when I was ten and helped dig it out of its 3,000-year-old Mesopotamian grave. Just once, Jon took me to India to meet Mother's family. Neither side was impressed with the other, so we spent five of the six weeks we were there travelling around on the railways, sitting on the roofs and eating with the local folk. Why would I have wanted to play with other girls or with a Barbie doll with such mysteries on offer? I lived in paradise.

Everywhere we went, Jon taught me about the local religions—old and new—and I would imagine the gods and the prophets *in situ*. I read ancient texts and devoured the stories of ancient heroines and talked to them when I needed older sister advice. In my mind, they spoke back. I bundled them up into an imaginary friend—a kind of guardian angel called Hero—and I lived in a cocoon of contentment.

Jon taught me astrology which he had studied in his twenties. He didn't mind one way or another whether I believed in it; the important thing, he said, was that people in ancient times *did* believe in it and you couldn't understand anything about the past unless you thought the way the ancient peoples did. He also taught me about reincarnation. I mentioned both in religious studies at school, once, which was not one of my smartest moments even though, as I was half-Hindu, technically it should have been allowed.

We weren't entirely without family in the UK but Jon avoided them as much as possible. 'They'—when they turned up at Christmas or holidays—said I was 'fey' like my mother because I talked to fairies and had invisible friends. I didn't like 'Them' much because they were always dismissive of how Jon was raising me and thought I should be in a proper family like theirs. Jon said that was because we both had inherited our parents' money and I could be used as a milch cow but I have no idea if that was true. 'They' only came for the first few years and then we fell, happily, by the wayside.

At school I was rubbish at everything but languages and mathematics but, by the age of twelve, I had made two good school friends who were fellow nerds, Josie and George, and I could hang out with them when Jon wasn't home during any holiday time we had in the UK. The three of us became obsessed with Douglas Adams' *The Hitch Hiker's Guide to the Galaxy* after Jon bought me the audio books for my thirteenth birthday. He had loved the original radio series as a young man and once he had inducted us, Josie, George and I dived into the delights of the books, the radio recordings and the original scripts for the radio series. Together with Jon we would act out the scenes together and invent more. Jon usually took on the role of Marvin for us and had us in fits of giggles.

George had passionately Christian parents which, with my agnostic-Hindu background, was intriguing to me. I went to church with them once but only once. To pass the time in a ceremony that seemed dry and uninspiring, I imagined an angel in robes by the altar who winked at me when the others took communion.

That glorious childhood ended when I was thirteen and just about to get on board with teenage hormones. Jon, in his late thirties, had started to get tired and put on weight. Eventually, he was diagnosed with congestive heart failure and put onto a cocktail of drugs that only seemed to make him fat and increasingly unhappy. In five years he aged about forty and I became a primary carer as well as studying for my exams. Those were not the best times but we remained friends (you don't have a lot of time for teenage existential angst when there's a real danger that the one you love more than anything is likely to die). Our love of the ridiculous, of languages, of gardening and cooking kept us sane as Jon's health declined. He would worry, 'What will become of you, if I die?' We both know the question was not 'if' but 'when.'

He made it until my final school exam results came in and he knew that I would be off to university and starting my own life. Then he died, politely and quietly in his armchair while we were watching television. Just one little jerk and a sigh and my dearest friend was gone.

I drove off to university in his old blue Fiat Panda and continued driving it until it literally fell apart. I devoured more ancient languages, got a first as well as getting myself laid and I continued to travel, working on archaeological digs and writing papers. I even got a doctorate. Apparently, I got married (but I still can't remember that bit)… but I don't believe anything in any of those following years meant as much to me as being hugged again by my big brother, Jon.

*

Then there were the sharks. In retrospect, I suppose I learnt a lot from the sharks—including the unexpected benefit of how to recognise a demon. Number one happened at the Barrier Reef in Australia just after graduation. I went out with Josie and her boyfriend which suited us just fine because three was company when I needed it or if they'd had a squabble but they were more than happy for me to go off on my own and leave them in their love-soaked paradise if they hadn't. We flew into Cairns and hired a 4x4 to drive up into the Northern Territories. But first, of course, we had to go snorkelling at the reef.

That was an off day for me. You know the sort: you're grumpy, probably hormonal, you haven't got a relationship, everyone you love is dead; you drank too much the night before and you actually believe the thought that surfaces that wishes you too were dead... and I was finding Josie and Ben's lovey-dovey ways totally annoying so, like a prat, instead of staying in the coral and fish-filled shallows on the correct side of the boat, I decided to swim around the ship into the deep waters.

It wasn't a very big shark, more of a medium white than a great one and I have no idea if it was just there by accident or if it was hoping that a tourist would be as stupid as I was. Whichever it was, it was hungry.

I only had a couple of seconds even to spot it in a 'What the...?' kind of way, before it was heading for me at speed and pretty much all I could see was teeth. Medium white sharks still have bloody big mouths and terrifying teeth.

I thought, 'But I want to live.'

They say that time slows down in moments of crisis and I believe it. It becomes *Kairos* rather than *Chronos* and, when you're in Kairos, some part of you opens up to the impossible.

For me, the impossible was a voice in my head that said, clearly, 'Swim *towards* it as fast as possible, make as much noise as possible. Do it *now!*'

I obeyed. I took in a great mouthful of air and yelling my head off into the water, I swam at it. The shark and I met at speed. At the last moment, *something* made me jack-knife and hit it in its cold, dead eye as hard as I could with my fist. The collision drove me backwards and—I think but I don't know—out of the water. It wasn't my strength that counted, it was the shark's own weight and speed as it met my fist. I gather that's how it only managed to bite and break my leg instead of taking it all.

It didn't seem to hurt. But the terror had hit me in such a way that it would have blocked pain anyway. And I was out of air. My blood billowed scarlet and the shark, a little bit hurt and maybe slightly confused, let go and turned to take a bigger bite as I began to sink. By the Grace of Something I was, briefly, in the blind spot behind its head so it had to regroup to attack again.

'Eye! Fist! Again!' said the voice and, through the descending mist, something guided my bruised hand so that I punched down into the other cold, dead eye as it turned. I swear I saw a bright human-shaped light in the water beside me before I blacked out.

That's all I remember before waking up in hospital. By the greatest of blessings, one of the people on the boat saw the turmoil in the water and raised the alarm. God knows how they got me out. God knows how they stemmed the bleeding before the helicopter arrived to fly me to hospital. God knows how it managed to pick me up. God knows what happened to the shark.

That time, I woke up before they moved me to the mortuary and then it was weeks of surgery, steel pins, skin grafts from my other thigh and learning how to walk again. Josie never forgave me for causing so much fracas and told me it was my own fault which, to be fair, it mostly was. The travel insurance, fortunately, didn't work that out and paid for me to be flown home where I emerged from hospital weeks later with a limp, a stick and a very scarred leg which scared the shit out of any lover who wanted to go down on me.

I can't tell you much about the second time, in Eilat, as the visit there is still shrouded in non-memory mystery but I do recall that this one was a *very* small great white shark that wanted a nibble while I was scuba diving in the Red Sea. Obviously, I wasn't alone that time as only utter, utter idiots go scuba diving alone and, this time, I was bloody furious when it bit me lower down on exactly the same leg and I punched it properly in that soul-less eye. At least, I think that's what happened. But then I banged my head on coral or rock and had to be rescued by my companions. Again, I don't know what happened to the shark but I only needed a few pints of blood that time instead of a whole transfusion.

This is what I learnt from sharks:

1. Miracles happen.
2. Harness the strength and the speed of the other whenever you're attacked. It's basic martial arts, of course.
3. Watch out for dead eyes in every living thing or, for that matter, in things that aren't, technically, living but might seem to be alive.
4. Every now and then, even taking a bath can be scary.
5. There *is* such a thing as a guardian angel.

This is what I didn't learn from sharks: how in the name of all that's holy, I'd managed to become a vicar.

Chapter Six

THE NEXT DAY didn't begin well.

First there was the police. And then the bishop. For a while, it seemed to get better but, in retrospect, it probably got worse. And that was before the Parish Council turned up.

I'd finally fallen asleep at about six o'clock, having checked the wardrobe and drawers and found clerical shirts and even vestments as well as my mother's beautiful saris. Running those old, still vibrant silks and velvets through my fingers was the brief escape I needed and the glorious textures were comfortingly familiar. I wondered if I still wore them. If I didn't, I thought I might start.

I'd looked at the disregarded mail on the table and noticed the title "Reverend" before the misspelling of Amabel.

I'd sworn a lot. A LOT. I had no idea how or why I'd become a vicar. There hadn't been anything further from my mind from the time I could remember. Heck, I was hardly a Hindu, let alone a Christian.

Presumably I had a vocation. But, if so, where did it come from and where was it?

'You're working to heal the dead,' said a Voice in my head. Yes, but that's hardly *vicaring* is it?

I finally fell asleep to be woken by the sound of the doorbell. Obviously, in a house this old, it shouldn't have gone *ding-dong* but it did. And it dinged and donged like crazy until I'd dragged on a dressing gown and staggered downstairs, heart in mouth, knowing that I was *a sodding vicar* and would be opening the door to a total stranger who *knew* that I was a sodding vicar.

It was actually a relief that it was the police.

Briefly.

The hospital had alerted them, of course. I was a missing

person, having left without telling the authorities. That was Bad. 'Discharge Against Medical Advice,' it's called.

At least there was only one policeman but he was cross. Before he even spoke to me, he radioed in that he had found me, alive and apparently okay. He did it crossly.

I felt guilt and just a tad of panic. What was I going to say if he asked how I'd got home? I could hardly tell him I'd been picked up by a ghost in a blue Panda and dropped off outside my gate.

Luckily, he was more concerned with telling me off (crossly) for wasting police time than finding out what had actually happened. I think he read me the equivalent of the Riot Act but I'm afraid I simply zoned out after saying 'sorry' about six times. I was pathetically grateful that he didn't seem to know that I was vicar. I expect a vicar would have got two Riot Acts because she really, really ought to know better.

I made tea when he'd gone and sat by the Aga and found that I couldn't stop shaking. I wished there were some kind of a pet—even a hamster—for unconditional company though what would have happened to it while I had been away didn't bear thinking about.

Food. That's what I needed.

There was a freezer. It contained frozen slices of hand-sliced bread, probably made in the bread maker by the window. There were eggs in a kitsch egg-box shaped like a hen house. There was butter in the fridge. I made scrambled eggs on toast and scoffed it. Then I had more toast with raw honey which, apparently, came from this very village. And I made more tea, noticing that the teabags were getting low and that there was coffee; proper coffee beans and a grinder and a cafetière by the kettle. I knew I didn't drink coffee. Or had I turned into a coffee drinker, too?

I was incredibly grateful that the day was a Wednesday. Maybe by Sunday I'd have worked out how to do a church service… Maybe, if I were lucky, They (whoever They might be) wouldn't let me.

Fortunately, I was just about dressed when the bishop arrived.

In my defence, he didn't *say* he was the bishop to start with and he wasn't dressed like a bishop. In fact, he was as scruffy as I was—I'd put on last night's sweatshirt and jeans. I simply couldn't face a clerical shirt.

I answered the doorbell to a furious man in his mid-forties who started off with, 'What the hell, Bella? *Seventeen* messages left unanswered and you simply vanish off the face of the Earth. I've been worried sick!'

His face was like thunder but I could see relief in his eyes.

That expression changed when he saw the dressing on my head. 'God in heaven! What's happened to you?'

'Car crash,' I said. 'I've been in hospital the last two weeks. I've lost my memory. Excuse me, but who are you?'

You'd have expected him to have said something like, 'Oh I'm sorry. I'm Fred/John/Colin/Whatever' but his eyes narrowed and he said, 'Holy Mother of God. It's true then. Get inside, love. I need to take a look at that.'

'Are you a vicar?' I asked, not moving. The references to Divinity seemed to be a bit of a clue although he wasn't wearing a dog collar. But then neither was I.

'Yes,' he said. 'Apart from other many things, actually, I'm your bishop. Okay, the lost memory explains a lot. Where do I start? Um.'

'Could you just *précis* for the moment?' I said. 'Everything's a bit overwhelming right now. You're probably not the right person to tell but I don't even remember becoming a vicar. I thought I was a Hindu.'

'Oh Bella!' he said and I could tell he wanted to give me a hug. I stepped back. I'm not good at being hugged by strangers, even if he, technically, wasn't one.

'Okay,' he said, putting his hands up. 'But I can't varnish the *précis* because this is serious. You and I are exorcists, Bella, and you went to Worcester to help release some troubled earthbound souls and vanished. Thank God you're back and you're safe but this is not good news. Let me inside please.'

So I did.

He drank two cups of coffee, so that explained the cafetière. And, for a bishop, he seemed to be on very easy terms with one of his vicars (but what did the new me know about bishops or vicars?). There was no chance of even trying to call him 'my Lord' or 'your Grace' or whatever the correct term might be. There was very little chance of anything until we sat down with our drinks as he kept putting his finger to his lips to shush me every time I tried to speak.

Once we were sitting, he took both my hands and said a prayer. In Latin. It was powerful and strangely familiar and it made what hair there was left on the back of my head stand up. This was not your ordinary sort of bishop.

'There,' he said. 'That should keep us safe for the moment. Now, tell me everything.'

'Well I can't, can I?' I said. 'I don't remember. Apparently, another car hit mine in Worcester. I don't know why I was there: frankly I don't know anything from the last ten years or so. Nothing at all.

'Hmmm.' He pondered for a moment while I looked at him. Not a conventionally handsome man; not particularly tall, greying, curly brown hair and dark brown eyes.

'Will you let me look at your head?' he said, eventually. Not, 'How did you get home?' or 'what happened to your car/the other car?' or anything else you might expect.

'Okay,' I said doubtfully.

He stood up and pulled gently at the dressing.

'Are you hurt anywhere else?' he asked. 'Bruises?'

'No,' I said slowly, realising that that was odd. Surely I should have other injuries? I'd not thought of it before (but to be fair, there had been rather a lot going on). I was going to add 'I think I bruised my arms when I woke up in the mortuary,' but thought that might be too much information for now.

Instead, I sat silently, pondering, while he carefully removed the dressing and stood, looking down at my head. I waited for what seemed to be a very long time.

'Bugger,' said the bishop, sitting down abruptly. I realised that I had no idea what his name might be so 'the bishop' he would have to remain for now.

'Bugger?' I queried anxiously.

'I don't think you *have* been in a car crash, Bella,' he said. 'Or if you have, it's not because another car hit you. I think you've been hit with some kind of cosh. Your skull has been cracked from behind.'

'What!'

'Have you got a mirror?'

'Erm... I don't know. There's one in the downstairs loo. On the wall.'

After about ten minutes of rummaging we found a portable mirror and the bishop showed me the wound on my head by using the two mirrors. To be honest, that was fairly pointless as I didn't know what I was looking for. But I could certainly see that there was fading bruising, a three-cornered operation scar and some bristly hair coming through which, frankly, was a relief.

'I could have hit my head in the crash,' I suggested.

'You could,' he agreed. 'I just don't think you did. You probably don't remember that I was a doctor in my past life but, to me, that does look rather suspicious. Why a head wound on the back of your head and nothing else? How was your car hit? Do you know?'

'Side on, they said. I was taken to hospital in an ambulance after the car crash. They said it was a car crash. And anyway, why would they lie to me? What the hell do you think is going on?'

I was getting pretty agitated by now. Life was confusing enough without the thought that someone might have deliberately attacked me.

Come to think of it, what evidence did I have that my visitor actually was a bishop? Or even a friend? To my shame, I began to cry. This is me, who *never* cries in front of strangers (I'll tell you the real reason for that another time). Somehow, I felt safe with him. And once I started, I couldn't stop.

It was a long-overdue reaction to all the shock and fear of the last few... well how long was it? I didn't know. I didn't know anything.

I let him hold me because I needed the feeling of some kind of love and he rocked me like a baby, handing me an enormous soft, old-fashioned, cotton handkerchief to dry my tears and blow my nose.

'I'm sorry, Bella,' he said. 'I didn't mean to make it all worse. But there is a reason for doubting this. Do you actually remember anything about the accident at all? Or the ambulance? And do you have your mobile phone?'

'No!' I almost shouted. 'I woke up in the mortuary. In the *mortuary!*' And more tears began to flow.

The bishop (alleged) took me by the shoulders and looked me in the eye.

'And where did you go when you were dead, Bella? Do you remember? Did you get an assignation of any kind?'

I didn't know what to say. I must have watched too many spy TV shows; who knew who I could trust? Who knew if I were actually mad? I gulped and said nothing. I couldn't meet his eyes.

'Okay,' he said, patting my shoulder and getting up. 'I'm pressuring you. I'm sorry. Let me tell you a couple of things. Would that be okay?'

I nodded, sniffing. Almost absentmindedly, he put the kettle on again.

'Right. My name is Paul. Paul Joans.'

I looked up. 'That's unusual spelling,' I said automatically.

'It is!' he said, his face lighting up. 'It *is*. You *do* remember!'

'No, I can hear it in your voice. I can do that. It's a… thing.'

'Okay,' he made tea for me and more coffee for him. 'Oh, you're nearly out of tea bags. Sorry! Irrelevant.'

'No, it isn't,' I said fervently. 'I've got no mode of transport to get some more.'

'We can sort that.' He sat down again. 'Okay, I'm going to start again from the very beginning. Bear with me. Oh, have you got biscuits?'

There was a brief pause while we investigated the cupboards. I had Jaffa Cakes. Life suddenly looked better to both of us.

Two Jaffa Cakes in, he began to speak.

'I was a doctor. A surgeon. Not an actual brain surgeon but I know brain trauma pretty well. And some of my patients died, as they do.

'But the thing was, Bella, that some of them didn't leave after they died. I could tell. We've discussed this before; does that aspect feel familiar to you at all?'

'Yes.' It did but I didn't want to say more.

'Okay, well, I started studying what was known about what are called earthbound souls. There's not a lot of literature about it, obviously, because what *is* known—or I should say *was* known—was a subject for the Church. I didn't know about Shamans and mystics at that time.

'But that information, or rather I should say, knowledge, is being lost, *particularly* in religious institutions which were meant to be the places where death was understood. And the problem is compounded with the world getting more and more secular, more and more electrically-spiked through technology. Then there was the virus... and that was the tipping point.'

'The virus?'

'Yes, covid-19—you don't remember?'

'No.'

'In 2020. It was a flu-type virus that literally closed down the world for a while and killed a lot of people.'

'Golly. You'd think I would remember that.'

'Well... it's not top of your list of priorities! Trouble was, a lot of people got immured in conspiracy theories—and conspiracy theories lower vibration and humanity's vibration was low enough already. Worse, funerals became 'chuck them in the furnace with the odd word and no congregation' for a while—and, with the death toll and the anger and the lack of knowledge, there was a build-up of what's called 'the etheric' which created a kind of slough of despond. Hard for the dead with no knowledge of an afterlife to get through. And now more and more souls are forgetting how to leave. Are you still with me?'

'Yes. Yes, I am.' Surprisingly, I was.

'Okay, well that was the start of my vocation. I wanted to find a way of helping them. I wanted to know more about it. I was a Christian anyway and I left my job as a surgeon and studied to be a priest. I am now a bishop—your bishop—and I train certain people (and only certain people) to do exorcisms and release earthbound souls. I don't make a big thing about it; it's certainly not orthodox behaviour.

'I've been training you. You came to me, worried about one of your parishioners who'd been exhausted all her life and you had an inkling that something was wrong that had nothing to do with medicine. You told me that she had a twin who died at birth and you wondered—you were so nervous talking to me about it but I am *so* glad you did—you wondered if the dead baby's soul had become attached to her.

'You were right and, together, we were able to release the soul. And your parishioner got better.'

'Did we tell her?'

'No. Sometimes we can tell them but mostly we don't. We're not in this for the kudos and we're not in it to frighten the horses, as it were.'

'Oh…' I felt myself start to relax. I had a companion. Someone who would know what I was talking about. Someone who wouldn't mock or deride me. It was *such* a relief.

'The thing is…' he paused and got up to take my tea bag out of the mug and pour milk. 'Oh, you need milk as well. The thing is… someone or something has got wind of what we are doing and they don't like it. There was a big article in the *Church Times* about vicars who thought they were shamans or witches. Very disparaging. And there's going to be some kind of a clampdown. I've had word. Someone in your parish has complained that Robbie—do you know Robbie?'

I nodded.

'Good. He's with us—the complaint was that he had been, I quote, 'acting weird.' Robbie, has been moved by the Archdeacon to a more orthodox parish at no notice whatsoever. I may be bishop but I don't deal with the appointments at that level and *I* only found that out two days ago.

'Bella, you were in Worcester to help with an exorcism. I don't know what happened—the other priest was called Celeste. And I say 'was' because after she let me know that it had all gone well and that you had decided to go away for a few days on your own—which is why I didn't come and look for you—she *was* killed in a car crash. It was on the news and I saw the car. You weren't in it.'

'Shit—oh, sorry,' I said.

'Shit is *exactly* the right word,' said this very unusual bishop. 'Anyway, I heard nothing from you and there's been a problem with our *WhatsApp* group so, when I didn't hear, I wasn't particularly concerned to start with… but time moved on; you didn't answer your phone; no one knew where you were, and now, this.

'But what's this got to do with *my* accident, or whatever it was?'

'I don't know. I've just got a bad feeling. For God's sake, one exorcist is dead and another nearly died. That's suspicious in itself. But, anyway, here we are you're alive and recovering. Did they say anything about the brain trauma and memory?'

'Only that it would probably come back.'

'Hmmm. Well, the thing is, it may not. No one knows. And you may find that you are everyday forgetful too. Either just for a while or forever. Sorry to be depressing. I think the only thing is to start again from today, if you can.' For a moment, he looked so sad that I almost took his hand in mine. Then he brightened up.

'So, do you think you *could* be a vicar?'

That made me laugh.

'I don't know! I didn't even know I was a Christian!'

'Well, there's a new assistant vicar arriving tomorrow, apparently. Which is very quick work. So, she'll be able to help while you find out. We'll just let people know you are recovering and you can take your time.'

'Thank you. It is all very confusing.'

'One more thing. Where *is* your mobile phone?'

'I have no idea. I wasn't sure I had one.'

'Oh, you do! They have become epidemics nowadays. You've forgotten that, obviously! The problem is the messages that are on your phone—we have that *WhatsApp* group on exorcism and I'd hate that to get into the wrong hands.'

He showed me his mobile phone, which looked like a skinny, small, flat TV. I had some recollection of seeing something quite like that before.

'Well, it's not in my bag and no one gave it back to me.'

'Bugger,' said the bishop again. 'Oh well. You're perfectly safe if you've lost your memory. You can say quite honestly to anyone who asks you about exorcism that you've no idea what they are talking about.'

'But why's it a problem?'

'Because anything apart from orthodox Christianity is viewed as heresy, even in this modern, secular day. The law wins over love nowadays, nearly every time. And there are genuine forces of darkness on the rise.'

'Jesus!—Oh, sorry.'

He laughed. 'No problem. There's nothing we can do about any of it right now. You simply need to get better. We'll get together with the others and talk again then.'

We finished our tea and then he took me shopping because, apparently, that's what bishops do. I didn't protest. We found some lint and sticking plaster for my head and a baseball cap (Really? Me? Twice in two days?) to cover it and went to Waitrose which felt like a bit of a treat.

Paul insisted on paying—'We are quite good friends, Bella, and I know what your bank account is like,' he said and I stocked up on food and essentials for at least a week. It was a huge relief.

Then we had lunch at a local café and, on the way home in the safety of his Toyota, I risked telling him everything else. *Everything,* including the world-between-worlds, Holly, Sam and Callista. Everything, that is, except about Jon, the blue Panda and the solar system which were too valuable to share.

He was a good listener and just nodded and went 'uh huh,' to encourage me. When I'd finished, his eyes were shining.

'This is brilliant, Bella. Bloody brilliant!' he said. 'I know of a couple of others who had a death experience and are doing the same. Oh, that's great. Maybe it *was* a car crash and I'm completely wrong and it was arranged so you could do this work. There are very few folk who can straddle worlds.'

'You mean it was God who crashed my car?'

'Not quite!' We both laughed. It was all beyond me but I felt safe again. And happy.

Paul hugged me when he left. I didn't want him to go but I knew he had to. He probably had a family, for all I knew, and bishopping work to, do.

'Take good care of yourself,' he said. 'We have to be careful, of course. But the work has just gone to a whole new level now. Thank you, Bella.'

'Nothing to thank me for! I didn't do it deliberately.'

'Your soul did,' he said and kissed my hand. 'Call you tomorrow!' he said and my heart lifted.

I waved goodbye and went back into the house so grateful that I had a friend.

I would never see him alive again.

Chapter Seven

I WAS SITTING at the laptop in the dining room, ignoring emails and staring at my Facebook page with increasing incomprehension. Outside the window the early evening sunshine lit up the clock face on the church's tower, catching my eye and making me ponder whether I could clear my brain by walking over and taking a look around.

Then the doorbell rang a third time.

I sighed. Visiting the church had seemed an attractive prospect. It and its graveyard were right behind the house, on the other side of a brick wall from a surprisingly neat vegetable garden containing what looked like brassicas and onions amongst other things (me, a vegetable gardener! That was almost more surprising than being a vicar).

The church was a small, square-towered Norman building, pretty as a picture. Directly behind it stood the majesty of the Dartmoor hills. It was a stunning view. When I looked at the church, I thought I had vague memories of a couple of knights' effigies in a chapel by the altar. The archaeologist in me was interested in how much of the building was original and the beauty-lover in me wondered how I had come to live in such a bucolic paradise.

But answering the door would most probably give me more keys to this life, so it had to be done.

The man outside was one of those people who manage to be both shockingly ugly and incredibly attractive at the same time. It's hard to explain but, if you've met someone like that, you'll know just what I mean. He had beautiful, Arabic, tanned skin but the proportions of his face were all over the place and his eyes were small. He seemed vaguely familiar which was hopeful. His smile of greeting showed white, even teeth.

'Hello,' he said. He seemed nervous.

'Hello.'

'I'm sorry to disturb you. Could I come in for a minute?'

'Um. I suppose so.' I stepped back.

He walked in as if he knew the place well. He probably did. I followed him into the west-facing living room, which was tinted golden in the afternoon sun, softening the scruffiness of the sofa and the chairs and gleaming off the—to me—rather over-large flat screen television.

'You've still not upgraded your TV!' he said, in direct contrast to my thoughts.

'Money,' I said. It seemed the easiest answer. 'None of your effing business' was probably out of order for the vicar. Obviously, whoever he was, he'd not been here for a while but that really didn't give me much of a clue. And for some reason I wasn't telling this stranger that I had lost my memory. At least, not yet.

He sat down. I didn't. Neither did I offer tea. Not everyone gets tea; only people who are comfortable in kitchens.

'How can I help?' I said.

'I was just passing,' he said. He was lying.

'Well I'm glad you stopped,' I lied back. 'What do you need?'

'Well... I just wondered...' Here it came. I braced myself.

'Would you, possibly, be willing to...' Pause. I didn't help. I sat down with my hands folded in my lap, smiling politely.

'To... well, to Christen Felicity?' It came out in a sudden rush.

'I don't see why not.' (I'm sure I can learn how to baptise a baby; there must be a book somewhere).

'It's just that you *are* the vicar and, well, Rachel would really like her to be... Oh!'

He had finally stopped and heard what I said.

'Oh, thank you! Thank you. I'm really grateful. I wouldn't even have asked if Rachel hadn't...' he tailed off, obviously under the impression that it was best to shut up now.

I was a little intrigued. There was obviously some mystery here which it might be useful to discover in order not to put my foot firmly in it some other time.

'And Rachel is sure she wants me to do it?' I said.

'Oh yes. She's never had a problem with you.'

And obviously you have. Curiouser and curiouser.

'When were you thinking?' Oh shit, is baptism like marriage? Do you have to do banns or something? And was this man actually a Christian? He looked more Muslim (but who was I to judge?). Did it matter?

'Oh, whenever you could manage it. Sooner rather than later.'

'Is Felicity ill then?'

'Oh no, she's fine. Thank you. It's just that Rachel… Rachel…'

'Is pregnant again?' I suggested, rather wickedly.

'Yes! Oh, thank you!' He said again, adding, 'I thought you might mind.'

'I don't mind,' I said, because I didn't and I didn't see why on Earth I should. 'Congratulations.'

'Good, good,' said. 'Thank you.'

'Well, if you want to have a party as well and invite people, it had better be a couple of weeks off,' I said. 'I don't have my diary to hand right now—' His eyes swivelled to what was immediately and quite obviously a large Church diary on top of the bureau. 'Oh! There it is! Silly me. Right.'

I got up to get it, which was stupid really, as it gave him the first sight of the back of my head.

He jerked upright and reached out toward me. 'Amabel! What's happened to you?'

Amabel. Hmm. He was a fairly close acquaintance then. Or a formerly close friend.

'I had an accident. It's fine.' Suddenly, I wondered. Could he be…? But surely not?

'Oh, I hope it is fine. I'm sorry.'

I brought the diary back and leafed through the pages.

'What day of the week? A Saturday?'

'Please. Look, Amabel, are you really okay? I do still care, you know.'

'I'm sure you do,' I muttered, immersing myself in the book. What else could I say?

'There's Saturday 19th. It's nearly three weeks away but the Saturday before is fully booked.' It was; there was a blue diagonal line through the page. God knows what that meant. 'Morning or afternoon?'

We settled on 2pm so there could be afternoon tea—to which I was, of course, cordially invited. Now came the problem of what I should actually put in the diary. 'Felicity' wouldn't be enough.

'Her full name?'

'Felicity Beatrice.'

'And presumably your surname? Or hyphenated? You never know nowadays.' Nice one, Bel. Now will it work?

'Yes, hyphenated. Nazam-Burn.'

Nazam…? Fortunately the ridiculousness of it all hit me right in the gut and I began to laugh.

'What's so funny?' He was offended.

'Oh, not the name, sorry,' I was gasping now. 'Just the whole situation. Just my odd sense of humour.'

The man who was almost certainly my ex-husband recovered his composure and stood up. He grinned awkwardly in acknowledgment.

'Well, if that's sorted then…'

'Yes. Yes. Thank you for stopping by.' I stood up and put my hand out to shake his. 'I'm sure you know your way out.'

After he'd gone, and I'd stopped laughing, I sat down with (yes, another) cup of tea and worked out what I could remember. I got a few inklings although, for the life of me, I couldn't work out *why* I had married him. However, I knew we did have a few happy years before it all went pear shaped.

So, a divorced vicar then… Interesting.

'Cheer up, Bel,' I said to myself. 'It may be scary and ridiculous and stupid but at least you're not a *boring* country vicar.'

It was nearly dusk by the time I got to the church to look around. It was locked, of course, so I had to trail back up to the house to look for the key. Which was right behind the front door on a rack, together with several more, mostly made from cast iron and fairly ancient. There was an air rifle, too. Interesting.

I took all the keys, just in case, and let myself into the cool calmness of the most beautiful church in the world, Or, at least, that's how it seemed to me. *St. Raphael the Archangel*, it was called, according to the old wooden sign at the gate. I pondered that for a moment; it struck me as unusual. For some reason, I locked the door again behind me and put the key in my pocket (and thank goodness I did). I can only suppose that I wanted to make sure I wasn't discovered as a pseudo-vicar while I explored.

The church had stone walls and floor (as they do), plaques commemorating the dead on each side, a lovely old wooden font by the door, bell ropes at the bottom of the bell-tower—it looked like a full peal of seven bells—old and dark wooden pews with kneeling pads, obviously lovingly embroidered by parishioners who, for some reason, thought that grey was the most appealing colour possible and two side chapels which did indeed contain tombs just as I had half-remembered. The altar was locked away behind a rood screen but one of the other keys opened that so that I could go up to the altar itself and sigh with pleasure at the ancient, gold-painted triptych behind it.

The angel was in its usual place, looking rather dusty, to the left.

I reached up to touch the golden or gold-plated cross set with cabochon jewels. Deep red at the centre and green, yellow, blue and orange at the ends. Garnet? Citrine? Who knew? But I could find out. For some reason that I couldn't explain, I picked up the matches on the right-hand side of the altar and lit the candles on either side of it and spent a moment just breathing in its beauty.

Both side chapels had well-preserved stone effigies over the graves of the medieval knights and their ladies. I walked around both of them and discovered that the right-hand one was also an exquisite lady chapel with an old, dark, wooden-faced Madonna and child on the altar. I stared at them for a while. This must be a great treasure; where could it have come from?

Hang on a minute… my brain finally connected with my sight.

Carefully, I peered through the wooden screen that formed the boundary between lady chapel and sanctuary. Yes, it was still there.

It wasn't what most people would call an angel, which is exactly why I knew that it was one. It wasn't wearing a toga and it didn't have wings. It was a column of dusty-looking golden light.

'Hello,' I said cautiously.

It awoke, slowly and partially. It was aware of being observed and so was I.

'Can you understand me?'

It indicated, Yes. I can't tell you how it did that, it just did.

'Have we spoken before?'

It indicated, No.

'But I knew you were there. I don't understand.'

It waited. I got the feeling that if it could have shrugged a slightly exasperated shoulder, it would have done. Obviously, there was no comment it could make.

I regrouped.

'Are you the angel of this church?'

Yes.

Do all churches have angels? I'd stopped speaking out loud by now. There was no need. Somehow, it was answering inside me.

No, not all. They all start with one but most angels fade.

Why haven't you faded?

This church hasn't died. There have been enough priests who acknowledged me.

I haven't. And yet, I knew you were there. Did I know? How strange.

Pointed silence.

You don't chat, do you?

No.

Did I acknowledge you before?

No. Now you do.

Okay... um. What am I meant to do with you. If that's not a rude question?

What is rude?

Sorry. What am I meant to do with you?

I am a channel of Grace and healing for this church. USE ME.

That last bit was definitely in capitals. My whole body resonated and the angel glowed. It was no longer dusty.

Erm… exactly how do I use you?

You are a child of God. I am a servant of God. As the child of my Creator, I serve you as I serve Her.

Actually it wasn't 'her' it was a word that meant both 'her' and 'him' and either and both but it was such an amazing word that I translated it to 'her' in shock. Because, of course, the angel wasn't speaking English, it was speaking angelic. And I was understanding it.

How wide is your remit? I asked.

Clarify.

I mean, can you heal the world, this village, this congregation or just me?

All of the causes of dis-ease that the priest of this church knows of and that they ask through me to be healed that belong to this village. All the healing that they truly desire.

Can you heal my head?

I do not heal.

You just said…!

No. Healing comes through me. I do not heal.

Where does it come from, then?

The angel seemed to gather itself together and for a moment, the air was filled with an inexpressible feeling of love and joy and glory. The altar actually glowed.

This.

I was shaken. *Is that God?*

It is what you would call an atom of God. Not God. No human can see the face of God and live.

Okay. I regrouped and, with the customary selfishness of my species, brought it back to me.

So can you 'channel' (is that the word?) Healing from This?

Yes.

Then please do that for my head. Thank you.

No, I cannot.

WTF? You just said…

All of you has to want this healing to resolve it. Part of you is frightened that if you are healed you will remember. Part of you does not wish to remember. This is why you humans are so difficult. Complicated. Only that which all of you wants healed may be healed.

I thought for a while. Was that true?

It is true.

Then please heal the part of me that is willing.

I do not heal.

Okay, okay. Please will you channel the healing that I can receive?

Yes.

I stood embarrassed, waiting. Nothing happened.

Erm... was I supposed to feel something?

No.

Right.

There didn't seem to be anything to say. Self-consciously, I started to back away.

Would you laugh?

What?

We love your laughter. We can only laugh when you laugh.

You don't laugh?

We can only laugh when you laugh.

I hadn't really been thinking of a lot that was funny lately but the meeting with Whats-his-name-husband-Nazam had been pretty amusing. And the fact that I still didn't even know the given name of someone I had obviously slept with, let alone married, was ridiculous. I started to chuckle. How worried he'd been that I would refuse to Christen his daughter! Maybe the old me *would* have refused to Christen his daughter. Wasn't Nazam an Arabic name? Either Muslim or Urdu? Memory flooded in. Yes! Galel Nazam, 'The wave of God, discipline and order.' Those were his names and their meanings. Nothing else about him filtered through, though. How daft was that? I gave a sudden crack of laughter at the ridiculousness of it all, not least an agnostic-Hindu vicar married to, and divorced from, a Muslim.

The angel reacted to my laugh by flaring like a sparkler, flooding the church with iridescent light and sound and I felt my blood turn to champagne. It was a shock wave of angelic giggles and I was lucky not to fall down the altar step. As it was, I lost my balance and reeled sideways, holding onto the rood screen and still laughing until I tumbled into the entrance of the lady chapel.

Then the altar exploded.

No, I'm not making it up. The sodding altar exploded. It went 'wop' and then 'bang' and 'crash' and sundry other explosive noises (loud) and shot cloth and stone, candlesticks and cross in all directions.

I was vaguely aware that, had I been still standing in front of it, I could have been killed but I was still enveloped in angelic laughter so the sight of one, lone candlestick rolling down the aisle, just like the obligatory single wheel after a car smash in a movie, made me laugh all the more. You know those hysterical bouts of laughter when you simply can't stop? It was one of those. I was sitting on the floor surrounded by debris of a Norman stone altar and laughing so much that my jaw ached.

That was the moment that the Parish Council arrived.

The moment I heard the sound of the church door being unlocked, the laughter dried up in my throat and, from an instinct of self-preservation, I dived into the chapel and looked frantically for a place to hide. The only possibility was under the altar, *if* it were a table and not all stone. It wasn't a table but there was an open box-like space which had probably been a grave or a reliquary, so I curled up inside it, behind the altar cloth, vaguely aware that this was stupid, probably desecratory (is that a word?) but, for Christ's sake, an angel had been talking to me and the altar had exploded. How in the name of all that's holy was an amnesiac vicar with a head wound supposed to explain that in any way that was going to make sense?

They were definitely looking for me. Two of them called out, 'Reverend Amabel?' One called, 'It's Parish Council time. We couldn't find you at home,' while a fourth scolded, 'the door was locked. She'd hardly lock the door behind her.'

How little they knew me.

But I wasn't going to be their focus for long.

'What's that smell of burning?'

'Oh my God!'

'The altar!'

'What's happened?'

'Is it a bomb?'

'A bomb!'

'Of course it's not a bomb! The door was locked.'

And so on, and so on. I stopped listening because I started to feel really weird and light-headed and the space under the altar seemed to have contracted. It took a moment or two to realise that was because the angel was hiding under the table with me.

What the...?

It shushed me with a touch which, somehow, I knew was a warning. And then the space got even tighter and I felt even more weird but this time it was a powerful, deep red kind of weirding. Can't explain it any better than that.

At that moment, someone pulled up the altar cloth and stared right at me. It was a middle-aged balding man in a sports jacket, the very epitome of a Parish Council, and now I had *so* much explaining to do.

Or not.

'No one here,' he said to the person behind him, dropping the cloth back down.

Two angelic beings currently wrapped around me seemed to exhale with relief.

'Are you sure?' said another voice, female this time and as melodious as a waterfall. It was the kind of voice that promised strawberries and cream with Pimm's and lemonade. It was the kind of voice that would sing a child to sleep after playing with it all day and not minding for a moment that it had broken her favourite ornament.

'Look for yourself, if you can't believe me,' he replied, waspishly. 'I could hardly miss a whole human being, could I?'

Well yes, actually, you could...

The person with the beautiful voice laughed like a cascade of stars. 'Of course not,' she said. 'I'm so sorry.'

They poked around the chapel for a moment and then joined the others in the chancel.

Hang on. *Two* angels?

They both shushed me. A minute later, the altar cloth was lifted again and a face as beautiful as its voice peered in. All three of us held our breath. Which is a silly thing to say as angels don't breathe. But trust me, they were holding their breath.

All I could see were big, velvet brown eyes in a pixie face surrounded by blonde hair. Oh, and a dog collar. Then the veil dropped again and she was gone.

Chapter Eight

I DON'T KNOW how long we lay there, curled up together in the darkness, but it seemed like forever. Even after the Parish Council left we stayed silent and still until the angels deemed otherwise. I didn't protest.

It's not as if I didn't have anything to think about while I waited; my brain tried, somewhat cautiously, to collate the information received today and then flatly refused, stating overload and, it has to be said, a shed-load of resentment at even being asked to try.

At last, with what seemed like a sigh, the angels unravelled themselves and I could roll out of the under-altar box and get to my somewhat dusty feet. I made a mental note to talk to whoever cleaned the church (look at me, behaving like a vicar!).

The altar angel looked the same as before but smaller. The other... well, the other... I'm sorry, but he/it looked like Russell Crowe in *Gladiator*. But red.

There were a lot of questions to be asked but I suspected I wasn't going to get any answers. Nevertheless I tried.

What happened? Good start, I thought.

When? It was my angel, of course, seeking clarification. Mr. Strong-and-Silent-In-Red was just that.

Okay.

The altar. Why did it blow up?

Not known. We may have laughed too much.

I snorted with amusement. I couldn't help it; yes, things were pretty serious but the idea of laughter blowing up an altar was pretty entertaining.

Why did you hide with me?

Bad man. (again the gender wasn't specific but I heard 'man').

Bad man who can see and hear angels?

69

Yes.
So, a psychic?
Yes. There was more to it than that but it couldn't explain.
And who's your friend?
Friend? Clarify?
This angel, here.
Of Samael. Protective angel. I called for protection for you.
For me.
'Of Samael.' What kind of name is that? And isn't Samael supposed to be the same as Satan?
No. Now it was Russell Crowe speaking/resonating in a deep gut-tingling timbre. Not Satan. Protection. 'Of Samael' is... and it explained without words, showing me a kind of rising tower of angels from the least resonant to the most powerful, all aspects of one archangelic being working in a cosmic hierarchy. I saw and understood that humans could not bear the appearance of a full archangel as it was the size of one of the stars, so before me was an essence of the archangel as an angel low enough in vibration that it would not burn me with its presence. But it had full communication with all the other levels. I hope you got that. I'm not quite sure I did.
You made us invisible?
Yes.
Am I still invisible?
No.
What is your name? I turned to 'my' angel.
No name. Of Raphael.
And can a 'bad man' harm an angel? That seemed unlikely.
Human with knowledge can destroy angel. That one would.
Oh. That indicated serious power. And even worse trouble. Where was the bishop when I needed him? Oddly, I didn't feel afraid.
Okay, so what do we do now?
Clarify?
About the altar. About you. About... the 'bad man'...
Both angels looked blank.
Okay, do you have any advice?
No.

Yes.

The *yes* came from Of Samael.

Name me. If you name me, you can call me whenever you are in peril and I will come.

Of course, 'Russell' was in my brain before I'd consciously thought. And it was only later that I realised it was perfect: russ or russet for red and 'el' means 'of God.'

Rus-el said the angel and, strangely, it seemed to experience great content.

And me? Said the other angel, hopefully. It seemed that they liked names.

Good Lord, how many names do I know that end in *el?* Not a lot.

Ariel, I said. *The Tempest* had been my favourite of Shakespeare's plays.

Ariel, she said, pleased.

We stood there for a while, awkwardly. That is, if angels do awkward. I know I do.

'So…' I said out loud. 'I'd better get back to the house then, before they bring more people.'

Wait. It was Rus-el. Hold up your hands.

I did and it held out the equivalent to touch mine. A frisson of fire went around me.

If you need invisibility, name this.

Good grief, this is getting more like Harry Potter by the moment.

Good grief.

Hang on a minute! I didn't mean…

Good grief is the name by which you call invisibility.

Yes, of course it is… hang on, you mean I can actually *make myself invisible by saying that?*

Yes. For a few moments only. Use it wisely. It will fade.

Erm… okay. Thank you. I'll… er, see you another time then.

Yes.

I didn't want to leave the church but it had to be done. Outside, it was dusk and the lights of the house did look inviting across the churchyard. But, hang on, I'd left in daylight; had I actually left any lights on?

71

No, I hadn't and, as I got closer, through the French windows I could see the members of the Parish Council gathered around my dining room table. Bloody cheek! Who said they could just come into my home without a by-your-leave?

Common sense suggested that it must have been me but the new (not improved) me wasn't impressed. And it had been a very long day.

Mustering the last of my strength, I marched round to the front door, drew myself up to my full five feet four inches and walked into the hall, almost absentmindedly picking up the air rifle as I passed and, as my body remembered, even if I didn't, both cocking and loading it with a pellet from a tin in the brown waxed jacket by the door.

'Ah,' I said, pointedly, as I walked into the dining room. 'Not burglars then. What are you doing here?'

There was a susurration of surprise.

'Reverend Amabel!'

'Vicar!'

'That's me,' I said cheerfully.

'We weren't expecting you.'

'Obviously.'

'Er… there's a situation in the church. We were having a meeting…'

'And do you actually have permission to walk into my house just like that?'

'It's the Rectory!' The one now speaking was the balding man in the sports jacket. The 'bad man?' He looked more like a tortoise.

'Actually not,' came a voice from a memory I didn't know I had. 'This is my house. It's the *old* Rectory. My property. The parish house is one of the modern ones down the road. Where Robbie lived.'

'But you've always…'

'Well, I think that changes now.'

'But Reverend Amabel, something terrible's happened. Mere semantics don't matter right now.' This was a blonde woman in her forties who looked terminally worried.

'Is somebody sick? Dying?'

'No.' They were all on the back foot now, being faced with an unexpected and furious vicar with a gun. Apart, that is, from the clerical beauty standing to one side. She just exuded goodwill which was particularly annoying right now.

'Well, if no one is dying then I think it can wait until tomorrow, can't it?'

'But the altar. In the church. It's broken. We were taking Reverend Lucie in to show her the church—she's your new assistant—and the altar is broken.'

Reverend Lucie (definitely with an 'ie' not a 'y') and I looked at each other. God, she was gorgeous. Why on earth would a woman that lovely want to confine herself to a black clerical shirt? Black technically shouldn't have suited her with that fair colouring but she just darn well went and outshone it anyway. There were two large, soft holdalls on the floor behind her.

'How do you do, Reverend Lucie,' I said politely. 'You'll be living in the new house down the road then?'

'Oh, of course,' she said, with a smile that spread around the whole room. 'But for the moment, these kind people had suggested I stay here, as that house isn't actually ready.'

'While I was away? Without asking me first?'

'Er… yes,' said Angst-Ridden Lady.

'It's an unprecedented situation,' said Tortoise Man. 'We didn't know where you were and Robbie moved away so suddenly and the Archdeacon brought us Reverend Lucie today. But Amabel, the *altar*…'

'Can wait until tomorrow,' I said. 'I will go and take a look myself but, unless something is actually on fire, it can all wait.

'Point one, all of you have homes and I'm sure you have spare beds if, as you say, the church house is uninhabitable. Though why Robbie should have left it so is unclear. Point two, as none of you seem to know, I have been in a car accident. I am only just out of hospital and I need time and rest. I've seen Bishop Paul today and he knows all the details. I am now going to have some supper and an early night and get some rest so I would appreciate it if you would all leave. Perhaps ten o'clock tomorrow morning, in the church, would suit?

'Now, excuse me, I need to discharge the gun in the garden.'

'Vicar, this won't do,' said another man, tall and dark with an aristocratic nose.

'Won't do?' I was tired and exasperated. 'You come into my house knowing I'm away and expect to put a total stranger up in my spare room? Even if there is a disaster in the church, even if she is a cleric, even if I have been enough of a doormat in the past for you to think that is acceptable it is, in fact, presumption of the highest order! I will not have it. You leave now!'

'That is not the kind of behaviour I would expect from our vicar,' said Aristocratic Nose Man.

'Well you'd better start expecting it,' I said. He was probably right but I didn't care. 'Out!'

Reverend Lucie actually dared to put her hand on my arm.

'I'm so sorry,' she said. 'I can see you have a head wound. You are almost certainly not yourself. Yes, we should go.'

In one fell swoop she had taken charge, made me look petulant and simultaneously justified and patronised my behaviour to the Parish Council. She would get big Brownie points for that. But not from me.

I managed (just) not to shake her hand off my arm. Instead, I said, 'Please excuse me,' stepped away to open the windows and walked out into the garden, discharging the air rifle safely into the earth. I stood in moonlit darkness, taking long, deep breaths of the night air.

Then I leant the gun against the hedge, stepped through the slightly-crooked little wooden gate into the churchyard and began to walk. From the churchyard there was a footpath around the edge of a small field and onto the moor. I knew this path so I wasn't afraid to walk in the dark—and, anyway, three-quarter moons offer quite enough light for the foot-sure. I wove my way through the three yew trees that tradition had planted in the churchyard to repel the devil and round the field onto the moorland itself.

I have always loved desert places and a moor is its own kind of desert. These spartan lands are the bones of the Earth; the kind of places where the veil between heaven and Earth is very thin.

Tonight, as I walked, I took deep breaths of the spring air and managed to clear my mind of its nagging fears and worries enough to be able to appreciate the range of greys around me and the panorama of stars shining through patchy cloud. The moon was dressing and undressing herself as if trying on new clothes. Each time a wisp of cirrus crossed her light, she gave off a spectrum of colour, a kind of aura, and then she was her pearl-white self again with the deeply mournful grey-and-silver face gazing down on humanity and our stupidities.

I found myself mouthing a blessing that I didn't know I knew. It was a benediction for the devas and spirits of the land, the air, the fire and the waters. It came from some part of my mind which knew this routine of blessing the night and, somewhere, I knew that the spirits welcomed it and received it. I felt as though a wave of unseen presences acknowledged me as I walked. For sure, I was a very odd sort of vicar.

Even though I knew this land, I was sensible and stuck to the path and, after about fifteen minutes of brisk walking, I turned back on exactly the same route, smiling involuntarily at the beauty of the church and the village in the moonlight before me.

When I got back, the people were long gone. The freedom of the moor had receded and I found myself tensing up again, so I locked and bolted the front door behind me and made a mental note to discover who actually had a key or whether there was another one under a different flower pot. Then I went to the kitchen to search out some supper. I thought I deserved something really nice. Today had been a helluva week.

There was salad in the fridge and salmon and bacon and eggs and a couple of ready meals. To my credit, I didn't go for the ready meals automatically but, after checking that I had soy sauce, I stir-fried the salmon in garlic (in the fridge and edible even though sprouting) and ginger which I sensibly kept in the freezer and—amazingly—remembered. Sandwiched with salad in fresh sourdough bread, it was almost enough to keep anyone sane. Rashly, I opened a bottle of cider and drank the lot.

I was replete and slightly squiffy when Jon walked through the door. That's *through* the door.

Now you might think I ought to have been mad at that but (a) continuity is not my strong point, (b) it wasn't the Parish Council or (c) an impossibly beautiful new vicar, it was *Jon*.

'I need a hug,' I said, staggering to my feet, and he wrapped his long arms around me as substantially and physically just as though he were still alive.

'Why didn't you tell me, I was a vicar?' I said. '*Really*, Jon!'

'You'd have killed me,' he said, laughing. He was probably right.

Chapter Nine

THE BISHOP AND I had bought plenty of chocolate biscuits that day, so Jon and I sat down and had tea and he ate four. He said he had come to take me out again but, as he could only eat and drink in the company of a living human, he liked to take what opportunities he could. It didn't sound too fantastic given the rest of the previous twenty-four hours.

'I think I've gone mad,' I said

'No,' he said, definitively. 'Crazy, maybe, but there's no harm in crazy. Mad can be a bit of a problem.'

'So, what is going on? It's all so confusing. I don't even know why I'm a vicar. Hell, I don't know *how* to be a vicar even if I wanted to be one! And the altar in the church exploded. And there's an angel. No, two. And that's not to mention riding through the stars with you in the blue Panda and helping souls retrieve themselves.'

'We'll talk on the way,' he said. 'It's back to work when you've finished your tea. Remember, we still have a soul to reunite.'

'What, now? But I'm exhausted!'

'Yes, now.' That sounded like the old Jon telling me it was time for bed. He remembered that too and we both laughed. 'Come on,' he said. 'There's spare energy going among the stars. You'll be fine.'

He was right. As soon as we were outside and I could look up into the starlit sky, I felt better. I locked the front door, carefully, although who knew who else had a key?—and climbed into the blue Panda which Jon had parked on the verge.

We drove off, down the lane and then we were in the sky. I never saw the actual transition part in all the times we did it, no matter how hard I tried. I suppose it's like when you have an anaesthetic. One minute you're awake... and then you're awake again later.

'Okay,' said Jon as we accelerated past Jupiter. 'Reality is fluid, for a start. Quantum mechanics is just the start of it. Oh, that's Io, by the way.'

'Mmm-hmm.' I gazed at the icy moon and heaved a sigh of satisfaction. Even if I were simply bonkers, this was amazing.

'It may help if I put it like this: "The time streams are now very polluted. There's a lot of muck floating about in them, flotsam and jetsam, and more and more of it is now being regurgitated into the physical world. Eddies in the space-time continuum, in fact," he quoted wickedly and entirely accurately from *The Hitch Hiker's Guide To the Galaxy*.

'"Is he... is he? And who is Eddie, exactly, then,"' I quoted back, right on cue. We both laughed and squandered some happy time on more Hitch Hiker quotations about Slartibartfast, Sub-Etha Sens-O-Matics, Pan Galactic Gargle Blasters and how the first million years were the worst, and the second million years, they were the worst too.

'What exactly do you want to know?' said Jon, at last. 'Why you're doing this work? Who you are? Who you were? What the bishop's got to do with it? Whether Robbie is doing it too? Why you've lost your memory?'

'Yes.' That seemed to be the most appropriate answer.

'There is a team of you, on Earth, doing this Work because the number of souls who don't get through safely has risen tremendously over the last decade or so. The pandemic of 2020 was the tipping point? You remember that?'

'No, but the bishop told me about it.'

'Right. Well, the whole of the Universe—seen and unseen—relies on balance and this is an imbalance. The whole ecology of the Earth depends on souls leaving and taking their etheric existence away with them when people die.'

'Etheric existence?'

'All the baggage they accrued on Earth. It has to be lifted up and transmuted so it can be recycled into future energy fields. If it isn't, it becomes cosmic pollution.'

'I see,' I said. I didn't.

'Well, be that as it may,' said Jon. 'There is also opposition to the Work.'

'That's Work with a capital W then?'

'It is. Truly, existence depends on the balance.'

'And there's opposition to existence?'

'To clarity in existence, yes. That's because the etheric energy carries a form of basic consciousness and that feeds on similar energy. The more negativity there is in the lower astral field, the more it can be used for destructive purposes. It can be used by unscrupulous beings as a form of control or chaos. Evil is essentially chaotic and chaos can be very harmful.'

'Are you actually talking devils and demons?'

'Sort of... but *mostly* those are only semi-conscious forms. The drive behind this *is* definitely demonic and it has infected humans, including discarnate humans. Some souls which were so incredibly damaged in life can remain in the lower etheric and learn to operate there. They appear to be demons but they are human demons. Conscious and up to no good. They attach themselves to living humans who are already weak.'

'So, what do they get from opposing soul retrieval?'

'Food. They eat the negative and get stronger. 'It's something which has been going on since the beginning of time but, up until now, the celestial forces have always been the strongest—with glitches such as the Inquisition, Hitler, slavery, war and the holocausts of course.'

'Glitches?!'

'Yes, horrible, horrible glitches. And there will be more and more of them if the darker forces get their way. Since the virus caused a tipping point, everyone who can do this Work on Earth is now being called to do it. Unfortunately, the opposition is starting to have a lot of fun in fighting back.'

'And my car accident was part of that?'

'Your 'accident' was certainly part of that. Your memory loss is not coincidental. You and Celeste were onto a big patch of lost souls and about to help them let go. Paul has taught you a very powerful exorcism which works extremely well. You'll have forgotten it at the moment?'

'Er... yes, I have. Um. No, oddly, I think I've still got it. Um ... *Exorcizo te, omnes spiritus immunde, in nominee Dei Patris*

Omnipotentis, et in nimine Jesus Christi, filii, ejus, domini et judicis nostril et in virtute Spiritus... blimey. There's a lot more of it too. Well how about that?'

'Okay, well so far, the people who have had near-death experiences and who can work between the worlds have been safe, so we've just upgraded you to do that. You should be relatively safe, especially if they believe you have lost your memory and can't do the work on Earth any more.'

'That's *relatively* safe?'

'Yes.'

'And "upgraded." What exactly does that mean?'

'It means communing with angels; seeing demonic forces and being able to discern between them—remember, Bella, evil *cannot* get anywhere when it appears as unattractive. It has to be glamorous and beguiling in order to tempt people. You were "upgraded" by dying and being returned to Earth. You did agree to it of your own free will, I promise you. But I guess you don't remember that.'

As I pondered this, the Starship *Heart of Gold* drifted by, followed by the U.S.S. *Enterprise*.

Jon barked with laughter. 'Sam has sent those images to greet you,' he said. 'Nice touch!'

'Yes, but how the hell am I supposed to know what's real and what's not?'

'Well look closely,' said Jon and I did. Neither starship was real; it was obvious when you looked consciously. But then, they couldn't be real, anyway, being fictional...

'And the vicaring bit?' I asked, as we landed on the driveway as before and decelerated.

'It's called working from inside the box,' said Jon. 'You became fascinated by the first few centuries of Christianity, before it was overtaken and made an extension of the religions of Rome and used for war and control. You believed that you could be part of a movement to bring it back to its original concept of mysticism, love and healing and that it would be better to do that from inside the box. Let's face it, seminary was going to be a doddle for someone who already understood ancient Greek, Hebrew and most of the writings of the Early Church Fathers—that was your second doctorate, in case you've forgotten—*Merkabah And The Divine Feminine Of The First Temple In The Early Christian Church*.'

'Really? Who has the time or energy or even need for a *second* doctorate? And what is Merkabah?"'

'Chariot riding. From the Book of Ezekiel. It's a code for how to ascend to the heavens while in a physical body. What we're doing right now, just updated to include the Panda so you wouldn't feel scared.'

'And are you really Jon?' I *was* suddenly scared.

'Yes,' he reached out and touched me under the chin, just as Jon used to do as a gesture of affection. 'I'm really Jon. I chose this work after I died. The Panda isn't real but it'll do.

'We're here,' he added, somewhat unnecessarily. 'Oh, and the bishop is one of the leading lights of the Work in the UK and, yes, Robbie was—and hopefully still is—doing it too.'

'What happened to Celeste?' I asked, hoping I didn't already know the answer.

'She's still in hospital,' said Jon. 'On this side. We have hospitals on this side too, for those with particularly difficult deaths.'

'She was murdered?'

'Not exactly.' And he would say no more.

We drove up to the Georgian house in silence. Sam was standing at the open door. He looked more human and less spirit than he had the first time I saw him. Or maybe I was just adapting.

'Bel,' he said with a smile that stretched from ear to ear. 'How are you feeling now?'

'Bonkers and bemused,' I replied proffering a hand to shake. I still wasn't quite up to hugging.

'Well, we can work on that,' said Sam smiling and shaking my hand vigorously. 'Guaranteed to be more bemused by the time you get home, at least.'

'Oh thanks!'

Tonight's job was to be slightly different. Actually *radically* different. This time, we were taking Holly's soul with us into the etheric lands.

'This is a technique we use when the ego has proved to be powerfully resistant,' said Sam. 'She was strengthened by her contact with you so it's worth a try. It's something we use more frequently nowadays but it's not without its dangers. It needs three of us for the Trinity Recovery because the Law of Three holds the soul safely inside the container and it's even more powerful with a living human.

'The Law of Three?'

'Yes, when there are two there are often opposites or, even if there's unity, it can be broken apart. When there are three, it can become a divine dance or circle and that creates a fourth—a new possibility.'

'Erm…'

'What *do* they teach them at these seminaries?' said Sam with a grin. 'Trinity is meant to be foundational to the whole Christian religion.'

'It's more something that's respectfully ignored,' I said, ruefully. I remembered that out of nowhere.

'Quite. Well, don't worry, you'll see. But please, Bel, do *exactly* what we tell you. It's quite safe if you follow our orders. We know what we're doing. You don't yet.'

As I've always been someone who yelled, 'don't be such a dickhead!' at every movie when the hero or heroine broke away, thinking they knew better, and got everyone into more trouble, I didn't have any problem with that instruction. I do realise that the *Harry Potter* books would have been less than half the length if Harry had just gone to Dumbledore every time he was worried but it might have saved everyone else a lot of trouble.

And yet…

There was no sign of Callista; apparently she was on another mission, so it was to be Sam, Jon and me—and the blue Panda.

Before we set off, all three of us put on a dark, gossamer-soft hooded cloak, to make us less visible but not *in*visible because the one we had come to find had to be able to perceive us. We had sturdy boots that fitted beautifully and we each had what seemed to be a metal bottle of some kind of fluid that tingled when you touched it. It was nicknamed Prozac so I had a clue what it might do.

'It's pretty heavy energy down there,' said Sam. 'But even so, don't drink until we tell you to. Really, it's important.'

I nodded, half excited and half nervous. The last thing we had to do before setting off was collect Holly's soul.

She came down to us in a kind of sparkling wind and, to my surprise, asked permission to come inside of me. *Inside* of me?

'Of course,' said Jon with a grin. 'How else would you carry a soul?'

'Will it hurt?'

'Not at all. It's just a bit tingly.'

'Have you done it then?'

'No, that was hearsay. Only living humans can carry a soul inside them. We are souls who just sometimes carry a bit of human outside us.' Both he and Sam laughed. A bit of an in-joke then.

Permission given, Holly's soul slid inside me through my brow, throat and heart. She felt icy cold; not tingly at all.

'No tingle,' I said, anxiously. A quiet voice inside me said, 'Sorry,' and for a second, I thought I heard an echo. Maybe that was the tingle?

'She's still quite weak,' said Sam. 'Are you comfortable?'

'Yes, no. It's fine.'

'Quite comfortable, thank you,' said Holly in a whisper through my throat. To say it felt odd wasn't the half of it. My brain seemed to be trying to connect to a series of completely unfamiliar memories, colours and textures.

I climbed into the blue Panda and onto the back seat.

'Strap yourself in,' said Jon as he and Sam got into the front and did just that. 'It may be a bit bumpy.'

It was. We drove down a different kind of wormhole which twisted and turned and felt like crossing a cattle grid. I found myself wrapping my arms around my body to keep Holly safe inside me as if she were in danger of falling out. She felt the concern and whispered, 'thank you.' Again there was a kind of echo.

In about five minutes we were through and driving along what seemed to be a perfectly ordinary road, probably somewhere in America. That surprised me as I hadn't detected an American accent from Holly.

'This is where I lived,' she whispered inside, reading my thoughts. 'We souls speak in all languages and all accents. You hear as you are, not as we are.' Then, I did feel a tingle and it was really rather marvellous.

If it hadn't been for the fact that we started driving through houses, it would all have seemed perfectly normal. 'I'm just showing you the landscape,' said Jon. 'At this level, it's all pretty much the same as on Earth. If we only had to pick people up from this level, it would be a doddle.'

'Mostly a doddle,' said Sam. 'Do you remember...?' And he was off on some story. I probably should have listened but I was too interested in what I could see through the windows. I wished I could have sat in the front so as to see more clearly—at least I did to start with but oddly, I seemed to lose interest and found myself thinking about my head wound and what on Earth I was going to do about being a Goddamn vicar and, without realising, I sank slowly into a kind of low-grade depression.

Unexpectedly, some kind of dark, winged apparition battered on the windscreen and I jumped.

'Just a washing line,' said Jon. 'Don't panic!'

It was, too. We were driving through a back garden but now it was getting steadily darker and the Panda was definitely slowing down.

'Can you feel it, Bel?' said Sam. 'It's not you, by the way. It's outside.'

I could feel it. There was a heaviness in the air and a susurration as though thousands of people were whispering, 'It's not fair; there's nothing you can do; it's all right for *them;* what's the point? I hate them; it's all *their* fault; you don't care; why should I?' It was a huge relief to realise that it wasn't emanating from me but even so it was shockingly debilitating. I wrapped my arms around myself again, remembering Holly. I thought I could sense her weeping.

'No, I'm all right,' she whispered, but there was weeping somewhere.

'Is this hell?' I managed to say. It was like speaking through grey wool.

'No,' said Sam. 'Not yet. Take a sip of the spiritual Prozac. It's really tough the first time you come here. But make sure you put the top back on as soon as you have drunk.'

Shakily, I unscrewed the top of the bottle and drank. It was like inhaling silver light. I paused to appreciate it.

'Lid *on!*' shouted Jon as something big hit the car from the side, jolting a tiny drop of silver out of the bottle. Another jolt and I dropped the top on the floor. Another, and the car rocked.

'Bel!' Both Jon and Sam were yelling now. 'They want the Prozac. Put the top on the fucking Prozac!'

'I dropped it.' *Bang.* Something else hit the car and another few drops flew up.

'Cover it with your hand or your mouth. Hide the damn Prozac!' Sam sounded furious and I felt a searing rush of resentment. But I put the bottle to my mouth again and closed my lips around it as I leant down to scrabble for the cap. That silvery water was the elixir of life because imbibing just one more drop dissolved all resentment.

Even so, it was a huge relief when I found the top. And yet, that extra time gave Holly a chance to drink some of the water too. I could feel a thirsty soul drinking deep.

'It's back on,' I said, screwing the lid tight. 'Sorry.'

'I'm sorry, too,' said. Sam. 'I didn't mean to shout at you. It wasn't your fault.'

The banging and bumping stopped as swiftly as it had started and Jon drove on through walls and houses and gardens.

'Erm…. can't you go round by the road?'

'There isn't a road here! It's a land of memories and stasis. Not a lot of people's memories are formulated on roads. Apart from the homeless, of course and that's a whole other story… You'll see that one another day.' Jon swerved round a group of children staring vacant-eyed at a television and drove straight through their mother. 'Oops. But she won't have felt it.'

I looked back out of the rear window. The woman hadn't moved; there was a visible stream of sickly green passive-aggressive misery pouring out of her mouth towards the man who was sitting at the table behind her, black despair wrapped around him like a stole as he hunched in front of his laptop. And then they were gone.

'So, this is the land where the habitual lower self lives? Are these people conscious? Are they separated from their souls?'

'They're conscious but they're not conscious of *being* conscious. Only the soul can do that. They can't change anything, they just go around the same old circle again and again.'

'A bit like life on Earth then.'

'Well no. There's always the possibility of waking up on Earth. Agreed, most people never do it, but it *is* possible.'

'So, what *is* waking up?'

'Stepping outside the same-old, same-old,' said Sam. 'Realising that it's not *what* happens but your *response* to what happens is what creates the experiences of your life.'

'Oh, New Age stuff.' I didn't mean to sound dismissive but Sam almost snapped back.

'No! It's foundational teaching at the heart of *all* the religions before they got wound up into the controlled ego-centric versions most people know. It's self-responsibility. Consciousness. It's what the soul is *for*. Dammit, Bel! That's why you became a vicar. To teach exactly that!'

'Oh. Well, I forgot.'

'Ex-bloody-actly,' said Sam. 'Except, of course, you've got another chance now.'

I left that as it was because Holly was stirring anxiously inside me.

'Are we nearly there? Holly is agitated.'

'Yes,' said Jon. 'We're there.' He stopped the car and put the handbrake on.

We were in an open-plan house with a kitchen, a breakfast bar and a living space. A couple, probably in their thirties, were sitting watching the television. At their feet a little girl, probably about six years old, was holding tightly to a doll with long fair, curly hair, and rocking back and forward, murmuring endearments to it. The atmosphere felt both threatening and sticky.

Jon, Sam and Holly all tensed so I did, too.

The woman, a rather faded little thing with fair hair and dark roots, got up.

'I'm off upstairs then,' she said, slightly awkwardly. 'You'll put Holly to bed, then.'

Her partner grunted. The little girl turned big, frightened eyes to her mother. 'Mama...' she said.

'You be a good girl, Holly,' said the woman. 'Daddy's special little girl.'

And she left.

I was shaking. I knew exactly what this was. Holly inside me was quivering. Strangely, she too seemed to be holding the doll in her soul-arms; I could sense it.

'Bloody hell!' I said. 'She's just going to let this happen? Jesus!'

'It's same-old, same-old,' said Sam, softly. 'Here, she has absolutely no ability to stop it.'

'But we do?'

'We do. But we have to pick our moment. Trust us on this, please, Bel. We know what we're doing.'

I closed my eyes and put my fingers in my ears as the father leant down and picked up his little daughter. But I still heard her voice saying, 'please, Daddy, no. Please...'

Holly inside me was tense as a coiled wire. My heart was pounding.

'Wrap the cloak around you, Bel,' said Jon softly. 'It's time.'

He and Sam stepped out of the car. Shamefully, I kept my eyes on the ground as I climbed out of the back seat. I could hear whimpering and grunting but I didn't want to know; I didn't want to know.

Jon and Sam held my hands so we moved in a kind of circle.

'Trinity,' whispered Sam. 'Trinity. Just say it. It has power.'

'Trinity, Trinity, Trinity,' I muttered.

Somehow, we half-passed through the man and the little girl so we were surrounding them. Still I kept my eyes shut but nothing could shut out the sound, nor the urgent, erotic energy. I felt disgusted to my very soul. Holly kicked inside me like a baby in my heart.

She shot out of me just as her six-year-old self mewled like a kitten and then began to scream. Her father had finished and pushed her away and she had fallen against the lit electric fire. The smell of burning hair filled the room and, simultaneously, a bright golden-silver light exploded into the atmosphere and a tall, shining woman stood before the man and snatched up the screaming child.

'Holly!' she said in searing tones. 'I'm here. This stops now. I have you.' And she gathered up the little body, pulling it away from the fire and wrapping it in all-loving arms.

The little girl began to sob and sob. But she put her arms around her saviour and the sobs of pain were mingled with those of relief. I saw a pale shadow around them and realised, with a jump of my heart, that it was their guardian angel. It could only connect with them when they were united and now, all would be well.

'Back to the car!' Sam and Jon pulled at my hands. But I stood stock still, as a feeling of biliousness built up in my stomach. Something else was inside me; something heavy and resistant. I could feel it, eating my energy. I couldn't move.

Holly looked directly at me and then shot a flash of light into my heart, enabling me to pull my hands away from Sam and from Jon.

'No!'

'Bel!' they shouted, together. But I was driven out of the door and up the stairs, every step becoming more and more difficult until I was in the bedroom where Holly's mother lay in the bed sleeping. I felt subsumed with hatred.

'You bloody bitch!' I yelled. I wanted to hit her but my hands were too heavy. I sank down on the floor, a sudden fluttering sensation in my heart. And then I knew. Holly had smuggled her mother's soul inside her own, hoping that she could save that other lost woman too. The soul was reaching for its missing persona but it wasn't strong enough and my anger hadn't helped. A haze of hopelessness foamed around me, coating everything and dissolving all rational thought. There was nothing I could do. Out, in that atmosphere, I was locked in a cage of despair and bitter misery. My bottle of Prozac was back in the car and this world was too, too heavy.

My last conscious thought was one of being trapped, alone and lost and then the dreamtime began.

Chapter Ten

HOLLY'S MOTHER'S NAME had been Sharon and, with her soul still held (just) within mine, I dreamt her life as though it were running through my own memories. And oh, the weight... Everything was contaminated by the drabness and pain that had been Sharon's life experience. Had I had the energy I would have understood her lack of fight over her own daughter's abuse; it simply mirrored Sharon's own childhood. It was 'how things were.' There was nothing that could be done about it and the only spark of power was the anger that could be held within and the dreams of revenge—glorious revenge—that could be fantasised over. In Sharon's life, too, was the bitterness of unanswered prayer. Her father had been a church-going Christian and, every week, she would pray and pray and pray for deliverance which never came. Who would not give up on a God like that?

And yet, even in the depths of that never-ending horror, I saw the moments when a kind neighbour enquired, her teachers looked at her with questions in their eyes, her friends asked her what was wrong. But it was 'our little secret.' Children don't reveal those little secrets so Sharon never spoke out. And who can blame her? In the time between telling and whatever the social services equivalent over there might have been had started to investigate, she would still have lived at home and faced the possibility of being beaten, even killed by her father.

Cycles within cycles within cycles creating a living hell for hundreds, no, thousands, no, millions of men and women and children and animals. Hell without end.

But this is hindsight. I felt it all but I couldn't view it with consciousness. It was just a spiral of hopelessness and betrayal, dotted through with re-ignited grief and fury at the death of my own parents. I was aware that this was, somehow, being drawn out of me to be fed on by something dark and dangerous at the bottom of this land which was trying to claim me too.

And yet… Somehow, my soul still existed. A sliver of light, still holding the other tiny, fading soul and trying to protect it. How, I don't know but occasionally I felt strength flowing in. I half-heard Jon's voice: 'Bel, we have to get Holly back. But we will come and fetch you. I promise. We will come back.'

I didn't believe him. He would abandon me just as Sharon had been abandoned.

No, I was here. She wasn't abandoned.

I half-felt the shadow Sharon, the one who lived in this land, woken sharply by her partner. Some energy shift had occurred and he was angry and confused. Hazily, my mind remembered that Holly's soul and shadow had left so he had nothing to abuse any more. Apart from Sharon.

He was conciliating at first. He wanted her to tell him where their daughter had gone. He wanted her to reassure him that she hadn't told anyone. He wanted to know that he was still safe.

I felt her terror of him; remembered his violence towards her. Remembered her brief relief, years before, that someone seemed to love her; remembered her offering the only thing she knew that a man wanted and her later horror at the realisation that she was pregnant and trapped. *That* had been the pivotal point at which she had given in completely. She was so pathetically grateful that he wanted to stay with her, 'to give it a go' even though she knew already what lay ahead. It was just too hard to walk away, to be an unemployed single mother; to risk the shame, to risk the streets. And I understood. This pathetic apology of safety in a relationship was all she had.

In that moment of compassion, I heard rustling. Rustling? Rustles? There was something to do with rustles. My mind and heart were searching for something to do with rustles.

It persisted and it gave my consciousness something to focus on. Something to lift me out of this hell.

Rus-el!

I cried out with all my strength and the world turned scarlet as blood and fire exploded all around me.

90

*

I woke in my own bed. The Gladiator stood in the corner of the room, hand on the hilt of a sheathed sword. When he saw I was awake, he nodded to me and dissolved into the ether.

Dear God! How had I got back? What had happened to Sharon's soul? Did Jon know I was safe or were he and Sam searching for me in that God-forsaken land?

I reached out, blearily, for the bedside clock. It was seven o'clock. At least the Parish Council wouldn't be knocking on the door quite yet.

I turned onto my back, assessing. Part of me hoped that it just been a dream. No, it was real. Shit. What did I do now?

I staggered to the bathroom for a pee and looked, unimpressed, at my reflection in the mirror as I washed my hands. The dressing on my head had fallen off and, when I reached up to touch my scalp, I felt the fuzz of the re-growing hair. Probing gently, I couldn't find any pain, so that was good and, if I was lucky, my shoulder-length straight hair would fall over the wound point, at least partially disguising it.

I found myself smiling at my vanity at that moment and rediscovered that I had dimples.

Then I saw the image in the mirror behind me. Shock kicked in but, before I could panic, a gentleness touched me. I turned but there was nothing there. Back to the mirror and, yes, an echo of an image. A female of some kind. It didn't feel threatening but even so...

'You are?' I said.

'Hero,' she replied. 'You know me. Guardian.' A frisson of shock and recognition ran through me. I had named my childhood invisible friend Hero but I had long forgotten her. Somehow, I knew this was both that Hero *and* the being who saved me from that shark in Australia.

'Safe. Sharon is safe,' she whispered. 'Jon is safe. Sam is safe.'

'You were real?'

She just smiled and I realised that guardians speak even less than church angels. Hero never had during my childhood. I had just started forming her from sacred stories a few years after my parents died. She was someone who helped me get my toys out and play with them. I sometimes called her 'Mummy' by mistake when she held me in her arms like my mother had. She was company that didn't expect anything of me; didn't say 'don't cry,' as so many adults did (even Jon sometimes). I knew she was called Hero because she told me. And she was clear that it was 'hero' and not 'heroine.'

Had I always been this fey? I hesitated to use the word 'psychic,' it had too many connotations of contacting the dead. And then, of course, I almost fell over laughing because I'd done pretty much nothing else but contact the dead for the last couple of nights.

Hero smiled at me in the mirror and faded away. Of course, I turned again to look for her but there was nothing.

I felt blessed and peaceful which was just what was needed because, this day, I was going to have to do some vicaring.

I showered and dressed in a clerical shirt and dark trousers. Imposter syndrome hit me like a 4x4 but that was the least of my potential problems that morning.

I was hungry but headed over to the church before breakfast. I wanted to see the damage to the altar in daylight so that I could at least say that I had seen it and maybe make vaguely intelligent comments.

The church door was unlocked. Good grief, what now?

I stepped in and will be perpetually grateful that someone had oiled both the lock and the hinges because the first thing I saw was Lucie standing in front of the almost-reconstructed altar. She was waving her arms gracefully and the stone and cloth and gold were obeying her.

I must have made a sound because she turned, startled—and looked straight through me.

And I mean straight through me. She didn't see me at all. A crease appeared between her beautiful brown eyes and then she turned back to the job in hand.

WTF? Simultaneously came the knowledge that I had said 'good grief' and that I must now be invisible. Really? This was just too surreal… And what was I supposed to do next? I didn't know

92

how long invisibility would last and I didn't want to be appearing suddenly out of nowhere.

And what the hell was going on with this beautiful assistant? Wasn't there *anyone* normal any more? I watched open-mouthed as she waved her arms one more time and the altar was whole again.

Now I really was in a quandary. Had 'the vicar' actually seen the altar before it was restored? Was I supposed to believe it had never been damaged? What did I say? What did I do?

There's a very good adage that telling the truth is always the simplest way because then you don't get your stories mixed up but it wasn't going to work this time. 'I know the altar exploded because I was there and you couldn't see me because the church angel and I were invisible' simply wouldn't cut it.

Except, of course, it might with Lucie. Presumably she was one of us? Maybe she was here because of the 'bad man,' which I presumed was Mr. Tortoise.

But then, it struck me that angelic doesn't actually distinguish between genders. It could just as well have been 'bad human' and my assumption that it meant male. And Lucie is incredibly close to 'Lucifer.'

I'd never believed in the devil. But it's not as though nearly all my beliefs have been proved to be utterly wrong lately, is it? When you actually meet something it's hard to keep disbelieving in it. I'd always thought that the legend of Lucifer was just a story and like all great stories, it had a message: that evil will present itself as goodness and as beauty if it can't beguile you with power.

I slipped out of the church as silently as I could and ran back to the house.

Tea. Tea was the thing. I found my hands were shaking as I filled the kettle.

I had made pretty creditable cinnamon French toast in perfect time for when Lucie rang the doorbell.

It was only as I opened the door that I remembered that I was invisible.

Damn.

'Hello,' she said. 'I hope I'm not calling too early?'

Phew. Mental note: invisibility lasts for a maximum of half an hour.

I welcomed her in, invited her to join me for breakfast and asked if she were vegetarian. If not, I could happily fry some bacon. She said she was a veggie but not vegan and she would be delighted to join me. Her laugh wasn't quite as musical as I expected but I guess 100% perfection can't be guaranteed all the time whether you're a human or a demon.

I set myself on 'willing to be enchanted' mode. I hadn't remembered that I had got one until that moment but I have and it's incredibly useful. It laughs and listens and makes all the appropriate responses while a watcher observes carefully.

And she *was* enchanting. She asked how I was, told me how lovely the house was and complimented the front garden. She chuckled when I told her that I had no memory of doing any of it and might well have a cleaner and a gardener who would show up out of the blue—and how much I was starting to enjoy having haphazard memory lapses as I was getting so many interesting surprises.

'Surprises keep you awake, don't they?' I said. 'It's all too easy to get lost in habitual thinking. I can't say I like all the surprises I've had but some of them have been utterly delightful.'

'Such as?' she asked, seemingly genuinely interested.

'Oh, that I still have a head full of wonderful recipes from my mother's books. That I am meeting so many people for the first time—again.' And I told her that I suspected I'd agreed to Christen my ex-husband's daughter without even realising who he was. 'Perhaps if we all lost our memories on a regular basis, the world would be a far more forgiving place,' I said.

'Well that's a sermon!' she said. 'And yet, surely there are things we shouldn't forget?'

'Well, yes, of course. The big stuff, obviously, wars and discrimination and faith and all that,' I said. 'But I didn't mean those. Personal relationships could often do with a re-boot. You might just remember what made you love the other person in the first place.'

'And did you?' she asked? 'I mean, did he seem attractive?'

'Er... no, not really. Rather the opposite. But I don't suppose

I'm still the same person as the one who fell in love with him. I didn't feel that pull, if you know what I mean.'

'Oh yes, I do.' She had an impish smile and, if I hadn't been tired, nervous and watching myself, I think I would have fallen in love with her.

'So, tell me about you, Lucie. If you're my new assistant, I'd like to know something, obviously. Apart from anything else, you've got a big burden on you being with a rector with a spotty memory. I don't even know why Robbie left but it's incredibly bad timing. He knew everyone just like I did. He could really have helped.'

'I don't know either,' she said. 'I'd just got back from six months travelling the world with some friends and had started looking for a new parish and I got the call out of the blue.'

'From the Archdeacon?' I prompted.

'Yes. I've not met the bishop yet. Is he nice?'

'He is. Very nice. Well, I like him.'

'I'm delighted. That helps. I didn't get on all that well with my last bishop—or rector either, I'm afraid. I hope that doesn't make you immediately think I'm a troublemaker.'

'Why would it? These are crazy days for Christianity. There are all differing levels of beliefs and views, especially about women and homosexuality let alone the concept of a Universal Christ.'

The words came out automatically; I seemed to know what I was saying and I certainly knew that I believed in a Universal Christ. I filed that away for investigation later.

'Oh yes, thank you. My last parish was a little bit old-fashioned. And there were some lovely gay people who just felt *so* excluded. St. Paul has a lot to answer for sometimes. Oh! I hope you don't mind my saying that!'

'No, of course not. But we can read Paul very differently nowadays if we understand the society he lived in and, of course, if we can read him in the nearest we can get to the original Greek. They didn't even have a *word* for homosexual one-to-one relationship in those days. Male rape was a power issue. In Romans 1, he just talks of 'unnatural acts' and makes them no worse than gossip or being rude to your parents. And we don't even know who wrote *1 Timothy* but it certainly wasn't Paul.'

I knew exactly what I was talking about. Exactly *how* I knew what I was talking about was another matter.

'Oh yes! I do wish I knew as much as you do. I've read *Mother of God*, of course. It was a real thrill to be posted here with you!'

Memory flickered. Oh good gr—good Lord! (phew, that was close) I'd written a book. That was a nice boost to my ego… However, fun as all this was, there was still the elephant in the room. It was really rather a large one, covered in mud and it was about to start trumpeting.

I started cautiously.

'Where did you stay last night, in the end?'

'At the church house. It was fine. I don't know what all the fuss was about. It's a bit basic-boy, of course, but I'll soon sort that out!'

Hmmm. No clues there.

'Did they lead you to think you would be living here?'

'Um. Not *living*, no. But they thought it might be a good idea if I stayed while you made a full recovery.'

'Ah, so they *did* know I'd had an accident then.'

'Oh! Yes, I think so. I can't think of any other reason they'd want you not to be alone. Can you?'

I thought I probably could, but who knew?

The elephant loomed nearer. I ignored it. Let's see if she had anything to say. She had.

'Have you been into the church today?'

'No. I thought it best to wait.'

'Oh good. You see…'

I waited with great interest while she appeared to search for words.

'They—we—rather exaggerated the destruction, last night, I'm afraid. I think some youngsters must just have got in and thrown some things around. They made it look as though the altar itself had been damaged quite a lot more than it was. I've just been there and, once I'd put the altar cloth back on and replaced the cross and candles and put away the kneelers (they're grey on one side; look a lot like stone in the dark, don't they?) it's fine.'

'Oh. Weren't the police going to be called? That was very kind of you but it rather removed the evidence, didn't it?'

'Gosh, I didn't even think of that! Oh, I am so stupid! I just couldn't bear to see it in such a mess! It was instinctive.'

I noted that she did rather like her exclamation marks.

'Oh… but there is one thing. The big garnet in the centre of the cross *is* missing! I couldn't find it. I do hope it's just hidden under something. We could have a better look later?'

I wondered how she knew that it was a garnet that was missing.

'Well, I'm very glad to hear that it's not as bad as everyone thought,' I said, innocently. 'And perhaps we could do with some more colourful kneelers. Let's go over after we've finished our tea and take another look, shall we? I wonder how they got in? Oh, come to think of it, how did *you* get in?'

'It wasn't locked,' she said, swiftly. 'I assumed you'd unlocked it.'

'Curiouser and curiouser. Must have been one of the others then. I assume it *was* locked when you left last night?'

'I think so. I don't think I really noticed, to be honest.'

We sat in silence, finishing our tea. I looked as innocuous and bland as I could. Lucie tried to do the same but it was impossible. She shone.

So, the beautiful, tall and elegant girl and the short, knackered, dimension-travelling and slightly bemused vicar walked out into the autumn sunshine, through the wicket gate into the graveyard and across to the beautiful Norman building. I took the church key, in case the door was locked, which it was. Lucie didn't seem to notice so I said nothing. Whether she was on the side of the angels or the demons, this was either a pretty powerful mage or a piss-poor liar. My money was on both.

The morning sun streamed in through the rose window over the altar, gilding the lovely little church with pale gold. Lucie sighed.

'It's so beautiful, isn't it?' she said. 'My first church was a modern one in Portsmouth. A great place but very 1960s.'

'It is very special,' I agreed. 'And set on the crossing of the Michael and Mary ley lines. There will have been another place of ritual or worship here long before this building existed. The land remembers.'

'Mmmm. I'm not sure I'm on board with ley lines.'

'You mean mystical lines in the landscape as opposed to an imaginary Holy Spirit?'

'Well, if you put it like that… but the Holy Spirit *isn't* imaginary.'

I sighed. 'To imagine simply means 'to picture to yourself.' And the original Greek of 'mystical' means 'the hidden things.'

'Orthodox Christianity covers up so much of the original marvels, the perennial wisdom that has existed longer than time. As St. Basil said, 'a whole day would not be long enough for me to go through all the unwritten mysteries of the church.''

Good Lord, I really *was* a minister and, what's more, one with the potential to be a colossal bore. This stuff, I guess, is lodged in a different part of the brain from the mundane memory and it was certainly a step too far for the everyday vicar because she ignored me. 'There,' said Lucie, turning my attention to the altar. 'Look!'

I contemplated the altar. It looked just like an altar should look, apart from the hole in the cross where the garnet cabochon had been and, to be honest, I only noticed that because she had drawn my attention to it.

The rood screen was still open and the lock was unharmed. That had been me, of course, but it was going to look strange if/ when any police showed up. But what the hell, no one was going to believe the truth anyway. I was in it (whatever it was) up to my neck. All I could do was roll with the punches, try and remember what I'd said and bluff my way through to whatever happened next.

At which point, I noticed that Ariel wasn't there.

Are you hiding? I asked inside my head.

'Why would I be hiding?' said Lucie.

We stared at each other for a breathless moment and then tried to pretend that nothing had happened. Suddenly, Lucie's face didn't seem quite so beautiful.

The garnet, said Hero, in my head.

'Did I say that out loud?' I said. 'I was talking to the garnet.'

A second of uncertainty passed and then Lucie laughed. 'You are funny,' she said. 'Fancy thinking it was hiding!'

If it was, I couldn't blame it.

Chapter Eleven

I WAS BEGINNING to understand why Harry Potter got into quite so many scrapes. What would have happened if I'd simply told Lucie the truth, that I was talking to an angel, that I was there when the altar exploded and that I saw her put it back together?

Not going to happen.

'So, are we meeting the Parish Council here or somewhere else?' I said, instead. 'I don't think they'll exactly feel welcome at my place.'

'Um. Here, in the church. At least that's what Mr. Phillips said last night. So that they could examine the damage properly.'

'We'd better find that cabochon then.'

We searched high and low and I kept an eye out for Ariel. Was it Lucie she was avoiding? Was Lucie the 'bad man'? Finally, I looked under the Lady Chapel altar and, sure enough, there was an angel hiding there.

I made the universally understood FFS? gesture and she mimed *shhh* and held out the garnet. I thought I felt a slight tingle as it dropped into the palm of my hand but I could have been mistaken.

I stood up, allowing the altar cloth to drop and then acted out spotting something on the floor under a pew. I'm not really sure why, but then, you don't want people thinking that angels hide under altars, do you?

'Here it is!' I bent down as if to pick it up and took it over to the cross where Lucie joined me, all of her sparkling with exclamation marks of delight.

The garnet slotted neatly into the space and then fell out again.

'Are you allowed to glue precious stones?' I asked, perplexed, catching it before it rolled off the altar.

'I don't know! But at least we've found it.'

At that point the Parish Council arrived.

I suppose I'd better stop calling them that, firstly because very few such entities deserve capital letters and secondly, they were probably five perfectly reasonable human beings. Probably.

Understandably there was a lot of milling around and confusion at first because they were all quite certain that they had seen a lot of damage the previous night. But when it comes to the crunch, most human beings believe what's in front of their eyes *now* and Lucie was profuse in her apologies for putting it all back together again. 'I just couldn't bear to see the altar profaned,' she said.

We all poked around the structure for a while but couldn't see any problems apart from the garnet which, apparently, *could* be glued and Colin Phillips (Tortoise Man) offered to sort that out for me.

'If you would, Colin,' I said. 'And I'll bless the altar with holy water when it's done.'

'Holy water? That's a bit high church isn't it?' said Diana Henderson (Angst-Ridden Lady) but I was so excited at the fact that I remembered the recipe for holy water that I wasn't going to rise to that bait.

The other three councillors were David Jackson (Aristocratic Nose Man), Joe Cartwright (Friendly, Ruddy-Faced Man) and Sara Cummings (Rather Jolly Redhead with the more unusual spelling of Sara-pronounced-Sarah).

I asked if they would like to come back to the house for coffee/tea and the meeting. David and Diana put on 'oh so it's all right *now* is it?' expressions and I hastily added, 'unless we can meet somewhere else? I'm afraid that's the kind of thing you will have to help me out on. It's my short-term memory that's affected, not the long-term one.'

It turned out that we often used the church hall, a small and dumpy building on the other side of St. Raphael's, which had a meeting room and an open area for village events and Sunday School. Sara went straight to the kitchen and put the kettle on and Lucie helped her put out cups and saucers that looked as if they had been in workhorse service for more than forty years.

There were Jammie Dodger biscuits and those thick fingers of alleged shortbread which would be fine if they'd just call them something else. My paternal grandmother gave me a recipe for Scottish shortbread which melts in your mouth. Oh, I am so glad I remember that! Cornflour is the secret—it makes all the difference in the world.

Lucie didn't have any biscuits because we had just had breakfast. 'Reverend Amabel cooked the most wonderful cinnamon toast!' I had biscuits. Obviously.

We sat there for nearly two hours with very bad tea (note to self: get better quality tea bags for the church hall and hang the cost) and thrashed things out. It turned out that I wasn't just a vicar, I was the Rector of a group of churches. There were a couple of other, older vicars around—mostly retired—who helped out and we had a group of readers who took services when they, or I, couldn't.

So that explained how I could have such a beautiful church in such a small village. I had been wondering how on earth my wages got paid. It seemed I was in charge of seven churches, in all, within about a twenty-mile radius. No pressure there, then.

The councillors were, understandably, concerned about whether I could do my job properly without a fully operational memory. Foolishly, I asked them whether I'd been able to do the job properly *with* a fully operational memory. Sara, Joe and Colin chuckled. David (Nose) would have liked to have said, 'no' and Diana did actually say it.

'So, what's the problem?' I asked her, rather suspecting that at least one part of any completely truthful answer would have been 'this is Devon and you're really rather brown.'

You can't grow up mixed-race in a predominantly white country without these echoes of Colonialism and systemic unconscious racism creeping into life at odd intervals. I was more than blessed in that I was part of the middle class—and an academic—so I got a lot less of it than many folk my colour and probably nothing like that of my full-blood Asian, Arabic and black brothers and sisters. I once overheard my childhood friend George's mother, saying to her husband, 'but Amabel isn't *really* brown, darling,' by which she meant that I was of sufficient good breeding for my skin tone to be discounted.

Some people actually assumed that Jon had adopted me because of our ages and as our colouring were so different—and later on, some even thought that I was a child bride that he had fetched from abroad. Occasionally, we rather wickedly had some fun with both those scenarios. It is what is. I'm coffee-coloured in the still very white Western World. Mostly, I don't bother about people's views, sometimes I laugh at them and sometimes they make me feel discouraged and sad.

Today, I was simply interested in how they would get around this potential minefield.

'Well, if you really want to know, vicar,' Diana said after a noticeable pause. 'Many of us find your sermons far too radical and too ... *interfaith*. We were a comfortable congregation before you came here.'

'And how long ago did I come here?' I asked, refusing to rise to the bait.

'Two years ago, nearly three,' said Colin. 'You have certainly been a much-needed breath of fresh air and that's often uncomfortable for our more established members.' One in the eye for Diana there! She bristled.

'"I come not to bring peace, but a sword,"' I quoted, gently, again slightly impressed at how much I knew. 'The world doesn't need any more dying Christianity. Congregations are dropping like flies. "Comfortable" means stasis and anything in stasis will die.'

'You sound like the Bishop,' said Diana, sniffily.

'Good,' I said. 'Now. Why did Robbie leave? While I'm delighted to welcome Lucie, an experienced assistant is what's needed right now. Can we get him back just for a week or so to keep things on an even keel?'

'Oh, I don't think so,' said Diana. 'Reverend Cole was found with his fingers in the till.'

'Diana!' That was Tortoi—sorry, Colin.

'Nothing was proved,' said Colin. 'But there had been... irregularities. Reverend Robbie was... well, his face simply didn't fit.'

I wasn't going to get any further than that for the moment.

'He came to see me in hospital,' I said. 'That was kind of him. I'd appreciate his new contact details; I may need to ask him a few things.'

'You take your time,' Colin reached out and patted my hand. I hadn't realised that I was flicking my middle finger with my thumb, a sign that I was feeling stressed. His gesture wasn't patronising, rather meant to comfort. 'Apart from communion on Sunday morning, there's nothing you need to do for the rest of this week other than getting your bearings back. If you're up to doing communion, it might be a good way of getting back on the horse.'

'I love the analogy,' I said, laughing. 'Yes, I'm sure I'll be happy to get back on the horse.'

And, strangely, I knew that I would. I was almost excited about the prospect. Odd, really, but then I was a vicar. I must like *some* of the proper vicaring at least. It couldn't all be about haring around in the shadowlands.

From there, we got down to the real parish business which made it obvious that vanishing, memory-loss, slightly-too-brown vicars were simply a minor inconvenience. What *really* mattered was pews.

Pews, you might think, have been a fixture in churches since the beginning but no, until the Catholic Reformation, people didn't sit down in churches or, if they did, they sat on chairs or on the floor. Mostly they milled around staring at the stained-glass pictures. It's entirely possible that pews didn't really become a thing until parishioners got bored enough by sermons to start falling asleep. Pre-Reformation, sermons really weren't much of a thing but post-Reformation they became long and intense and probably terminally boring.

The first pews were all posh boxes where the aristocracy sat. I expect the *hoi polloi* were still milling or, if they were lucky, they had a backless bench.

Having a box was serious kudos in those days; it was all about being seen *not* to be seen. You swanned up the aisle to your high-walled pew box and then could pretty well do what you wanted .

without anyone spotting you. It was probably fairly important for one member of the family to stay awake—probably the maiden aunt who lived in the attic—so that they could poke anyone who was actually snoring.

You paid rent for your closed box pew which was good income for churches and I can't recall how that practice died out; frankly, I'm amazed I can remember any of it. But the point was that St. Mary's down the road has had the utter nerve to suggest removing the pews so they could use the church for different events, including a version of Shakespeare's *Twelfth Night*.

This was Not On for the councillors. Pews, you would have thought, were sacrosanct, Norman and vital to the health and well-being of every church.

Oddly, it seemed that it would be all right to erect a stage *over the top* of the pews—at substantial cost—but the pews themselves must not be attacked by any modernist, sacrilegious heretic. If one church gave in, the pestilence would spread everywhere! Over their dead bodies was the only way that was going to happen in this series of parishes.

Almost as bad was the leaving of a quarter of St. Raphael's, St. Mary's and St. Saviour's churchyards unmown to encourage wildlife. It was 'messy' and 'objectionable' and 'someone visiting a grave might fall over.' Yes, but if I remember correctly (and oh joy, I do), the wildlife part of all three graveyards is where the occupants are all more than a hundred years old. If anyone's visiting their great great grandmother regularly, perhaps they need to get a bit of a life? Luckily, I didn't say that out loud and Lucie seemed, currently, not to be reading my mind.

There was also quite a spirited debate about whether anyone had contacted the police about the damaged altar. Technically someone should have but, as Lucie had put it back together— oops, sorry, it wasn't badly damaged in the first place—there was no evidence. Riot Acts were read about leaving the church unlocked, assuming that one of us had done just that. I considered mentioning the old rule of sanctuary: that a church should be kept open so fugitives and those in need could find refuge there but, wisely, I kept shtum.

Of such stuff is the life of the parish councillor. I ate a lot more biscuits than I intended in order to pass the time, was more tactful than I wanted to be and tried not to roll my eyes at any of it.

What was fascinating to me was which memories were returning and which were not. It seemed to be a complete hotchpotch. During the discussion as to who should replace our last, now deceased, member of the council, I couldn't identify any of the possible candidates so I spent that time wondering if I could remember any church services. I know vicars generally read them but I'm a linguist; surely some of it would have gone in? I could remember the words of the exorcism, after all, and they were in Latin.

Once we had finished and I'd declined to join any of them for lunch (too many biscuits turned out to be a great excuse), I made my way back to the church.

Carefully, I locked the door behind me and looked for Ariel. She was still under the altar.

Why?

She intimated that she was unable to move until her purpose was re-established. It was an inexplicable-to-humans angel thing.

If I say communion, would that do it?

Yes.

Okay, I'm going to give it a go.

I found my robes in the vestry, surprised to see that I wore a white alb, not a black cassock with a white frilly tent on top. Perhaps the Church had staggered into a new century then?

I took some communion wafers and poured a little wine into the silver chalice I found in a cupboard and, with a service book under one arm, went up to the altar. I ignored the table below the rood screen where the priest faced the people. It might well be the done thing to face the congregation but I knew I wasn't going to do it. I would face the altar, leading the congregation to God, not blocking their view.

And yet...

No, not the main altar. Not the one that exploded and then fitted back together. I would say communion in the Lady Chapel.

I lit the candles there and, opening the service book, haltingly

I began the words of the communion service, finding that I did remember them amazingly clearly.

And as I spoke, the angels came.

First, Ariel was upright again, this time in the corner of the Lady Chapel, and then a few other presences seemed to arrive like vertical plumes of soft light. But the big one came straight down from above and this was unmistakably a being of power. Pretty darn scary, to be honest.

I stopped and queried it.

Of Michael, it said. Archangel Michael, the patron of priests. Not the whole archangel, obviously, as he's about the size of the sun and one exploding altar a week is more than sufficient. Just 'Of Michael.'

It said nothing else; just waited for me to continue.

I ploughed on.

The communion service, in its earliest remembered form of the Tridentine Mass, followed a sacred ritual of rising up that is believed to date back to the Last Supper. Some theologians actually place it before the first century, as far back as the First Temple of the Hebrews, and suggest that the Christian ritual was a return to this ancient rite. The Church of England version is pretty watered down, considering, but still, it has been used for centuries and momentum builds up. It just works. Maybe it works because angels attend it?

I could observe, as I spoke the sacred words, how very well it works. I have no idea if I had sensed that before, in the same way I was experiencing it now, but as I spoke and, as the well-known and well-loved words wove themselves together, the angelic presences brightened and began to sing in harmony. It was glorious.

At the moment of the sanctification of the bread, the Christ Spirit flowed down to the altar as the Dew of Heaven, flooding out in a colour that tasted like silk and velvet and I knew it was all true. I knew in the depth of my being that God loves things by becoming them; that Christ was, is and will be; that this was a portal to Grace and, simultaneously, that there were many other portals that Christ would use also where people knew him by another name.

'Holy, Holy, Holy, Lord God Almighty,' I sang as the angels accompanied me in paeans of joy. Glory flamed across the altar and throughout the church and that dry, tasteless offering and the cheap communion wine were transformed into pure spirit; not the physical body of Jesus but the eternal body of Christ in all power and mercy.

Okay... *now* I knew why I was a vicar.

After the Mass was over and the angels, apart from Ariel, had gone, I sat down on the altar steps and remembered. I remembered quite a lot. It came in patches with huge holes torn into them but the basic story was there.

The vicar thing started after my marriage break-up. I'd been visiting Tunisia on my own; a ridiculous-seeming thing to do, really, when your heart had been broken by a Muslim to go to a Muslim country but, on the other hand, I was at least familiar with the hijab and, being fairly dark-skinned, would pass for an Arab woman so there was less chance of being hassled continually like most of the white women I saw over there.

One day, I took a tourist trip to the Grand Mosque at Kairouan simply because I was bored. In my salwar kameez with a veil covering my hair, I passed quite easily for a Muslim so, once I'd moved away from the others, I was assumed to be a pilgrim. This is one of the four great Mosques that all Muslims are encouraged to visit once in a lifetime. At that stage of my life I had no faith in particular; lazy agnostic would have summed it up best, I think, and yet something pushed me to ask if I could go into the prayer room. I washed my face, hands and feet in the fountain and waited patiently by the door until a group of young women came up and spoke to me. Ascertaining my wishes, they went to find a man (of course!) to let me in. He was doubtful but bowed to their pressure and my appropriate clothing. He opened the door for me.

How do I explain the awe that struck me as I walked into that wide-open space in which no one had done anything but pray or dust for nine hundred years? I can't. Even the word 'awe' is tainted by everyday usage now. But awe it was. I fell on my face on the floor because there was no other proper response. It was spine-chillingly extraordinary.

I've no idea how long I stayed there; I had no thoughts, only experience. Eventually, I realised I had to leave and got up onto my knees where another five minutes of colours and sounds engulfed me before I could pull myself together sufficiently to get up onto my feet.

Once I'd staggered out and looked at my watch, everyday life came back in one panicky judder and I ended up running flat out after the coach as it pulled out of the car park to leave. They had, apparently, looked everywhere for me and the tour guide was furious, not to mention the other passengers as we had another location to visit and were now late.

I didn't care; I don't think I even went more than thirty yards from the coach at the other location, whatever it may have been. I remember having a peppermint tea in a café by the car park and reassessing everything. There definitely was something bigger; something holy; something that radiated love and it was trying to communicate with me. But what was I meant to do with it?

Being entirely human and dealing with all the fallout from divorce, I did nothing. It faded away. I did return to the Mosque that Galel occasionally attended and sat with the women for one prayer session but there was nothing there that I could feel at all.

The following year, I went to Spain with a friend. We visited Cordoba and, while Gail was shopping, I dropped into the old Synagogue there. It was full of Japanese tourists so I could barely see anything. So I just sat on a stone block at the side and waited in case the crowds would clear. They did and, for just a couple of minutes, I was there alone... and it happened again. It wasn't as dramatic an experience as before; this space was muddied by the secular but, even so, I had a sense of awe so powerful you could almost cut it and eat it.

I blissed out.

The return, this time, was brutally harsh as another battalion of tourists tumbled in, all selfie-sticks and noise. I felt quite disoriented but the phrase 'this transcends all religions' stuck in my head.

From then on, I was on a "Children of the Book" pilgrimage. The Holy Spirit was in Islam and Judaism. Now I wanted to see where its abode might be in Christendom. It wasn't anywhere in Spain; it wasn't in St. Peter's, Rome; it wasn't in St. Mark's, Venice; it wasn't in Canterbury Cathedral nor in St. Paul's. The only place I ever found close to it in Christianity was a small chapel on the Lassithi Plateau in Crete. I was sitting in the shade, resting, on yet another tourist trip, but alone this time, and the local custodian of the tiniest little church I had ever seen asked if I would like to see the icons. My Greek being excellent we were able to discuss how rare this chapel was because it was full of mural icons of women. He unlocked the old wooden door and I went in. The awe was not present but the hope and yearning for it and the remembering of it was. I experienced a great feeling of desire. 'Who will return the Spirit to us?' it said.

I suppose it was a bit like that famous bit in Isaiah: 'Who shall I send?'

My reaction was swift: 'Not me! I'm no good; I'd be rubbish. I don't want to.' And then there was a strange feeling of heat throughout my body—a fire of roses is the nearest I can get to it—and I said, 'Here I am. Send me.'

It's called a vocation and it is mostly inexplicable. After all, who in their right mind would want to become a modern-day social outcast wearing a tent for work? And how can one mixed-race woman, who's rarely been to church but now wants to attend Church of England seminary where she would find more to repulse her than to attract her, change the world?

The answer is that you don't try to change the world; you do try to change you but I was too fired up to know that then. I did know that I hadn't found the Spirit in Christianity because, at heart, I hadn't believed it was there. Once I knew it could be, I was on a hot-footed quest to reveal it.

Oh, I had such pride! Something certainly happened at my ordination; there was a breathless wonder throughout but before and after, to be honest, it was uphill all the way. 'Amabel Ransom, stubborn as a stubborn thing in stubborn town,' as Jon so often said. 'Just *give up* will you?' But I wouldn't.

I became a curate in a church in south London and battled with disappointment from day one. It was such a slog! So much of it was just listening to people repeating their problems; very little inspiration or revelation. I wasn't any kind of trained counsellor; I was a linguist! I'd got depths of social and cultural knowledge to the background of the Bible that I thought would be *so* useful but nobody wanted to hear it; they just wanted me to fit in with the tribe and not rock the boat. Pride may go before a fall but it also gets a thorough kicking over a hundred cups of over-milked tea and a mouldy mini-roll.

I thought about quitting within a couple of months—that was the day of the mouldy mini-roll. I pocketed it when the lady wasn't looking because it would have broken her heart to know what she'd given me... and then she commented on my being greedy for having scoffed it so fast. I thought I couldn't bear years and years of parishioners' reiteration of habitual complaints about what life was doing to them without any interest in the concept that they might, just *might,* be the pivot point in said problems.

Of course, my pride was my own pivot point of all the problems that I was experiencing and I assuaged it by starting to write. I could bear the struggle of the daily life as long as I could let my fingers flow in the evening. I got a great book deal for *Mother of God* and my ego kept on growing. Of course people couldn't understand me on the street level. I was just *so* clever, wasn't I?

When I was fully ordained and promoted to my first church, I had such hope that when I led my first communion, the Holy Spirit would descend on me and I would be transfigured. But nothing at all like that happened. I was far too involved with my own self-aggrandization.

I won't go on. Suffice it to say, I became a successful vicar but a sad, depressed and lonely one. If Bishop Paul hadn't seen some untapped potential for humility in me and hadn't drawn me in to the Work, God knows what would have happened.

There had to be some reason why he had but, for the life of me, I couldn't remember it. That memory hole was still empty.

And as for the car crash (or whatever it was), well what Grace! Dying brought me to my senses, not my intellect. Instead of the proud, successful imposter vicar, I became a cracked vessel, knowing nothing and knowing that I knew nothing and that was why I could see angels; the energy of a broken or somehow lowered person who is simply holding together with nothing much to give is a type of spiritual archetype for transformation. It was also why this true first communion had worked for me. As both Rumi and Leonard Cohen wrote, it's through the cracks that the light can come in. Unrealising, and uncertain, I had, for the first time in all my ministry, stood humble, truthful and naked before God.

The rules are that you can store the sanctified bread but have to finish off all the wine. As I'd been a tad too generous with the appalling vinegar-vintage that I was henceforth determined to restock with a nice Shiraz, I was also just a tiny bit drunk.

Chapter Twelve

BOTH THE BISHOP and the doctors were quite right about the returning memory being haphazard—I'd go so far as to say seriously clunky—but, post communion, I did at least have quite a few more important patches of myself back.

But when you've had a mind wide open to wondering what you *might* think about things, finding out what you *do* think can be quite a shock and I wasn't sure I liked myself very much.

You might assume that, after that revelatory and alcoholic communion, I'd be blissed out in prayer or meditation for the rest of the day but, instead, I did what the modern person does more often than not in such cases. I went and retrieved my mobile phone from its hiding place at the back of one of my dressing table drawers.

I did that without even thinking; I simply remembered. You see, I hadn't taken it with me when I went to help Celeste with the dark power in her parish because we already knew that there was opposition brewing and a mobile phone is one of the easiest ways to trace people. It was scary to realise that the dark energy problem was the same both sides of the veil between life and death but the least I could do was continue to try to be part of the solution.

As might be expected, the phone battery was flat so I set it to charge via my computer (things were suddenly *so* much easier now I remembered what all those leads were for). However, some semblance of sanity made me go and put the kettle on the moment the phone was plugged in. I knew that once it had started up, there would be a cascade of pings and I'd be on our *WhatsApp* group and that would be the rest of the day gone. A mug of tea was the least that would require.

I remembered that there were nineteen of us in the group, exchanging information and stories and working to release earthbound souls. I'm rubbish at it, to be honest and, even if I weren't, I'd be an absolute beginner compared with Nigel, who's cleared battlefields of lost soldiers or Louise, who's a hospice chaplain in a hospice without a chapel.

'It's now called a "peace room",' she said at the first meeting I attended. 'The chapel was the pathway that the dying used to use whatever their faith or none. But now it's clogged up with political correctness. You think I'm joking? There's a *lot* wrong with religion but churches, temples, synagogues and the like all have their angels and angels know how to get a soul through.'

It would appear that politically correct peace rooms, and the like, where there's no prayer pattern or ritual lose their angels faster than I can finish off a packet of Jaffa Cakes.

I had enjoyed the meetings even though I was the most sceptical one. Earthbound souls and exorcisms had still seemed more like fantasy to me. But having had invisible friends as a child and breathtaking experiences in Mosques and Synagogues it was good to be with other Christians who would acknowledge both—and more—as viable experiences. So much of Christianity is locked down in Jesus instead of being liberated by Christ. We worship him (which he never asked us to do) instead of following in his footsteps (which he *did* ask us to do); we turned him into a mere religion, excluding those who didn't believe what we believed, instead of a journey towards union for us all.

Those kind of statements can get you in a lot of trouble if you're a vicar which, if you think about it even for a moment, is ridiculous. Sometimes I wonder if *any* Christians actually read the Gospels. Being a linguist and an historian, I tend to read the Bible in the old languages—but the world is full of something called *the Mandela Effect* where whole groups and societies of people are absolutely sure something was said or written when it never was. Religion is a prime mover in that. The lion never lies down with the lamb, for example, in the Book of Isaiah. It's quite clearly a wolf, but *everyone* thinks it's a lion. And everyone seems to think that Jesus requires us to worship him.

It's mostly Rome's fault; the Emperor Constantine took a religion that focused on the poor and the needy, on shared meals, love and healing, changed Jesus into Jupiter and made it a religion for people who wanted to be right and who loved going to war.

So, anyway, there I was with a spotty-partially-restored memory; more than two hundred and fifty unopened emails and God knows how many messages about to come in on *WhatsApp*. What else could I possibly do but put my jeans and sweatshirt on, take my cup of tea out into the garden and do some weeding?

Just that one decision probably saved everything.

Jon joined me in the garden. There's this weird reality/non-reality thing that I can't even begin to explain in that he drove up to the house in the blue Panda, parked outside and was corporeally real enough for a next-door neighbour to say to him, 'If you're looking for the vicar, she's in the garden at the back. Side door'll be open.'

The neighbour didn't seem to notice when Jon walked through it.

Note to self: I must have a word with that neighbour. A vicar in the garden should be allowed to remain undisturbed in the garden. Firstly, because she may be hiding, secondly because she may actually have gardening to do and thirdly because she might have to share Jaffa Cakes.

'It's ineffable,' Jon said every time I queried something weird like the neighbour being able to see him. I could sometimes give it a whole load of effs but I digress.

We debriefed about the events of last night and I was momentarily chuffed when Jon was impressed that I seemed to have my own protective angel capable of diving into the shadowlands and taking me home.

'Bloody hell, Bella,' he said. 'That's amazing and awful simultaneously.'

'How so?'

'It's amazing that you've got your own personal aspect of Samael and awful that you're obviously going to need one. They don't get assigned willy-nilly, you know.'

He was astoundingly unhelpful about exploding altars, angels hiding and beautiful vicars who were capable of reassembling said shattered altars and possibly reading minds.

'I'm sorry but I have no remit in these lands anymore,' he said. 'They are none of my business and I can't explain anything that goes on here.'

'But you're here now. And you were talking to me about our life together.'

'Only because of the spiritual connection with you; because of the work we're doing and because we share actual memories. I'm here now so you know that we got Holly safely back and that we did come back for you but you'd already gone. We were a bit miffed about that for a moment. But let's face it, you couldn't exactly tell us and we were so grateful you were okay.'

'Was it my fault, Jon?'

'No, absolutely not. It was your first time there and you were carrying a cosmic hitchhiker—you did absolutely fine. I'm just sorry we didn't spot Sharon's soul in Holly. But you die and learn.'

We discussed how a soul, which I'd thought was pure and incapable of deception or hiding stuff, had managed to sneak another soul down into the shadowlands.

Turns out that was pretty ineffable too. Apparently our next task would be to retrieve the mother and—oh the resistance I felt to this!—the father too.

'Radical Grace,' said Jon.

'What?' I said, accidentally stabbing an onion seedling with the trowel.

'Where religion gets it wrong—*all* religion,' said Jon. 'Grace is. No matter how good or evil you may be, Grace is. Everyone who is open to it can receive Grace and it's our job to ensure that souls have that option.'

'Even Hitler?'

'Even Hitler. However, to receive Grace, the soul has to be open to it and some souls are so damaged that it could take most of eternity for them to be able to perceive it.'

'I can see people would have a problem with that, even so.'

'They do. The human mind-set is still locked into the eye-for-an-eye retribution system. It wants punishment, not Grace.

And you know what's worse? Until he can perceive Grace—and through it, perceive from his own soul the enormity of what he did (and that will be no picnic, believe me)—Hitler's damaged soul is being cared for by the souls of people he murdered.'

'You are kidding me!'

'No, that's part of the perception of hell that he's going through; that those he judged as being inhuman are the ones showing him love now.'

'My God, they must have worked on the forgiveness.'

'Yes. They are admirable. But not all of those who have suffered so terribly have been able to do that—as you saw last night. The tragedy is that having experienced cruelty, despair, horror, a lot of humans are so wounded that they can't forgive and the darkness is perpetuated.'

'Bloody hell, Jon.' I stopped digging and rested back on my heels. 'That *is* tough.'

'Yes. It's *all* about resonance. What you resonate with. And if the soul and the ego are separated, it's incredibly hard to move on. But moving on is where the joy lies.'

'I find it hard to believe that Hitler even had a soul.'

Jon sighed. 'I know. His soul was laden with darkness. I gather it is still incredibly damaged. I have no idea how it separated from his shadow when he died but it did. He's now experiencing hell on two levels simultaneously. I can't explain it but it's still going to be a long time before that work of reunification can begin.'

'Did you have problems when you died?' I was really curious now.

'Not a lot. Some residual guilt, some angst about being gay. You know I never really had any religious belief but that part was wired in. Remember, when I was born, male homosexuality was still illegal, let alone making allowance for the Church's stance on it.

'But in my case—as with the majority, thank God—I was more curious at what had happened; *was* happening. That death wasn't the end.'

'Um… and have you seen… er… have you…' I tailed off. But Jon is Jon and he knows me well.

'Have I seen God? Have I seen Jesus? Have I seen Buddha or Mohammed?'

'Yes,' I was grateful he understood.

'Nope. As Sam would say, they are all well above my pay grade.' Jon chuckled and I giggled too. 'But I do know that there *is* a Divinity, just not one which we can explain or understand; a kind of creative force of Love. And the souls of the great ones are either still working on earth or elsewhere. Some have gone through to total union which, to us, is scary because you lose all your individuality but not all of them have. Souls do get to meet them. I guess I'll get to meet them one day but it's not going to be any time soon.'

'I expect there's a pretty long queue.'

'No so long as you'd think. It's mostly the ego that wants to meet Jesus. The soul is already connected.'

We were interrupted then by Clive, the neighbour, who knocked on the side door and stuck his head round.

'Vicar? There's a man with a letter for you. Says he has to hand it to you personally.'

'Not a writ, I hope!' I stood up and dusted off my hands, making a mental note to do some watering later.

'I'll get off,' said Jon. 'Good to see you Bella, as always. I expect you'd like a night off? If so, I'll see you tomorrow.'

'That would be nice. I could do with a bit of a mental catch-up.'

Round at the front of the house was a gardener's van and a red-headed man in mud-covered trousers, holding a white envelope.

'Reverend Amabel Ransom?' he said. I was impressed.

'Yes.'

'The bishop said I must hand this too you in person. I'm his gardener. Um. Sorry, but do you have proof of who you are?'

'She's the vicar all right,' said Clive, who was obviously curious.

'Come in for a moment,' I said, just as much to get rid of Clive as to find some means of ID.

Jon waved and drove off as I led the gardener back through the door to the garden and in through the French windows.

I showed him my driver's licence and he handed over the letter and showed himself out.

What on earth could be so important that it couldn't be done in a phone call? Or that needed to be handed over directly?

I reached out for my paper knife; something this important deserved respectful treatment.

The note inside was short and succinct.

> Bella,
>
> *If you find your phone* **don't**, *whatever you do, turn it on. The WhatsApp group has been hacked. It is seriously compromised and there's big trouble brewing. They can't implicate you if you've not accessed any messages and your memory is lost. If you find the phone, immerse it in water and throw it away. This is IMPORTANT.*
>
> *Burn this. I'm not being melodramatic.*
>
> *You must keep on with the Work.*
>
> *Blessings,*
>
> *Paul.*

Oh shit. What the hell now?

Bugger, bugger, bugger. I had charged my phone. It would automatically be on and connected to the wireless signal. My heart sinking. I went over to pick it up and pressed the touchpad. Nothing. Of course! The laptop lid was down; I'd forgotten that no charge would go through if the lid were down. Oh phew, phew, phew.

Even so, it took me a few moments to even begin to come to terms with what might or might not be happening or what any of this meant.

It was incredibly tempting to turn the phone on; it was incredibly tempting to ignore the instruction. This was a virtually newly-purchased iPhone for God's sake. I'd be paying for it for at least another year on the contract.

I sighed. And then brightened up, briefly. Maybe all the data was on the sim card? I could just take that out? And anyway, what kind of thought police were going to turn up and investigate my phone?

At that moment the doorbell rang.

To say I jumped out of my skin would be an understatement. Of course it could have been anyone but the shock decided me. I walked out through the French windows and across the garden to the cover on the septic tank. I heaved it up and threw the phone and the letter down into its depths. In a moment of uncharacteristically breath-taking intelligence, I ran back to the house to retrieve the phone lead and threw that in too.

It was only a couple of minutes before I could get to the front door but the bell rang again twice before I was back there, already berating myself for such a shocking waste of money. It was probably going to be someone selling dusters.

It wasn't; it was two serious-looking men and one woman holding warrant cards. Behind them was a black car, parked. A very big, very black car. This was not just the police; this was the *Marks & Spencer* of police.

'Reverend Annabel Ransom?'

'Reverend A*m*abel Ransom, yes.' They weren't bloody well getting away with that.

'May we come in?'

'Why?'

'I'm afraid we have bad news.'

'Oh.' I stood back and held the door wide. All three walked into the hall and there was that usual, uncomfortable moment of people milling around, not knowing where to go. I was trying to catch some breath in a throat that felt like dust.

'In here,' I led them into the dining room and indicated that they should sit down at the table. I sat at its head. Well, you have to do something to try and get some inner control back when you are *bouleversé*.

They introduced themselves; I didn't listen. My mind was racing round in circles. Was this about the altar? Was it about the car crash? Was it…?

'I'm sorry to have to tell you that your bishop, the Right Reverend Paul Joans, is dead.'

My heart plummeted.

'But I…' Oh dear God, I was *so* close to saying that I'd only just received a hand-written note from him.

'Yes, Ms. Ransom?' This was the lead man, I think his name was Johnson. He was not a nice cop. He was suspicious of me.

'But I only saw him yesterday.' That couldn't hurt; loads of people must have seen us shopping. 'What happened?'

'He took his own life.'

'He what? He can't have…'

'I'm afraid he has.'

'When?'

'This morning.'

But that *couldn't* be so, could it? He was fine yesterday. Wasn't he? He just wrote me a letter. Didn't he?

'Who found him?' I stuttered.

'He dialled 999 and reported a death. Police went straight round, it being the bishop's palace. He hanged himself.'

'What?'

'He hanged himself,' the man repeated.

'A note?'

'Yes. A note apologising. I'm afraid I have to inform you, Ms. Ransom, that Mr. Joans has been under investigation for some time as the head of a paedophile ring. He must have felt the net closing in.'

No, said a voice in my head. Hero's voice. And I *knew* it wasn't true.

And now I was angry. Now I was flaming with rage. Hold it, Bel. You can't afford to let anything show.

'It's not Mister Joans, it's *Right Reverend* Joans,' I said, waspishly. 'And I don't understand.' I wanted to say that I didn't believe a word of it and demand their evidence but, just in time, I remembered that I wasn't supposed to be remembering anything.

'May we see your phone, *Ms.* Ransom,' said Detective Chief Inspector Johnson.

'No, I'm afraid you can't,' I said. 'I don't have one at the moment. Why do you want to see my phone?'

'*Mister* Joans had a *WhatsApp* group of mostly clergy who helped him groom the victims,' said the Chief Inspector. 'I find it very convenient that you don't think you have a phone as we have it on record that you are a member of that group. Do you mind if we search your house? I can have a warrant within the hour and I warn you, we won't be leaving in the meantime.'

I looked at him clearly for the first time. His eyes were colder than you'd expect in someone whom you had never met before and I had that sinking feeling that comes when you know that you've already been tried, convicted and sentenced for something you'd never even conceived of, let alone done.

Oh boy, do I miss being dead...

Chapter Thirteen

LET'S RECAP FOR a moment.

It's barely two weeks since I woke up dead. I lost years of my life in a car accident (or not).

I was taken back to the heavens to help retrieve souls by my brother, Jon, driving his old blue Panda, and then deposited back at my home in Devon.

During fifteen of those missing years, this agnostic linguist had miraculously become the Rector of a series of Devon Parishes.

Said Rector had an assistant who got moved while she was in hospital and replaced by a woman of striking beauty and fabulous figure; the kind of annoying person who can probably find Manolo Blahniks in Oxfam for a fiver and can wear them without her feet even hurting. Hell, she can probably even spell Manolo Blahnik without having to Google it first. She can also restore destroyed altars.

I've become acquainted with a number of angels, one of which appears to have exploded said altar, one that turns Christian communion into the experience it was probably always intended to be and another which seems to be able to drag me out of hell, which has already proved handy.

I've been to the shadowlands (which I just inaccurately-accurately referred to as hell) to help a soul reunite itself with its persona for reasons I've still yet fully to understand.

I can make myself go invisible simply by saying 'good grief.'

I've been looked after and taken shopping by a sweet and kind bishop who may, after all, be a paedophile and who is now believed to be a suicide. I'm rather upset about that.

I've just thrown a nearly-new, fully-working iPhone that I

couldn't afford in the first place into a septic tank and I'm rather upset about that too.

I now appear to be on the verge of being arrested for aiding and abetting paedophilia. I am *deeply* upset about that.

The only reasonable response in the circumstances would appear to be 'I'm sorry, I can't help you. I've gone mad.'

'I don't understand,' I said, again, instead. 'What is a "What's Up Group"? And what are you accusing me of? I'm very confused. I only met my bishop for the first time yesterday. You probably don't know that I have memory loss from a blow to the head. I have only been out of hospital for forty-eight hours and I have no recall whatsoever of the last fifteen years.

'You can check with the hospital about my memory loss quite easily,' I said. 'While I can't tell you which hospital it was, right now, because I can't remember. I think it's in Worcester. Anyway, your local police sergeant can. He came round to tell me off for checking myself out without permission and finding my way home.

'Go ahead and search the house. I'd be delighted if you found my phone. It wasn't in the personal possessions that were given back to me at the hospital so I suppose it must be here. I haven't found it.'

Silence. I was not struck by lightning for outrageous lying-by-the-vicar, which was a small relief.

The police people looked at each other.

'How were you injured?' said the policewoman at last.

'I was told I was in a car accident,' I said. 'But I have no idea. I was in Worcester and I don't know why I was there either.'

'Should you be on your own?' said the policewoman. 'If you have a brain injury it's wise to have someone to care for you.'

'Probably, if I could have a minute to myself, I would agree,' I said. 'But I've barely had a moment to think since I got home. And now you tell me that the pleasant-seeming man I met yesterday has killed himself and I'm in some kind of "what's up" group he's in and I'm some kind of an accessory to child abuse. It's rather a lot to take in.'

'It's a *WhatsApp* group,' said the Chief Inspector, dryly. 'As I'm sure you know perfectly well. And yes, we would like to search the house right now.'

'*Thank you!*' I said waspishly.

'What?'

'You would like to search the house right now, *thank you,*' I said. 'That would be the polite response. It was a very polite offer and it warrants a polite response. And no, I *don't* know 'perfectly well' what you are on about.'

Honestly, you'd think I had brain damage...

'I think you should be considering your position very carefully,' said the Chief Inspector, standing up. 'Marks, Simonson, start looking. I'll call for a team.'

The next two hours were fairly hellish. Four more police arrived and searched the house from top to bottom. For a moment, I thought they were going to take my laptop (could I have stopped them?) but although they did check it and discovered that it didn't contain the *WhatsApp* app, even your basic policeman could spot that there were now three hundred and seventy-five unopened emails which made it fairly obvious that whatever I'd done or not done as a suspected enabler of paedophilia, I'd not been entirely active over the last two weeks. I thanked God, again, that I'd been too busy/lazy/overwhelmed to look at any of them.

I did not make them tea. I did not offer them biscuits. After I'd managed to stifle my outrage that they looked through my computer, I went back out into the garden and weeded and watered as though my life depended on it. They could search as much as they liked... but what if they planted something in the laptop?

No, Bel. Stop it. This isn't a TV detective show.

Eventually they left, having found nothing. As they left, I pissed them off royally by pointing out that they had just wasted a lot of their time but at least I'd got some weeding done.

DS Marks thanked me politely for my co-operation and advised me to get a family member to come and stay. Chief Inspector Johnson said they'd be back and DC Simonson said nothing at all.

After they'd gone, I opened a bottle of wine and cried to myself at the kitchen table. I'm ashamed to say that I cried just as much over the invasion of a police search and the loss of my phone as I did for the bishop but, in fairness, his death was so shocking I still didn't believe it.

I didn't call anyone because there was no one to call. It's not that I don't have friends; I probably do; I just couldn't recollect them. Even if I could, we all have different friends for different reasons and very few of mine would be able to handle what was going on in my life. The only people I could remember that I could sensibly talk to right now were all on that dratted *WhatsApp* group.

I watched the early evening local news which led on the sudden death of the Bishop of Exbridge. Police were not looking for anyone in connection with the death and all that carefully said stuff that makes everyone know it was suicide. They had some footage of him bishopping and a couple of photographs of him looking handsome and young and added in that he wasn't married with its usual implication that this made him gay.

Then I had another drink and another cry and cooked myself some supper. Just in case you wanted to know, yes it was comfort food: spaghetti carbonara; the Antonio Carluccio version where you don't need any cream. I probably ate far too much and I didn't care.

Next, it was time for some serious and slightly lubricated thinking.

Even with a clunky memory, I was pretty sure that the bishop wasn't homosexual or a paedophile. And that our *WhatsApp* group was only ever about earthbound souls. Which meant that either this was a complete fabrication or someone had managed to re-write the content and then told the police.

But who would do such a thing? And if Paul were innocent, why would he kill himself?

Had he killed himself or was it murder? After all, I'd had a strange accident and I didn't know what had happened to Celeste apart from a car crash.

I wanted to phone Robbie but I knew it wouldn't be safe. I had out-Harry Pottered Harry Potter with my withholding of facts from virtually everyone and the phones could even be tapped. Right now, there was nothing I could do apart from wondering who or what was behind this and why a group of people trying to help souls to go where souls are meant to go would constitute any kind of threat to anyone. I'd heard of the alleged Illuminati but this was surely too bonkers even for them.

And then I took the rest of the bottle of wine upstairs and made love to it in the bath. As one does when one's life is completely unaccountable, stupid and ridiculous. So there...

I slept, eventually and fitfully, to be woken by the doorbell at eight o'clock in the morning.

Jesus H. Fucking Christ and his black, bastard brother, Harry on a bicycle, what *now?*

(I'm sorry God, I really am. But I'm sure there must be times when even you are banging your non-existent head on a supernova or something at the sheer non-stop absurdity of things).

I couldn't face the front door so I wrapped myself in my dressing gown, went to the front bedroom, opened the window and stuck my head out.

Down below was an old Ford Fiesta, parked on the verge, a slight comb-over, two ears and one hell of a nose.

'Robbie?'

He stepped back and looked up. Lord, he looked tired.

'Hold on. I'll be right down.'

Dear, sweet Robbie who never harmed a fly; who was the darling of all the old dears in the parish and the world's most hopeless giver of sermons and one of the people I most wanted to see in the whole, wide world.

'Bel,' he said, as I opened the door. 'Do you know who I am?'

'Yes. Yes, it's okay. I do. Come in.'

He bumbled in like the world's most exhausted daddy long legs. His eyes looked dead—he must be traumatised.

'Tea,' I said. 'And food. Before *anything* else. How long was the drive? Have you eaten anything?'

'Six hours. No,' he said, collapsing into a chair at the kitchen table. 'But I had to come. I couldn't sleep. I heard about Paul.

I had the police come round. They took my phone. Bel, what's going on?'

I didn't answer. Instead, I filled the kettle, got out two mugs, put two slices of white sourdough in the toaster and began beating eggs with just a dash of water (which makes the scramble creamier, surprisingly).

Once we had tea and eggs on butter-laden toast inside us, we relaxed a little and began to talk.

Robbie had been my assistant for nearly three years. He's one of those hopeless priests with a heart of gold, tons of theoretical knowledge, the spatial awareness of a swinging cat and the social skills of a confused haddock. He could bore for England in the pulpit and out of it and his kindness and enthusiasm for local events were legendary. *Everybody* liked Robbie and everybody avoided him at social events because once he attached himself, you'd never get rid of him.

Over the years, I've learnt how to distract him into keeping to the point (it's an art) and we've always got on well. Robbie is love personified in the body of a badly-groomed stick insect; he always thinks the best of everyone and he would bend over backwards to help even the meanest of folk. The very idea that he would have a finger in any kind of till was frankly ridiculous.

Never, in all that time, had I seen Robbie angry. But once he had some good food inside him and was halfway down a second cup of tea, his eyes were alive again and blazing with a passion that transformed his very being.

'I know that I *don't* know anything, Bel,' he said. 'But I *know* that Paul didn't kill himself. I *know* he wasn't a paedophile. I *know* the group has been hacked. Have you seen it? Some computer wiz has turned it into a nightmare. There are pictures on there that no-one sane would ever want to see and entries, purporting to be from Paul, that are just hideous.'

'How long has it been like that? Didn't you notice before?'

'That's just it. It was fine two days ago. All this happened pretty much overnight. I posted a huge protest but it was deleted. I'm sure others did the same. And with this following my removal from the parish, I just knew something dreadful was happening.'

'Yes, tell me about that.'

'I just got a call out of the blue from the Archdeacon. She said that terrifying phrase: 'there have been complaints.' And she added that there was a desperate need for what she called 'a man like you' in Ely immediately and that my position here was terminated as of that moment and I was to transfer within the next twenty-four hours.

'I didn't know what to do. I'd only just been to see you in hospital. You didn't know me so I couldn't tell you...' his voice broke.

'About Celeste?'

'Yes. That she's dead too, Bel. Celeste is dead. She was killed in the car accident that nearly killed you. It must have been some kind of truck. Shunted you across the central reservation into oncoming traffic on the dual carriageway. Donald is in pieces, as you can imagine.

'I stayed over with him; tried to be some comfort, you know, but his family were doing a much better job than me so I came home. To the message from the Archdeacon.'

I sat with eyes closed, holding tightly to my mug with both hands. That didn't square with what the police had told me. They said I was alone in the car. And it didn't square with what Paul had told me either. But whatever the truth of the accident, two of us were dead and I had survived only by some miracle. It was like some dystopian nightmare. Was there some kind of plot? There must be. But none of it made sense.

'Robbie, did Celeste and I do the exorcism. Do you know?'

'No, I don't. Don't you remember?'

'No, my memory is still damaged. I don't even remember what we were sent to do.'

'Oh, right. It was a house just outside the city centre where every tenant in the last fifteen years had been diagnosed with glandular fever or chronic fatigue or fibromyalgia or something similarly debilitating. Is that a word? You know what I mean... something that takes all the strength and life out of you. Odd how almost the same thing— the inability to get up and live a life and persistent exhaustion and pain gets re-diagnosed and updated by the medical profession when to the outsider, it's obvious that it's different versions of the same issue. It's almost as though...'

'Robbie!'

'Yes, sorry. Well, Celeste was contacted when the landlord died and his daughter—also with chronic fatigue—inherited. She's one of those New Age types who uses crystals and the like and who obviously did have some real sense of something being out of kilter that she and her friends couldn't sort. She got a... dowser is it?... in and he said there were bodies under the decking out the back. Well, no one was going to do any digging on the word of a dowser but something had to be done. It was a real last resort for them to go to the Church, which is such a shame because isn't that supposed to be one of the things we're about?'

'Not nowadays, no, but yes. Go on.'

'Yes, anyway, Celeste thought it wasn't actual bodies so much as trapped entities or lost souls, so she got permission for the exorcism, contacted us and you went over to assist her in doing it. That's all I know.'

I tried *so* hard to remember, but it was a blank. And yet...

'I do remember something,' I said, slowly. 'Not the exorcism but when we were driving either to the house or back from it. It was like we drove into a dark fog. It was daylight but the automatic headlights went on. But that's all...'

What memory there was seemed vile, dark, almost slimy. The kind of energy that holds onto things...

I shook myself. 'Robbie, say the Lord's Prayer with me, *now.*'

It's not generally known but the Lord's Prayer is a strong tool in a minor exorcism. Just saying it cleared my mind and dissociated it from that negative force associated with the crash.

'What's going on, Bel?' said Robbie again, when I'd finished.

'I don't know.'

'Bel. I'm reeling. Could I have a lie down first? Just for half an hour on your sofa?

'Of course. But not the sofa. The spare bed is made up.'

'Thank you.' He smiled, weakly and I could see he was on his last legs despite the food. He climbed the stairs and disappeared into the spare room.

I sat with the remnants of my tea trying to make sense of things. I'd been thinking of something important. What was it?

Hero spoke in my head: Alessina.

Alessina! Of course. She was on the *WhatsApp* group, too, so I didn't dare call her. But she was only a few miles away and I had a bicycle. Of course I did! Didn't all vicars? I could leave a note for Robbie to drive round when he woke and I could cycle over.

I got dressed quietly so as not to disturb him and let myself out of the house. My garage was a separate building behind and to the side of the house and built of wood. It doubled as a garden shed. I unlocked the door and swung it open. And stopped dead.

There was my car. Totally undamaged.

What the actual fuck...?

So, Paul must have been right. It wasn't a car accident. Or, if it was, it wasn't in my car. And yet, hadn't the police told me it had been? But I remembered being with Celeste and they said I was alone. Oh my God, what part of myself could I even trust any more?

This was definitely a silver Renault Clio. It was *my* silver Renault Clio; I could see possessions I recognised inside it including my detachable satnav and a reusable bottle of water. So, had I taken the train to Worcester? Was it Celeste's car we had been in?

So where were my car keys? On the missing key ring with my house keys, I presumed. But there was a spare in the house somewhere. Even so, I didn't fancy driving and I pulled the bicycle out from behind the car, shut the garage door behind me and mounted.

Only then did I remember the bees.

Chapter Fourteen

ALESSINA LIVES IN a witch's cottage at the end of a rutted lane in the depths of Dartmoor. It has a thatched roof and a pond teeming with dragonfly larvae, water boatmen, newts and probably mermaids. All around the house grow herbs and vegetables, fruit trees and wildflowers, all woven together and tended by the bees that live in her hives.

Inside the cottage the roof is low, the floors are grey, uneven stone covered with old and slightly frayed rugs and there are feathers and bones on the shelves together with hand-made drums and home-made pottery. The living room has a spinning wheel and a great open fireplace where huge logs smoulder for hours on end. The fire is lit most of the year for the cottage is cuddled into a great, damp hillside and has probably never been completely dry in five hundred years.

Alessina lives with her husband, Stephen, her two young boys who, respectively, do a normal job (he's a carpenter) and go to school, just like ordinary people. But you can't be all that ordinary if you are married to a witch.

Alessina herself is elfin-featured with long black hair. She dances with the Black Morris at dawn at the solstices and equinoxes; she talks with the nature spirits; she rarely takes honey from her hives and, when she does, she needs no protective clothing because the bees know and love her and are willing to share their food with her. She sings to creation every morning as she walks through the glades and over the hills and she drums herself into the dreamtime to discover what ails the folk who come to her with troubles and questions.

You'd think she'd be at total odds with a Christian Rector and vice versa but three weeks after I moved down to the village, when I was still in the church house and finding my feet, I found her sitting in the graveyard under one of the ancient yew trees, playing cat's cradle. And waiting for me.

'The bees told me to come,' she said, smiling. That was her only greeting. I took one look at her, sat down and said, 'Tell me more.'

As a child I had read Elizabeth Goudge's *Linnets and Valerians* where the children were taught how to speak with and respect the bees. I had always wanted it to be true and now it was. Alessina and I talked for more than twenty minutes without even exchanging names, let alone the metaphorical bum-sniffing that new acquaintances usually do.

The next week, she brought me a small, hand-built hive. It was empty but she said that all I had to do was ask and a Queen would come, together with her children. She would tell her bees to send a swarm and, as soon as I was ready, it would show up.

We placed the hive in the overgrown part of the churchyard (the part that the parish council hates) where the wildflowers flourished in the breezes and, at least once a week, I would go and look in the hope of seeing bees. It took just two months and, as soon as I saw them, I did just what Elizabeth Goudge had written in her book. I sat by the hive and greeted them.

'Madam Queen, noble bees, I am Bella, the vicar of this church and custodian of this churchyard,' I said. 'I bid you welcome. You are safe here and I am glad you have come.'

They ignored me, of course, but I persevered. As the days passed, I told them about the people who came to the churchyard, either to visit loved ones or simply to walk their dogs. I told them about the bishop and Robbie and the parish council and anyone who came to stay. And as the months passed I found that, more and more, I would talk to the bees when I was perplexed or exasperated or discouraged. And also when I was joyful and at peace. In fact, I talked to the bees nearly every day.

How could I have forgotten them?

You might think this silly but I knew that if I could now talk with angels and travel through dimensions, I could definitely communicate with the bees. So I stopped, got off the bicycle and walked it back into the drive.

As I did, a huge, articulated lorry came round the corner at speed, taking up all the space on this quiet country road.

He blasted his horn and passed in a whirl of dust. Had I been riding, he would probably have hit me.

Thoughtfully, I put the bicycle back in the garage and made my way to the churchyard.

The hive was agitated; I could see that immediately. As I approached, half a dozen bees flew at me. I stood my ground and greeted them.

'Greetings, Madam Queen and noble bees,' I said. 'May you be blessed to the full extent you may receive the benediction of the all-Holy One.

'I have been away and I was injured. I expect you have felt something strange going on. I don't understand it but at least I am back now and perhaps you can help. I would like to see Alessina, please.'

The buzzing became less frenetic and the bees settled down a little. But there was still something wrong. They were restless, troubled. I wasn't surprised; the hive mind is a real thing and it is very sensitive to atmospheres. I'd been a bit of a walking atmosphere lately and being nearly hit by a huge articulated lorry *really* doesn't help.

It was a warm spring morning and such a relief to pause from everything. I sat down next to the hive and began to relax. Three bees landed on my hand and I knew better than to flinch. This was an honour, not an attack. I let them investigate my fingers and remembered the power of Trinity, the 'Divine dance' as Sam had called it.

After a minute, feeling drowsy, I lay down in the long grass and began to doze.

I was woken by a slightly breathless contralto voice singing:

> *Some velvet morning when I'm straight*
> *I'm going to open up your gate*
> *And maybe tell you about Phaedra...*

I sat bolt upright and saw Alessina striding across the churchyard towards me, singing the song for which I had been named.

'You'd sing better if you slowed down!' I said, shading my eyes with my hand and laughing.

'There's gratitude!' she said, hands on hips, her black hair tumbling over her shoulders. She wore a mid-calf length purple, layered skirt and a home-made felted jacket. Alessina never wore trousers. An old leather knapsack was slung over one shoulder and her brown boots were so old they were virtually shapeless.

'I'd already heard the news and the bees said you were home and that you were in all sorts of trouble besides, so I came as fast as I could.'

'And the song?'

'Your theme song? It just came into my head. I hardly knew I knew it. Do you think he meant 'sober' when he says 'straight?''

'I gather no one has any idea, particularly not Lee Hazlewood, and he wrote it.'

She sat down beside me. 'Okay, talk.'

I held my hands up. 'Where do I start?'

'Always a good idea, I find, to start at the beginning, find your way to the middle and then go on until the end.' She smiled and, when Alessina smiled, the sun came out.

'I don't want to be overheard.'

'We won't be,' she said, confidently, lying down on one elbow and pulling up a piece of grass to chew. 'The bees will ensure that. Madam Queen, we need your help not to be overheard, please. And so it is.'

It's hard to explain how it is that when Alessina says something like that, you believe her. So I lay back and gazed at the sky and started talking. Three times, while I was speaking, the hum of the bees rose and a group circled around us to warn us that someone was close to being in earshot and we lay silently side by side until the buzzing subsided.

I wondered if, before the accident, I would truly have believed in all this. Now it seemed second nature.

Alessina is the perfect listener. She raises a finger if she needs to interrupt, purely for clarification, which allows you to finish a sentence before she speaks. She makes slight noises of acknowledgment but mostly she just allows your words to sink into her consciousness.

I must have spoken for nearly half an hour. I told her everything. Not minute by minute but all that had happened including the confused awakenings at different times after the accident, about Jon, about working in the other world, about the angels in the church, about the altar and about Lucie mending it.

When I'd finally finished, and was feeling as if I'd been relieved of some enormous weight, she brought a bottle of home-made elderflower champagne out of her bag and offered me some. We drank together from the same bottle and she poured some on the ground as a libation.

'Okay,' she said, after a good couple of minutes of silence. 'May I meet Ariel?'

'I don't know. We can give it a go.'

'I didn't say 'can I?' I said 'may I?' She is your church angel and you are custodian of the church. She knows that. If you say I may meet her, I may.'

'Oh. Okay.' I got up. Strangely, I wasn't perplexed that this was what Alessina had focused on from all the story. She had a way of lightening anything without trivialising it; that was one of the things I loved about her.

'The door will be open,' she said, as I made a move to go back to the house for the key to the church. 'One of the things that's most interesting about this is how the church is responding.'

'What?'

'The door is open; the door is locked; the door is open. I would imagine that is Ariel or some other spiritual energy. And it certainly reacted to Lucie. Hmmm...'

She was right. The church door was *not* locked and there was no one inside. I called out a 'hello!' but felt a bit of a prat doing it.

Ariel was standing by the lady chapel altar, not the main one and, without even asking, I knew that was because I had activated it with the communion service.

'Ariel, may I introduce my friend Alessina?' I said, for want of anything more imaginative.

'Greetings,' said Alessina, bowing. Ariel bowed in return.

'Where is the darkness now?' Alessina asked.

Ariel indicated towards the main altar and separately in the direction of my house.

'Thank you.'

'Phaedra,' Alessina said incredibly softly. 'Do you remember the exorcism prayer in Latin?'

'Yes.'

'Then throw it at the high altar. *Do it now!*'

As she spoke I could perceive a greyness rising up from behind the cross and, almost in panic threw myself into the Latin of the great prayer of exorcism.

'*Per signum crucis de inimicis nostris libera nos, Deus noster. Amen.*

'*Exorcizo te, omnis spiritus immunde, in nomine dei Patris Omnipotentis, et in nomine Jesu Christi filii ejus, Domini et judicis nostri, et in virtute Spiritus Sancti, ut descedas ab hoc plasmate dei quod dominus noster ad templum sanctum suum vocare dignatus est, ut fiat templum dei vivi, et Spiritus Sanctus habitet in eo. Per eumdem Christum Dominum nostrum, qui venturus est judicare vivos et mortuos, et saeculum per ignem. AMEN.*

As I projected the prayer, my voice rising in crescendo, Alessina threw handfuls of the elderflower champagne at the altar and the grey film shattered and imploded with something that sounded to my ears like a sonic boom. Then it was gone.

Then Ariel began to sing. It was a silver flute of melody that rose and thickened until it seemed as though a hundred angels were singing in perfect harmony. Their voices filled the entire building with light and warmth.

The altar seemed to shiver in the light and I backed away in case it exploded again. Alessina laughed. 'It's all right,' she said. 'It exploded before because it was brittle with the darkness and angelic laughter broke it apart. Lucie put it back together again and it would have defended against what it already knew could attack it. But exorcism, it must obey.'

'Oh. Right.' I thought I saw but I wasn't certain. 'So, it's had a dark energy for... how long?'

'Who knows. All that matters is that it has gone now. But we must get back to the house; there's some there too.'

She bowed again to Ariel whose song had just ended. Ariel bowed back. I bowed too and was astonished to receive what could only be described as a distance hug. It was like being circled with light.

'She's grateful,' said Alessina. 'She has been weak for so long but now you know her and named her, she is strong again.'

'So why did you call me Phaedra?'

'Because naming is a complicated thing. Name an angel and you bind it to you. But if a dark energy knows your name, it can use it against you. That energy knew you as Amabel or just Bel. If I'd said, 'Bel, do you remember…?' it would have attacked you before you could speak. Song is powerful too. I brought the strength of the bees to you by singing your first name. Oh, and the elderflower champagne is infused with holy water. You taught me the recipe. I thought it couldn't hurt to bring some in disguise.

'But what's important now is getting to the house. Robbie's there, remember?'

'Oh Lord, yes. You mean there's a problem there?'

'Oh yes.'

We left the church (angels are like people on the phone in television programmes. They don't expect you to say 'goodbye' when you hang up on them, so we weren't being rude) and hot-footed it over to the house. In retrospect, I probably should have thought of checking the altar *was* still all right; it had been having quite a challenging time over the last few days.

The French windows to the dining room were open and through them I could see Robbie. *He was on my laptop.*

'Not a moment to spare,' muttered Alessina. 'HELLO!'

Robbie wheeled round to face us as we came in through the windows and my immediate thought was, 'That's not Robbie.' The face that looked at us was old and grey with dead shark eyes.

It started to speak in some strange language but that was its undoing because by using Robbie's vocal chords it enabled the soul inside to use them too.

'Help me,' he whispered.

You probably don't know this but you may never do an exorcism on a human unless the person possessed actually asks you to. As the grey thing rasped out its horrific language, Robbie's plea was the permission I needed. I grabbed a crucifix from the bureau and roared out the prayer of exorcism at the top of my lungs.

It sneered at me.

'Don't you by-our-Lady dare,' I thought, redoubling my efforts.

Beside me, Alessina began to say the Lord's Prayer and threw more elderflower champagne, I was in the zone by now and, gradually, the greyness cracked. It hissed like steam and then, like the energy at the altar, shattered and was gone.

Robbie slumped and began to cry.

'Oh God, oh God. It must have been me,' he said. 'I must have brought all this on us.'

'Rubbish!' said Alessina crisply. 'It certainly brought you here today but I suspect that's the limit of it. You must eat something to ground you. Bel, can you put the kettle on and I'm sure you've got biscuits. I need to go outside and deal with any fall-out.'

She left us alone together in the dining room. Tentatively, I put out a hand and took Robbie's.

'It's all right,' I said, as if calming a frightened horse. 'You're safe now. It has all gone.

'Come into the kitchen. I'll make some tea.'

I led him across the hall and sat him down at the kitchen table. He seemed to have lost weight but then, I guess, he'd been carrying something pretty heavy. Rather helplessly, I patted him on the back and got on with sorting out mugs and plates.

Alessina came back in just as I was pouring the milk.

'Not too bad,' she said. 'A dead cat, I'm afraid, and some rabbits. The energy had to go somewhere.'

'The Gadarene swine,' I said. She nodded. 'Christ knew the laws of physics even if they weren't called that then. Energy cannot be destroyed, only changed. Such a destructive force had to be discharged in some way. I'm sorry for the cat's owner. It didn't suffer. Ah, tea!'

She sat down and took a swig. One of the loveliest things about Alessina was that, at her house, you would be prescribed and served home-dried herbal teas for whatever emotions you might be feeling at the time. But when she came to your house, she was quite happy with a bog-standard cuppa.

'My God, what would we have done without you?' I said, my legs suddenly buckling as the adrenaline rush faded away.

'Almost exactly the same, I imagine,' she said, pushing the biscuit tin my way. 'And anyway, you wouldn't have been without me. The bees would always have brought me. Though, even if I do say so myself, the elderflower champagne was a touch of genius.'

'Elderflower champagne?' It was the first thing Robbie had said since blaming himself for everything. Good. Post exorcism, you can be pretty disoriented but now he was following the conversation.

'Yes. Bel taught me how to make holy water so I made holy elderflower champagne,' said Alessina. 'Worked a treat.'

'Golly,' said Robbie. He was holding his mug in both hands and looking very pale. But at least he looked like a pale Robbie.

'Eat,' I said, pushing the biscuit tin across the table. 'I know you're probably not hungry but you need the fuel.'

Obediently, he took a hobnob and chewed it methodically. Then another. And then, very daringly, a chocolate digestive.

'Are you okay to talk?' I asked, once he'd swallowed most of his tea.

'Yes, I think so.'

'Do you know when the energy got into you?'

'No... yes. I'm not sure. I was looking at the *WhatsApp* group last night after I heard about Paul and I felt incredibly angry. Rage even. Not really like me. But then the circumstances are nothing I've encountered before.

'I went to bed but couldn't sleep. I just knew I had to come here. It seemed logical—to be with Bel. I knew you'd be devastated,' he said, reaching out to touch my hand.

'Well, not necessarily,' I said. 'Though thank you. My memory is still patchy. I really hardly knew him before this week. But yes, it was a bit of a shock.'

For some reason, Robbie and Alessina exchanged glances.

'I didn't actually feel anything strange until you started the Lord's Prayer,' he continued. 'Then, I simply couldn't say it. I felt scared and really uncomfortable.'

I could have kicked myself. I'd noticed that he didn't join in and yet discounted it. You must *never* do that if you have any suspicions at all about possession. But then, stupidly, I didn't have any suspicions at all.

'I knew I had to sleep. And then, when I woke, there was this overwhelming urge to go to your computer. I had to go to a certain website and download a corrupted version of *WhatsApp*. I suppose it would have had the horrible stuff the rest of us had.

'When you surprised me, I felt...' he shuddered. 'Well, it was horrible. My God, some people must have that level of hatred all the time.

'But what if I have been carrying it longer and just didn't know? What if I am the one who has caused all this trouble in the first place? I couldn't live with myself.'

'Firstly, it wouldn't have been you, it would have been the entity,' said Alessina. 'Secondly, this kind of sustained attack on a group is rarely from one direction only and thirdly, entities can only use aspects that are already existent in the psyche. Whoever set up what seems to be a concerted cyber attack would have to have some technical knowledge. I doubt you've got anything like enough expertise to do that. You could click on a link, yes, and download something but setting it up on line? I doubt it.'

'Doesn't it depend on what the entity is?' I queried. 'If it's a dark soul with computer knowledge...'

'Yes, but it would still prefer someone with more competence,' said Alessina. 'I'm trying to be reassuring here. Help me out a little!'

We sat in silence for a while.

'Where's Mrs. Tiggy?' said Robbie, suddenly.

'Mrs. Who?'

'Mrs. Tiggy! Your secretary-cum-housekeeper. She's always here on Mondays, Wednesdays and Fridays. She should be bossing you around and despairing at how many emails you've ignored.'

I looked blank. No Mrs. Tiggy came to mind.

'Nothing?' said Alessina. 'But you do remember me. And you do remember Robbie. It's very haphazard isn't it? Did you really not remember anything about Paul at all?'

'No. He was like a total stranger. But I have a secretary? That's a relief. Someone who can tell me what I should be doing. Did you call her Mrs. *Tiggy?* As in Tiggywinkle?

'Exactly,' said Alessina. 'Mrs. Teague is her real name. Does that ring a bell?'

I thought.

'No, I'm afraid not. I'll look forward to meeting her.'

'Yes, but that's the thing,' said Robbie. 'She should be here now.'

'Maybe she thinks I'm still away?'

They both snorted. 'That wouldn't stop her,' said Robbie. 'Mrs. Tiggy is a force of nature. For a start, she's always Mrs. Tiggy. No one would dare to call her by her Christian name.'

'We can give her a call in a minute,' said Alessina. 'What is it, Bel?'

I was frowning. It had just occurred to me that it was strange that the police had come straight here after the bishop's death and that Robbie had been driven here, too. And now, it seemed that my secretary was either affected, too, or avoiding me. What was it that seemed to be making me a prime suspect?

I voiced my concern.

Again, Robbie and Alessina looked at each other.

With a sigh, Alessina took my hand.

'You're a prime suspect because of your relationship with Paul,' she said. 'My dear, I know you have no memory of this but you do need to know. You and Paul were lovers. He proposed to you last month and you said yes. *Now* do you remember?'

Chapter Fifteen

'OH. WELL THAT explains how he knew about the state of my bank account,' was all I could say for the moment. The bombshell that Alessina had dropped didn't stir even a sliver of memory. This was a colossal missing piece of my jigsaw.

Alessina and Robbie said nothing but sipped their tea. I was grateful that they gave me time to think; to consider. But try as I might, all I got was a blank.

All I felt was admiration for this man who must have been so utterly shocked and distressed by my not even knowing him but who had said nothing to frighten or knock me further off balance. That must have been so very hard.

You can't grieve if you don't remember the cause of your sorrow. But I knew that the pain had to be somewhere, hanging like a sword of Damocles that could fall on my head any time. That knowledge wasn't comfortable, to say the least.

We all sat for a few moments in silence.

'I'm not being heartless,' I said, slightly defensively. 'I simply don't remember. I can't explain any more than that.'

They nodded in acknowledgement.

There were only two things we could reasonably do in the circumstances, given that the sun had not passed over the yard arm: put the kettle on again and call Mrs. Tiggy.

There was no answer to either her landline or mobile phone but that in itself meant nothing. She could be out at the shops; she could have her phone turned off; she could be in an area with no signal (such places *do* still exist in the wild lands of places like Devon). She didn't *have* to be dead, possessed or avoiding us. I left a message after the automated voice that indicated clearly that Mrs. Tiggy had better things to do than record personal messages on telephones and was seriously unlikely to listen in to any that might be left.

We drank our tea.

'Why would someone who was, apparently, in love and planning to get married, kill himself?' I asked, both hands wrapped round a mug that said, appropriately enough, 'Don't panic.'

'And why would a practising Christian, let alone a bishop, who knows that suicide is against God's law, do it?' That was Robbie's contribution. I remembered that he was somewhat more orthodox than I.

'He might have been possessed,' I said, mildly. 'Wouldn't you have killed yourself if the entity had instructed you to?'

Robbie's honest, ugly face cracked open. I thought he was going to cry and bit my lip. It hadn't been my intention to hurt him.

'It is from within, from the human heart, that evil intentions come,' he said, quoting Jesus in the Gospel of Mark. Chapter seven, verse 21, if I wasn't mistaken. At some point, when it wasn't so important, I was going to be very interested in looking more deeply at why I could remember some things so clearly and others were a total blank. But then, Paul had already explained that.

I sighed. Sighing is a thing that, I think, women do particularly well. It can denote all kinds of things, from impatience or acceptance through doormat tendencies to simple exhaustion. In my case it was because this recalcitrant brain had summoned up a quotation from the *Zohar*, of all things, in response. Why did I know the *Zohar*—or even what it was?

I had a horrible moment of wondering whether Robbie and I had gone through whole evenings of just quoting religious texts back and forwards; *Bible Tennis* as my previous bishop had called it once.

I knew it wouldn't get us any further but the words pushed to come out.

'The ultimate objective of spirituality is not to remove the existence of evil or humanity's negative traits. Instead, we must confront and transform these dark forces, for it is only through the struggle of transformation that we ignite the spark of divinity within us,' I said. 'That's from the *Zohar* and no, I don't know why I can remember that when I can't even remember being in love.'

'Okay,' said Alessina. 'But what both of you are saying is an excellent summing up of the situation.'

'It is?'

'Of course it is. There are dark forces in the world—and perhaps the universe—but they are called into action and perpetuated by humans. They may not originate in humanity; they are more like viruses without what we would call consciousness. But once they are in touch with enough people with faulty spiritual immune systems they grow stronger and more powerful to the state of an epidemic. Worse, they can use the human ego state, as a *form* of consciousness, just like we do.'

'What?'

'Most of us walk around on automatic, right? We aren't really conscious when we make a cup of tea or even when we're talking to most of the people we know. We repeat patterns. How often do you say exactly the same thing to people you meet? Our brains are wired to repeat successful patterns—'

'And unsuccessful ones,' Robbie interrupted. 'Even more so!'

'Yes, exactly. We *think* we are conscious because we appear to be functioning normally but quite often we aren't even aware of what we are doing. *That's* the energy of the average kind of evil.'

'And the not-average kind? The Hitler and Stalin and closing borders to refugees kind?' I was intrigued. This seemed to be explaining what happened both sides of death.

'Well, I suppose those would be either a huge build-up of subconscious fears and hatreds *or* they could be harnessed and used by a human being who has consciously given their soul over to evil. You only need one of those to attract thousands of the others.'

It was a very sobering thought.

'So, if you find the one person and—um—destroy them, does the rest of it fade away?' asked Robbie.

'It will lose momentum, yes. But, it's back to that thing that energy cannot be created or destroyed.'

'Yes, of course! First Law of Thermodynamics,' interrupted

Robbie. 'Energy can only be transferred or changed from one form to another.

'So, what you're saying is that if a human chooses to take energy and use it for good or for evil, they are still using existing energy from the universe?'

'And as everything resonates with its own frequency, it will be drawn to other energies that are equally as dark or light,' I added. 'But how would something like that attack someone like Paul who was working at a higher level of consciousness—or, at least, I assume he was,' I finished somewhat lamely.

Alessina laughed. It was a rather bitter kind of laugh; one that was redolent with experience.

'Ah yes,' she said. 'Never hide your light under a bushel, as you Christians say. But what happens when you shine a bright light on a dark night? It attracts a lot of pests. As long as the lantern is fully sealed, all they can do is batter on the glass. But if there is just *one* hole in the lamp, then the pests will find it.

'There isn't a person on the planet without at least one flaw...'

'But I thought that the cracks were supposed to be where the light gets in, not the darkness.

'But... hang on...' Something was clicking in my brain.

'So, if there's a crack in the psyche that leads to an unresolved and maybe even unrecognised darkness, then the virus can enter and grow on that—it's a petri-dish; a kind of food for it. But if there's a different kind of crack where the deep humanity can wake up or look out and ask for help, then the light can get in. Just like Robbie having to ask for help before I could do the exorcism? This is all a bit bloody complicated!'

'No, it's really very simple,' said Alessina. 'Resonance. Like attracts like.'

'But how can that be if light attracts pests?' said Robbie.

'Oh my God!' I had it. Or at least, I thought I had it. 'Nobody is pure. Everyone has darkness in them and everyone has light. But it is like that annoyingly perennial meme on social media about the two wolves; the dark and the light one. It all depends on which one you choose to feed. Shining light makes you visible— and it also reveals all of you. But nothing can get in and harm you if you don't also have the dark cracks that maybe you don't even know you've got.' I shivered, involuntarily.

'But why would Paul feed the dark wolf? Did he actually have paedophile inclinations? *Did* he kill himself? I simply can't believe he did.'

'We may never know,' said Alessina. 'He might once have looked at a sexually-aware fourteen-year-old of either gender and, momentarily, found them attractive and fuelled that impulse with a ton of guilt.

'Or his light may have been fuelled by self-satisfaction and self-aggrandisement. Both of those look like pure light but just because something is bright doesn't mean that it *is* light. Glamour looks a lot like light and that's a very convenient trap for many of us.'

'Oh, how far have you fallen from heaven, O Lucifer, son of Morning,' I murmured. That time I was quoting Isaiah but I won't bore you with the chapter and verse.

'Yes, indeed. Lucifer. Myths generally carry a great truth within them. Doesn't "Lucifer" mean 'the light bearer?'

'It does! And the myths say that demons are *fallen* angels.'

'Indeed,' said Alessina. 'Paul might have *seemed* good when he wasn't (sorry, Bel…) '*Or* he might have been murdered by someone or something full of darkness that wishes to destroy a circle of light and is quite clever enough to make it look like suicide.'

Yes, said Hero, inside my head.

All three of us took a moment to digest the realisation that we might just be living in the kind of reality that TV shows and movies had been suggesting for years.

'Our group is supposed to be secret, isn't it?' I said. 'We truly believe that we are doing good and counteracting the level of darkness in the world but perhaps one of us has leaked what we are doing outside the group—maybe bragged a little? Or perhaps we are just getting really effective and someone; some *thing*, is powerful enough to attack through some small fissure we didn't even know about?'

And then I knew. A sudden flash of restored memory flooded my brain and I understood.

146

'We started protecting ourselves,' I said. 'At least, some of us did. We talked about how important it was to begin to defend ourselves against the darkness. There was a whole discussion thread on it. We couldn't agree as to whether the work itself was sufficient or whether we actually needed to put up magical barriers to counter any perceived outside threat. And by putting up barriers, maybe we actually attracted what we planned to repulse.'

Beside me, Robbie began to cry.

'You wouldn't agree to do that, Bel,' he said. 'And neither would Paul. Or you, Alessina. You warned us. But we went ahead and did it anyway. Oh God, I am *so* sorry.'

'How many of us and what did we do?' I noticed that Alessina did not say '*you.*' She was not handing out blame or separation.

'Two. Celeste and me. We created a circle of protection for us all. We thought we were doing the right thing. Oh God, oh God...'

'And by accident, you showed the darkness that we were afraid of it. Fear is its greatest ally,' said Alessina, grimly.

We both turned to Robbie, who was ashen-faced and about to start gabbling.

'Be quiet,' we said simultaneously as he opened his mouth. I grasped Robbie's left hand and Alessina, his right.

'This is not your fault. You had the best intentions,' I said. 'What *is* important is that you don't perpetuate any of it with guilt or fear or repetition, even thought. That is going to be *incredibly* tough, Robbie. But if you *have* been a crack, it or they will almost certainly try to use you again.

'But you know how to prevent it. Prayer, the Jesus prayer, the 23rd Psalm. St. Patrick's *Lorica*. They all work.'

'They do,' Alessina nodded. 'Even this heathen was shouting the Lord's Prayer at you!' She smiled and patted the still frozen Robbie on the shoulder.

'Did they send you to see Bel at the hospital in order to kill her?' she added almost as an irrelevancy.

'Oh *God!*' I didn't think Robbie's face could get any whiter. 'I don't know. I knew I *had* to go and see her. But she'd lost her memory.' The non-sequitur seemed to make perfect sense to both him and to Alessina, who nodded again. 'And I kept the accident secret. I didn't tell anyone she was even hurt. Why did I do that? *Why did I do that?*'

'Did you cause the accident, Robbie?' Alessina's voice was incredibly gentle.

'No,' he shuddered. 'No. At least, I don't think so. Oh God!' He put his face in his hands and wept like a child.

I wondered whether to point out that 'the accident' probably never took place but, at that moment, the doorbell rang and a key was turned in the front door lock. A small, almost circular whirlwind swept into the kitchen and, without pause for breath, refilled the kettle, started up the coffee machine, cleaned the sink, and berated the three of us to within an inch of our lives for practically everything we had ever done since the day we were born.

'Hello Mrs. Tiggy,' said Robbie but it was pointless until this miniscule force of nature had finished its diatribe.

It boiled down to the fact that I had neglected to tell her that I would be away *or* that I was back *and* that I hadn't told her about the bishop's tragic death so she had to hear it on the news; that a heathen like Alessina had no business to be in a Christian household; that Robbie should know that big boys don't cry but she wasn't surprised he was upset; that would be his conscience given that he had marched away and left the vicar willy-nilly and what was he doing here anyway now he had chosen another parish for his unwelcome presence? All that was neatly wrapped up in the side issues that the whole place was filthy; that Sarah at the hairdresser's was pregnant by that wastrel boyfriend of hers and that she didn't know what the world was coming to.

I wondered how many more people had a key to my house.

'Right!' said Alessina, briskly. 'Robbie, you are coming with me. We have a cleaning-up session to do. Bel, you'll be okay with Mrs. Tiggy to look after you? Good.'

She didn't wait for me to reply and I gestured hopelessly. I could see she wanted to get Robbie out of the house before he said anything that might be spread around the village and get him to her abode in order to do some shamanistic work with him to clear any unresolved energies. Exorcism in itself isn't always the end of the road; sometimes it takes two or three goes and some residual clearing and replacing of energies is required. This kind of stuff isn't always straightforward either side of the veil. I hoped she would be able to help Robbie with the guilt that was now almost subsuming him and I thanked God he was willing to go with her; when they first met, he had practically crossed himself at horror at the thought of knowing a witch. Much like Mrs. Tiggy was doing now.

Once they had gone, Mrs. Teague switched off her Craggy-Island-crazy persona with the flick of an internal switch and sat down at the table to take my hand.

'Oh, my dear,' she said. 'I am so sorry. I know you cared for him very much. I wouldn't have dreamt of staying away if Robbie hadn't told me not to come again until you were back from your trip. Of course, I should never have listened to him. Now, you don't need to tell me anything but I can see quite clearly you've been in the wars. And not only over the bishop.'

Honest, bright-blue eyes stared at me anxiously from a ruddy, cheery face topped with spiky brown hair, She was tiny; less than five feet tall and bustled even when she was sitting still. I didn't remember her but I *knew* I could trust her.

'I was in an accident,' I said. 'I've got a head injury. My memory is affected. I can't even remember whether I should call you Mrs. Teague or Mrs. Tiggy. I'm afraid I hardly remember you at all. And I hardly remember the bishop at all either. It's not really been a good few days and I suspect it's going to get worse.'

She nodded and patted my hand.

'I thought something must have happened,' she said. 'You're usually good at being in touch. I did telephone but you didn't call back. You are good at calling back.'

'I don't have my mobile phone any longer,' I said. 'And although I think I can remember how to be a vicar, I'm scared of all the emails and the messages because I don't remember the people.'

'Well, we can get *that* sorted now,' she said. 'And 'Mrs. Tiggy' will do very well.

'Now, if you've lost your memory, you won't have been in touch with the bishop's family? I think you should. They know who you are, even if you don't remember them.'

'Well, no. I only found out this morning that he and I were in a relationship. How many of his family do I know?'

'His mother,' said Mrs. Tiggy. 'Maureen Joans. She lives less than five miles from here. How about you drive over now and I'll have your messages and emails sorted by the time you get back?'

Oh, how wonderful to have such practical advice and help.

'But won't I make it worse by not remembering him?'

'Well, she'll need to know you've lost your memory for sure,' said Mrs. Tiggy. 'Or she'll be thinking very strange things about someone who loves her son. And, as you well know—or *should* well know—it's all about the listening not the talking, isn't it?'

Oh wise, *wise* Mrs. Tiggy!

'Should I call her first?'

'I'll call her now and tell her you're on your way. You can get yourself sorted and, if it's inconvenient, I can let you know before you start out. And I can tell her about your "accident."'

'Mrs. Tiggy, did you just put "accident" in inverted commas?'

'I did, dear. There's something fishy going on around here or I'm a Dutchman.'

That old phrase, beloved of my father, made me laugh.

'You're right,' I said. 'I ended up in hospital being told I'd crashed my car. But my car is in the garage. I may have crashed someone else's car but Paul didn't think so.'

'You've seen him then? When?'

'Yesterday. The morning I got back. I was totally confused and he only told me that he was the bishop and that we were friends. Not that... well, he didn't mention any more. But he said he used to be a doctor and it looked as though I'd been hit on the head with something rather than being in a smash.

'I liked him,' I added, somewhat inconsequentially.

'Of course you did! He's—was—a lovely man. Now, if I write down the directions, are you up to driving?'

'I think so.'

'Good. Now go and tidy up, there's a good girl. Clerical collar!

Decent trousers if you simply *can't* manage a skirt! Clean those shoes! Get along now, get along!'

Sarah Joans opened the door of her picture-perfect thatched cottage and ushered me in, silently. Her eyes were haunted. I touched her briefly on the shoulder and she patted my hand with hers in reply. In the living room was another, younger woman. Paul's sister perhaps?

We shook hands as Sarah introduced me as Paul's fiancée and her mouth trembled. I did the vicar thing of taking her hand in both of mine but said nothing. In a situation like this, the eyes have it every time.

I sat carefully on the edge of an armchair containing rather a lot of cat and accepted the offer of a cup of tea. For once, I didn't need one but it's part of the English mourning ritual, a little like a truncated version of the Jewish custom of sitting *shiva*.

I don't do fussy grieving stuff; never have. I don't say 'I'm sorry for your loss' because, to me, that sounds empty and meaningless. Instead, I sat with lowered eyes in a kind of receptive silence to discourage unnecessary breaking of the stillness of sorrow and, when Sarah had returned with my tea and some Rich Tea biscuits, I said, 'Will you tell me what you know, please?'

'What we know or what they say?' said Frances, Paul's sister, bitterly.

'What you know,' I said. 'The other can wait.'

Both women nodded and, taking turns, told me that Paul had been found hanging from a light fitting in his house. I winced, not only because that gave me a graphic picture but because I knew that a suicide from hanging might be problematical for the soul—but then, I didn't believe this was suicide.

Neither did they.

'Was there a note?'

'Yes, but we still don't believe it. Here, look...' I almost told Frances that I loved her as she took out her phone and searched for the photograph she had managed to take of the note before the police took it away as evidence.

I looked at the picture, recognising the handwriting from the message that he had sent to warn me.

I'm sorry. I can't go on pretending.
Please try to forgive me.
I love you all. Please look after Annabel for me.
Paul.

Okay, so now we knew…

Chapter Sixteen

BOTH WOMEN SAT up straighter at my sharp intake of breath.

'It's fake?' said Frances, almost in a whisper. 'It *must* be fake...'

'Yes, it's fake. It's not suicide, it's murder,' I said. 'Oh, poor man, they must have made him write it. Oh God.'

'Can we prove it?' asked Sarah, anxiously.

I leant back without thinking and was sworn at and scratched by a forgotten and furious cat. It jumped down onto the floor and stalked away in disgust.

'Ow.' I sucked the blood budding on my bare wrist. 'Well, I don't know if I can *prove* it, but I can certainly point out that a man in love would generally spell his fiancée's name correctly.'

'He didn't?'

'No. I expect he introduced me to you as Bella or Bel?' I said to Sarah. She nodded.

'Neither is short for Annabel and he must have known that very well,' I said. I peered at it again to make absolutely sure and blessed him for making sure that the two 'n's of *Annabel* were clearly written with space between them. There was no way they could be mistaken for an 'm.'

'I thought it was Annabel,' said Sarah. 'I'm sure I've called you Annabel.'

'And I'm sure I was polite enough not to correct you,' I replied.

'Why did you say 'he *must* have known that?' not 'he *knew* that'?' asked Frances.

'It's my memory,' I said. 'I'm so sorry. I had an accident. Lost my memory. Didn't Mrs. Tiggy—Teague— tell you? It's incredibly patchy. But I'm pretty ferocious about correct spellings of my name and everyone I love, or who loves me, would know that.'

We sat in silence for a moment and I felt the atmosphere become steadily cooler. Both women were looking at me as though I were more of a stranger than I actually was. The terrible truth is that as soon as the word *murder* has been spoken then someone has to be to blame and sitting in front of Middle England right now was an obvious scapegoat. I almost ate a Rich Tea biscuit just to break the chill, but I wasn't that desperate.

Several elephants in the room began to loom so I sighed and addressed the biggest one first.

'The police came round to see me,' I said. 'They had some ridiculous story about why they thought he might have killed himself.'

Both women looked blank.

Bugger.

Wrong elephant.

'Did they suggest anything to you?' I ploughed on before they had time to ask what it might be.

'They just asked if he was depressed or if anything had happened to upset him,' said Sarah. 'I wondered if you two…'

'If we had broken up? No, and even if we had, I know that wouldn't have made him kill himself. He's a bishop for goodness' sake! He has a faith. He had a purpose.' I noticed I was mixing tenses but you do when people die, especially if you believe in an afterlife.

'So, what did they suggest to you? What was the ridiculous story?' That was Sarah.

Metaphorically, I crossed my fingers. 'The same. That I'd been unfaithful or broken it off.'

'I suppose that was the logical assumption. But *murder!* Who would want to kill him? Oh, I'm not sure if that's not worse.'

Poor Sarah, her face crumpled as the realisation sank in, yet again, that her son wasn't coming back. Bereavement does that to you; you almost recover while you are talking about practicalities and about the loved one but then, in the spaces, the truth settles back down on your heart like a lead weight with slashing claws. A bit like a hostile cat, really.

I licked my wrist again. Interestingly, neither woman had offered me antiseptic or a plaster. In the silence, I considered the fact that neither woman had suggested moving the cat either. Was it simply that I wasn't that welcome here? They weren't required to like me, of course but I thought there might be more sisterly solidarity.

More elephants…

'There'll be an inquest,' I said. 'Have they said when?'

'No,' they both shook their heads.

I gave up and ate a biscuit. It seemed like the least I could do. I dunked it, deliberately, both for the sake of my taste buds and to see if that action made either of them despise me. It did.

It was one of those moments in every person of colour's life when we have absolutely no idea whether people dislike us for our character or our skin tone. Or both.

Now we had established that it was murder, the reason why *could* include the fact that a white British bishop in a predominantly white part of England wished to marry a woman who was brown.

A sudden wave of sorrow hit me because, somehow, I knew that Paul had loved my milk coffee skin and black hair. A half-memory of hands caressing me mingled with the clearer recollection of the gentleness with which he had looked at my head wound. My eyes prickled and I dug my nails into the palm of my hand to stop the tears from coming.

I have to own up now and say that the reason I don't cry in front of others is not because I'm afraid of looking ugly. Quite the opposite. I cry so beautifully that it looks totally fake and any noises I emit, for some reason, sound like laughter. Some strange genetic factor in both my make-up and my mother's meant that we cried like movie stars; no redness, no swollen eyes, not even a snotty nose, just big, showy, dewdrop tears falling one by one.

Unless you can cry like that, you can have no idea how much it pisses other people off. Especially if they think you are also laughing at them through your tears. 'Crocodile tears' is one pejorative term for the way I cry; so I don't.

I took a deep breath and addressed that final elephant.

'Do you think someone might have wanted him dead rather than see him marry a woman who is half Indian?' I said.

'Of course not!' they both said, too swiftly, and I forgave them instantly because they were horrified that I might realise that was exactly what they had thought.

I took my leave as gently as I could, asking on the doorstep as they showed me out whether it would be possible for me to see Paul's body.

They didn't know.

And just as they were closing the door, I found myself doing that clichéd thing of all TV detectives—turning back with one last question.

'Who found him?'

'His secretary.'

At least that was another avenue of enquiry.

Sarah stayed at the door to wave me off which was both kind and polite. I crashed the gears, probably as much as a gesture to demonstrate that I was upset as much as anything else, and drove away.

I suppose any respectable vicar-detective type, like Sidney Chambers or Father Brown, would hasten off to see the body, interview the bishop's secretary or hassle the police. My brain tried to convince me to do that, too, but no, in theory, at least, I had the ability to go to the horse's mouth. I was hoping I could persuade Jon to take me to see Paul's soul and find out the truth behind all this for myself.

In the meantime, I had a ton of administration to deal with as best I could. I was totally in awe of Mrs. Tiggy by the end of the day as she had deleted sixty per cent of the emails as irrelevant; dealt with thirty-five per cent of the rest of them, opened and discarded ninety per cent of all the outstanding mail and co-ordinated my diary.

We sat down together and went through everything that still needed doing and she guided me through the bits I couldn't remember with a brisk kindliness.

As dusk fell, she left, promising to return on Monday at 10am and I was, finally, left alone to ponder. I found myself wandering over to the church, hoping to sit in communion with both soul and source and maybe speak with Ariel. That went out of the window when I saw the altar, which had collapsed again. Talk about high maintenance...

With a sigh, I picked up the cross and placed it upright on the floor.

? I said to Ariel, who was shining nicely in the corner.

Demon held altar up. Demon gone.

How did a demon get in it in the first place? It's an altar. *It should be sanctified and protected.*

Demon sleep. Demon old. Demon activated. Many church altars have demons when clergy despise or hate.

Was it me that brought it? That activated it?

No. You did not see it. Is all. You did not see angel or demon. Now you can. Now is all there is.

I suppose I should have alerted the parish council or the police or something, but I just went back to the house and had some supper and an early night. There's only so much you can cope with in one day. I succumbed to a ready meal, in case you wanted to know. And yes, it was disgusting.

Jon woke me, gently, at about one o'clock.

'Mmmmgnff,' I said, as you do.

'Busy night,' he said. 'We have some regular work and, knowing you, you'll want to make a diversion.'

'May I?' I sat up at once.

'Of course. You don't get paid for all this work, do you? There have to be a few perks here and there. Mind you, he's very fresh across the line; you may not get all that much sense out of him. There had to be a pretty major death-moment rescue—no, don't ask. Currently above both our non-existent pay grades, I'm afraid.'

Trust me, there is nothing more surreal than considering what to wear when you're about to travel to the afterlife to greet a just-dead bishop who was also your forgotten lover. Sweatshirt and jeans it was, then...

We went a different way, this time—not through the solar system but down into a tunnel in the ground. The blue Panda bounced and bumped on what felt like cobblestones until it emerged into a great, softly-lit space the size of eternity, filled with planets.

'It's like the planet, Magrathea,' said Jon, knowing I would understand. Our mutual hero, Douglas Adams, might have been an atheist but he knew more about the mystical and the ridiculous than most of the priests on our planet.

'This is the hospital wing,' said Jon. 'Where souls who keep their connection with their soul but who have died from debilitating illness or who have had sudden, violent ends are brought. The former need time to rebuild their etheric body; not so much from the illness, frankly, as from some of the medicines, and the latter are in spiritual shock, sometimes torn between realities.'

I wasn't sure I quite understood but that didn't matter; all that did matter was seeing Paul again and finding out what had happened.

Jon parked the Panda outside what looked like a large island in the ether, containing a cottage hospital with people in muted colours wandering in its gardens. Their clothing varied from modern dress to what seemed to be togas.

John waited outside, admiring the multi-coloured flower borders, while I went in, suddenly wishing that I had bothered to dress better. No one greeted me but a kind of pathway of colours opened up at my feet and led me down the hallway to a room at the end on the left.

I'd expected a quiet, peaceful room but let's just say that heavenly hospitals have the best soundproofing in the world *and* the best entertainment. As I opened the door and slipped in I was engulfed by a cacophony of rock music being played live. I stood, rooted to the spot, while Jimi Hendrix riffed with Janis Joplin and someone who looked worryingly like Beethoven on one of those portable electric pianos. They were playing for Paul who was sitting, in teeshirt and sweatpants, on what looked exactly like an earthly hospital bed.

The music petered out as soon as they saw me and all three laughed at my jaw-dropped face.

'It's a live one!' said Janis. 'Roll over, Beethoven, we'd better give them some space.

'We were trying to get through to your man but he's still in shock. Maybe you can do better, babe?'

The three trooped out, taking their instruments with them. Jimi Hendrix high-fived me and I don't think I'll ever spiritually wash again.

Paul didn't register me for a few moments and I was able to look at him closely. I took both his hands and sat quietly, waiting. I could see that around his now not-physical neck there was a dark mark and his eyes looked both haunted and huge in a strangely-lined face but, when he looked up and recognised me, his features lit up and shifted back into pretty much the Paul I had—so briefly—known.

Some bitty scraps of memory jostled for space as my heart leaped. We hugged; he still had his own scent and I inhaled it deeply and said the most fervent 'thank you' of my life to the all-arching divinity that had allowed me to be here and to see him again.

Where to start? I sat on the bed facing him, holding hands again. Time passed and he came fully into himself.

'I saw your note,' I said. 'It wasn't suicide.'

'Nice to see you too, Bella,' he said with a twinkle. 'Good to know it is all true, isn't it?'

'What, Beethoven getting into rock music?' I said. 'I don't think I've ever heard a sermon on that one.'

'There's still time. Though I don't believe the new bishop would approve.

'Listen, darling Bel—what can you remember? You can't stay here long so I need to know what to tell you.'

'I know we were together but not much about it. Alessina told me,' I said. 'I know someone is trying to stitch us up as a ring of paedophiles. I know you told me it wasn't suicide by writing "Annabel." I know that Robbie has been infected—I exorcised him—and that there was a dark presence in St. Mary's altar. I threw my phone in the septic tank.'

'Okay, well it *was* suicide but I wanted the world to think differently. Can you work on its being murder?'

'What?'

'Darling, the forces behind this are pretty powerful. They *can't* get into you if you are clear and focused on good but they can if you let them. But they aren't as smart as they think they are. If you let them in consciously and allow your death, you get to take some of them, at least, with you.'

'Bloody hell!'

'Yes, it was pretty horrid and to be honest, I didn't do a very good job. There isn't exactly a text book. But at least some of the essence of what has been attacking us 'died' with me. There'll be some residuals but it should be alleviated, for a while at least.

'But Bel, dark forces *do* exist on earth, always have done and always will. They don't like it when we clear up the litter, as it were. They hide in plain sight in people and situations. Mostly they start out as mischief, I think, but human evil soon gives them more food than they ever dreamt of.

'Are there any humans I should be beware of?'

'Always. Watch out for the new vicar. And, I'm afraid, for Robbie. They bit him deep.'

'Alessina took him home with her.'

'Ah, well she should be able to get the taproot out, then.'

'What about me?'

'You're clear. I don't know if that was because of the memory loss or whether you don't have the holes in your psyche where they can gather.

'Celeste wasn't so lucky. She—or her possessor—was the one who tried to kill you. She hit you with a poker and then crashed her car with the two of you in it. It's only by Grace that you didn't die too.'

'So it was a car accident and it wasn't…'

'Yes.'

'And did she take that demon with her?'

'No, because it made her intend to kill another. You can only take them through—or transmute them—if you give your own life voluntarily. Story of the cross. That's what it means when it says Christ took away the sins of the world; he took on the demons of his time and transmuted them through his voluntarily-given death.'

'As you did.'

Heaven isn't a place with false modesty, so he just said, 'yes.'

We sat in silence for a moment. I was thinking.

'Was there a human there who made you do it? Or was it an energy form?'

'It was a both. An energy form in what was left of two humans.'

'Will you tell me who?'

'No, Bel, I won't. You see, much of this has come about because I was investigating claims of a genuine paedophile ring within the church. My death will bring that to light.'

'But they think *you* are in that ring or even leading it!'

'For now. But if you point out at the inquest that I didn't write that suicide note or that, if I did, I was forced to, then there's a good chance that it will be uncovered. If I tell you the names, you will think of them again and again and that's a clear line for a negative energy to follow. I'm not putting you in that danger, Bel. No, we have to let the mills of God grind. If you just pranced up to the police and say 'so-and-so did it,' it wouldn't help.'

I could see that. I didn't like it but I could see it.

'You have to go now,' said Paul. 'I have to move on. It's time. I love you, Bella, and I'm so grateful for the happiness you gave me. If your memory does return, try not to grieve too much. I'm off on an adventure and so are you. We will meet again.'

'But not yet,' I quoted *Gladiator*.

'But not yet.' He smiled. 'At least it wasn't another Douglas Adams quote!'

He kissed me, gently, on the mouth. It was lovely. And then he simply faded into the light and was gone.

I sat there, on that hospital bed, for a long time, not even thinking, really, just resting in the softness of the room. Eventually a youngish man dressed as a hospital orderly looked in and said there was a man with a blue Fiat Panda waiting for me outside.

'Of course,' I said, getting up, reluctantly.

'You like it here?' he said.

'I do.'

'We're always looking for staff.'

'Oh, I'm not dead.'

'Ah. Well, when you are…' He smiled and I chuckled.

He indicated which way I should go to find the exit (I would have headed off in exactly the wrong direction) and walked beside me, exuding the most glorious calmness. I felt as if I knew him from somewhere and sneaked a sideways look, but no. We reached the door and he gave me his hand to guide me down four very steep steps that I didn't remember being there before. It was the hand of someone who had done plenty of manual work and on the wrist was a scar. Startled, I looked into his eyes, saw the whole of creation and fell into it.

'Steady on, vicar!' he said, with a voice full of laughter as he stopped me from falling down the steps and then he was opening the door of the blue Panda.

'Hey Jon!'

'Hey Yourself. Thanks for finding her for me.'

'My pleasure.'

'P…p…pleased to meet you,' I stuttered.

'Oh, we are old friends, Bella,' he replied with a smile and stepped back.

I turned round to wave, just like a child waving goodbye to a parent, and he waved back. For a moment, his presence wavered and I saw pure light and then we were round a corner and he was gone.

'Um…' I said. 'I thought you said you'd never met him.'

'Met who?' said Jon innocently and ungrammatically.

I shut up.

That night we took Holly back to find the father who had killed her and bring him up to the hospital lands where he would go into rehabilitation. His soul and psyche found it incredibly hard to re-knit themselves (imagine what it must be like to an abuser who comes to comprehend exactly what you have done with no more blinkers, barriers or self-defence) but we managed it in the end. But what we took to the hospital lands was more a bleeding, charred body than a human being and it would be a long journey to recovery.

This time I didn't protest or question the quest to save someone who had done such evil. I didn't know how long it would last back on Earth but, for the moment, I finally understood the meaning of unconditional love. I knew that no heavenly soul could ever be totally happy while just one other soul was suffering torment or living in cruelty. The task was to heal everyone; no exceptions.

Jon dropped me off about ten minutes—or fourteen hours—after picking me up and I curled up in bed and slept.

In the dream, I was with Celeste in her house. We were talking over the planned exorcism and, while we did, Celeste kept getting bigger and bigger until she was twice my size. Her colour was darkening and the part of me that noticed (the rest of me was happily eating an omelette) was scared.

I seemed to be simultaneously inside my body and watching, so I saw her pick up the poker from the set of fireside implements behind me and smash me on the head with it. I saw the blood and my shocked face as I fell sideways onto the floor.

Then I watched as she dragged me (how did she have the strength?) out through the back door and into the garage and into her car. I watched from within the car as she drove out of her driveway and into the street and headed for the by-pass. As she hurtled the car out right in front of a truck, the dreaming me screamed and a great scarlet being with wings wrapped itself around my unconscious body so that time slowed down and I was cocooned as the accident happened.

I saw my almost unharmed body lying on the road, with the angel still kneeling over me to protect me and Celeste's smashed and bloody corpse trapped in the crumpled car. I saw the soul of the truck driver shiver and shake and work itself out of his body, collecting its psyche on the way and being met by an angel. I saw the horror and shock on the faces of people all around us... and I saw the hideous blackness that was the demon ooze itself out of Celeste's body and look around, seeking a replacement life to infest.

I burst into wakefulness, soaked in sweat and panting. It was seven o'clock in the morning and yes, as per normal, someone was ringing the bloody doorbell.

Chapter Seventeen

IT WAS THE police again. The equivalent of a dawn raid, I suppose, with a warrant. The thought of a lie-in was beginning to obsess me. This was a Saturday. Anyone with a sensible job at least gets a lie-in on Sunday but I guess that wasn't going to be an option here.

'Oh, good grief,' I said and started unlocking the door. The next half hour was awkward to say the least.

Five police officers came in, knocking me sideways which, until I realised that I was invisible, pissed me off no end. Still, at least, they didn't get to see me in my dressing gown.

Fortunately, they all started speaking at once which drowned out my voiced protests. They'd seen my silhouette through the stained glass and couldn't work out where I'd gone. For a moment, *I* couldn't work out where I'd gone. Three of them dispersed through the house, looking for me and shouting that they had a warrant. Sergeant Marks, the kind officer who had been concerned for my health, went through to the kitchen and placed a pile of paperwork on the table.

She waited until all four other police were with her and then started briefing them. I stood with my back up against the back door, trying to be as small and silent as possible, and wondering how soon I could get out of the house.

'No one here. Absolutely no one,' reported the three men who done the preliminary search. 'But the bed is still warm with the covers thrown back. She hasn't gone far.'

'That's very strange,' said Sergeant Marks. 'Dean, take a look around the garden and across to the church, would you? Oh, and in the garage, too.

I *just* got out of his way in time.

'Okay,' she continued. 'In the meantime, we are looking for the following:

'A mobile phone or several phones.

'Any kind of personal diary.

'Bank statements. The bank we know of is releasing her statements but there may be some we don't know of.

'Photographs. Both on computer and physical.

'Any evidence at all of ground, floor or walls being disturbed or repainted.

'Remember, this is a potential murder enquiry. We are, ultimately, looking for the body of Stephen Rivers.'

'I'm here.' It was a whisper but I heard it clearly. It was the voice of a child.

I've never felt terror like it. What if there *was* a murdered boy buried in the garden and even I didn't even know for sure if I were innocent? Of course, I thought I was but that counted for nothing. If they found him…

I felt Stephen's soul in a soft silvery waft. Though he had died as a child, his soul was the same size as a grown-up's and able to communicate.

Murdered? I thought.

'Yes,' and a picture of just how, came into my head. I shuddered.

Was I part of it?

Yes, I know, that was the single most selfish question I could have asked. But I really, really needed to know.

'No.'

Was it the bishop?

'No.'

Helpful but not exactly evidence. Surely, DNA would prove…? But that took time and I'd be in jail while they checked.

It's amazing just how selfish you can be when you're up against the wall, implicated in a paedophile murder ring and invisible to boot. Stephen was dead; his parents needed to know so they could start to grieve and the wheels of justice could begin but right now, I needed, *so* needed, his body *not* to be found.

Where are you?

'Rhododendron.'

Yes, there was a useful overhang of those bushes by the gate at the end of the garden. My God, he might not even be buried...

'Leaving now.' The soul's voice was soft as a cobweb in my ear. 'You hearing me opened pathway.' And it was gone. I managed, in my terror, to be pleased that it wasn't trapped on earth despite the manner of his dying. I wasn't quite as sure about knowing in advance where his body was, in retrospect, given my sudden lack of plausible deniability, but that was a problem for when I was visible again. For the moment, I just needed to be out of the way.

With the police turning everything upside down, I managed to sneak out of the back door. Yes, Sergeant Marks did look up and stare when the door appeared to blow open of its own accord but I couldn't help that. At least I had the sense not to close it behind me.

Out in the garden, I went to the rhododendrons and peered underneath them. Yes, there was earth that looked fairly recently dug. Shit. They were going to find that easily enough.

I sent up a stark prayer for help and, blundering slightly with the shock of it all, made my way to the church, remembering halfway there that I hadn't got the key.

It was open; of course it was. That church didn't do locks or keys in any normal manner. Standing in the half-open doorway I had a sense of *déjà vu* as I watched Lucie trying to put the altar back together again.

It was crumpled as though it had imploded rather than exploded this time and it wasn't having anything to do with her arm waving or whatever magical words she might be reciting.

'Who *are* you?' I said out loud, without thinking.

Lucie spun around and stared at... well, nothing.

Speak as me, said Ariel in my ear.

That might be a good idea. It might not. Oh well...

'I am the angel of this church,' I said, lowering my voice in a rather pathetic attempt to disguise it. 'The demon has been removed from that altar.'

Lucie's face couldn't have gone whiter.

'Who are you?' I said again.

'It's gone?' she whispered. 'Oh, thank God.' And she fell on her knees, covered her face with her hands and began to cry.

'I'm so sorry, so sorry,' she said, over and over, virtually dissolving into a sea of hiccups and snot. Uncharitably, I was pleased that she couldn't cry beautifully.

'Who are you?' I said a third time, wondering how long it would be before I was visible again.

'Just a very stupid girl who got in trouble,' she gulped. 'I didn't mean to do it.'

'Didn't mean to do what?'

'Any of it.'

Not entirely helpful. I looked at Ariel to see if she had anything to say. She made a warning gesture. Visible, she said.

I backed away. Manifesting suddenly in a church didn't seem to be a good idea, let alone manifesting in just a dressing gown (eat your heart out, Arthur Dent) but I did want to find out more. I backed out of the door and stood in the porch, trying to work out what to do next.

I could see two policemen in my garden across the churchyard and my heart jumped. But there was nothing I could do there. Instead, I walked back into the church and greeted Lucie as if I'd just arrived.

'Lucie? What's the matter? Oh my. What's happened to the altar?'

The girl turned a tear-stained face to me and wiped her nose with her sleeve. I handed her a clean tissue and sat down beside her on the chancel steps. Tentatively, I put an arm around her shoulder and she nestled into me. I rearranged the dressing gown to stop important stuff falling out.

'I'm so, so sorry,' she said. 'I don't know what else to say.'

'How about you start at the beginning,' I said. 'I know there has been some very strange stuff going on here. I know there has been demonic activity; I had to do two exorcisms yesterday and there is something very wrong going on. This is a concerted attack, Lucie, not just a set of coincidences. And you've been a part of it, I think?'

She looked at me through swollen eyes, misery oozing out of every pore. Then something else looked out of those eyes, two hands, like claws, clutched at my clothing and the world darkened.

Instinct and Ariel saved me. The angel sang a sudden sharp note that seemed to infuse me with strength and I jerked away from a strange kind of stickiness, twisting sideways just as Lucie reached out to pick up a fallen candlestick and struck at my head.

I fell off the chancel steps and rolled into the Nave. Above me loomed something that had finished being a beautiful woman, for the moment at least. It was still using Lucie's body but nothing about her seemed to be quite the right shape any more.

'You pathetic little runt,' said a distortion of her voice. 'You interfering little weasel. You should be dead four times over by now. You won't escape this time. They'll find everything we put here and you and your precious bishop's reputations will be in the filth where you belong.'

Out of the corner of my eye, I saw Sergeant Marks at the church door.

'Why?' I said, wriggling backwards as Lucie's body lunged at me again. She seemed to have little coordination, thank God. 'What did we ever do to you?'

'Interference! Stupid do-gooders.'

I knew I had to keep her focused on me; to try and get her to say something incriminating.

'What have you done?' I said, scrambling to my feet and facing the doorway so that she would face me. 'What have you put in my garden?'

'A child. A child we took. A child that gave us strength. And they'll blame you.' Lucie's mouth was all wrong as she spat out the words. If it hadn't been so terrifying I'd have been fascinated. It seemed like two beings in parallel; a parasite on a helpless host.

I considered speaking the words of the exorcism but I knew I didn't have the power or the strength to deal with this shadow-form alone, let alone in a dressing gown. All I could do was keep her talking so Sergeant Marks could hear.

'You got Bishop Paul accused of paedophilia. It was you. You killed him. I know it wasn't suicide,' I said.

'Yessss,' it said, with satisfaction. 'And now I will kill you.'

She lunged at me with the candlestick again, smashing it onto the rood screen as I managed to jump away. Pieces of wood splintered in all directions and suddenly I was furious instead of scared. Whatever this was, it was just nasty; vicious and nasty. And I had a secret weapon.

It saw my eyes flicker over to the door and turned to see the sergeant and one of her constables watching. I'd swear it snarled and then it threw itself at me.

'Rus-el!' I hissed, throwing up my arms to defend myself and receiving a nasty crack on the forearm from that dratted candlestick.

The air around me fizzed with noise and movement, both police officers recoiled as a grey shape roared in through the door and I fell to the ground with my arms over my head. Lucie screamed and screamed again, her body jerking as a swarm of bees engulfed it, causing her to crash down to the floor, convulsing.

For a moment, it seemed to me that the swarm was just one huge queen bee, looking at me.

'Kill?' it seemed to ask.

'Not the girl, just the demon,' I said. The Great Bee gathered herself and, lifting something intangible, it rose up, leaving the bodies of those workers who had sacrificed themselves to save me. In one swooping movement, the swarm looped around the altar and then dived back out of the door. Sergeant Marks didn't scream. Much.

Lucie lay unconscious, her face and arms swollen with stings.

After a few moments that were very cloudy, I was vaguely aware of the Sergeant calling for an ambulance. 'Suspected anaphylactic shock,' she was saying as she knelt down next to Lucie's body. 'And I think the vicar may have a broken arm.'

I tried to deny that but there's no doubt, that arm did hurt. All around me, the whole world seemed to be very vague and woozy. The last sensation before I fainted was of something red and strong holding me in its arms and I knew I was safe.

I woke up in hospital.

As you do.

I was a bit annoyed about that and also about the plaster cast on my left arm. Robbie was sitting beside me together with Mrs. Tiggy so that, at least, was slightly different.

Sergeant Marks was standing behind them.

'Ah,' she said. 'Are you *compos mentis*?'

'I think so,' I said. 'Hello Robbie; hello Mrs. Tiggy. I take it my arm is broken?'

'Yes, Bel, it is,' said Robbie.

'Are *you* okay?' I said to him, doubtfully. I didn't fancy encountering any more possessed clergy any time soon.

'Yes, I'm fine. Alessina saw to that,' he said.

'Rev'd Annabel?' Sergeant Marks stepped forwards. 'What did you mean when you said, "I know he didn't kill himself?"'

'The suicide note,' I said. 'If it were genuine, he would have spelled my name correctly. It's *Amabel*, not Annabel. He knew that. I wish you could remember that,' I added somewhat petulantly.

'I do remember that. I was just winding you up,' she said with a twinkle. I wasn't sure whether to believe her or not but it hardly mattered in the in the scheme of things.

'Lucie…?'

'She'll be fine. Once she has helped us with our enquiries, she may *not* be quite so fine. I'm afraid we are digging up your garden, Vicar. At least we will be when the swarm has finally gone.'

'Where is the swarm?'

'In your rhododendrons.'

Yes, it would be. Bees are truly magical beings.

'Alessina will move it for you. So, what happens now?' I asked, wondering if I were under arrest; if anything *had* actually been sorted or if the mess had just got even bigger.

'Hopefully, we find Stephen's body,' said Sergeant Marks. 'Then his parents can, at least, get closure. We test the DNA and we either clear the bishop and you of any involvement or you are in big trouble.'

'You didn't say it was a murder enquiry,' I said. 'I might have been a bit more cooperative if you had.'

'We like to let people's guilt give them away,' said Sergeant Marks. 'So far, I have to say, you don't seem to be displaying a lot of guilt.'

'There will be no DNA matching us,' I said. 'This is a huge, murdering set-up.'

'But by whom,' said Sergeant Marks, pulling up a chair. Robbie and Mrs. Tiggy moved back to give her space. 'And why?'

'I don't know,' I said. 'There's the car crash that killed Celeste, too. But that poor little boy... How old was he?'

'Seven.'

'Jeez. And this is a real paedophile ring? Not just something made up to frame a group of church exorcists?'

'Is that what you are?' Sergeant Marks was as politely disbelieving as most people who watch superhero movies seem to be. Suspend reality for fantastic fictional characters in tight-fitting clothes any time? Of course. Suspend belief for facts from a vicar in an ancient dressing gown? Not so much. Resurrect your hero or heroine? Natch. Accept he or she has a soul that might need to be helped? Nope. Forgive me if I sound a little bitter here, but I am in hospital *again* and broken arms are not exactly on my list of favourite accessories.

After all that, no body was found in the garden. The recently-dug earth under the rhododendron did contain something in what at first appeared to be a shallow grave. It was a tin chest with four well-made rag dolls stuck with pins. It was fairly easy to see that they represented Paul, Robbie, Celeste and me from the colouring and clothing.

'You've certainly got enemies,' said Chief Inspector Johnson who insisted on taking the tin away for forensic examination without removing the pins from the dolls first.

'You're being very superstitious,' said Mrs. Tiggy, disapprovingly, when I protested.

'Two of the dolls are dead and one is lucky to be alive,' I said. 'And the person who did this certainly believes that it brought us harm. Belief is very powerful.'

The hospital wanted me to stay in overnight but as I was, this time, willing to fill in the paperwork to say that I was a leaving against medical advice, they couldn't insist. And so it was that I took my first post-memory-loss services that Sunday with a broken arm, in a church with a propped-up altar, unassisted by a swollen-faced minister who was still helping police with their enquiries and with a police digger sitting in the ruins of my back garden. *I had vegetables in that garden!*

More than forty people showed up for ten o'clock communion which was a bit of a record; I suppose they wanted to be in the know as much as anything else. Paul's death was still a hot topic on the local news, as was the unsuccessful search for the missing boy's body.

I consecrated the sacrament at the hastily reassembled high altar facing the repaired cross and the beautiful stained window of the resurrection instead of facing the congregation at the table below the rood screen, as was the modern custom, and that gave everyone a contented month's worth of gossip and outrage, at least.

The parish ladies, without whom every church, temple, synagogue or mosque would collapse, made us tea and opened a new box of assorted biscuits as we mingled in the church hall afterwards. I couldn't remember most of the people who attended but you can discover quite a lot from people's behaviour when there are plates of mixed biscuits in front of them. Of course, you can learn a lot more when there's a cake and no one has cut it yet, but that's advanced vicar psychology.

There are those who take the biscuit they want (iced or chocolate covered) without compunction, wherever it may be located on the plate; those who automatically take the humblest plain biscuit; those who take the biscuit nearest to them because they don't care which one they have and those who take the biscuit nearest to them so as not to be thought fussy or greedy; those who reject all the biscuits because they're not nice enough; those who take two identical biscuits; those who take two differing ones and those who actually *like* pink wafers. There are, of course, people who genuinely don't want a biscuit but the less said about them, the better. So, having assessed all the biscuit-eaters and answered their questions appropriately (the best biscuit people want the juicy details; the dry biscuit people want to know there isn't a problem; the don't-care people only want to know what's relevant to them, etc. etc.) I said as little as possible, reassured and downplayed and turned the conversation back to them and their lives which were, understandably, far more important and relevant to them than the adventures of a vicar who really should know better. Part of me wanted to say what a wonderful communion it had been because the angels had shown up again but no one else seemed to have noticed and I wisely kept schtum.

The parish council members had to know about the altar, of course, so I showed them after everyone else had gone home. Mrs. Tiggy and Alessina had propped it up with some cardboard boxes and firewood from my shed and although its altar cloth was now too big, it *looked* quite usable which was all I really cared about in the circumstances.

Unilaterally, I'd come to the decision that I'd better tell them some of what had been going on. With the discovery of the dolls with pins in them buried under the bushes, it was quite clear that there was some Satanic involvement somewhere and people would understand that even if they didn't believe in the darker powers behind it.

'Bloody drug-fuelled hooligans,' was the general opinion.

We pondered for some while whether an exploded altar was claimable on the insurance or whether it counted as an "Act of God." I suspected that, as we hadn't reported the original alleged break-in to the police anyway, we were up a gum tree when it came to insurance. Lord knew how much it would cost to bring a stonemason in.

I did insist that the police came and took a good look at it, just in case Stephen's body was hidden underneath, and they searched the church from top to bottom, too, but he wasn't there. I couldn't help wondering why it was that I'd picked up the message from his soul that he *was* in the garden or why the being that had possessed Lucie was so sure it was. Nothing about that made any sense at all.

That afternoon I went to visit Stephen's parents. Apparently they were part of the parish, although not churchgoers, and it's the kind of thing a vicar is supposed to do: the impossible task of working out if there's any comfort we, with our ridiculous beliefs, can bring to agnostic or atheistic folk who are frantic with worry. There almost certainly isn't but it's the job at least to show up.

Nowadays, we can't use our stock-in-trade, 'Your child is in God's care.' That was rarely of much help anyway, because all people want is their loved one back, even if they do believe in heaven. This one was further complicated because I was the only one who knew for sure that Stephen was dead.

'He told me that he's dead and he's fine,' wouldn't hack it for a dozen different reasons.

Anastasia and Robert Rivers lived in a modern bungalow on the edge of the moor. Twins aged about four were playing in the garden when I arrived. It was a circular garden, all around the house, and I was met by a cacophony of barking as I parked outside the gate. I let myself in carefully so as not to give their Yorkshire Terrier a chance to escape and introduced myself in that self-deprecating way that all folk who have to visit people who really have more than enough on their plate without a total stranger arriving will know so well.

Robert was out but Anastasia seemed quite pleased to see me and asked me in. She had another child perched on her hip; a little girl with dark curly hair who chatted to her mother in Greek while she led the way to the kitchen.

I answered in kind and both mother and daughter lit up.

'You speak my language!' said Anastasia, in Greek. 'That is a treat for me. I try so hard but English is so tiring.'

'I only speak the old Greek,' I said. 'So, I will seem very archaic. But yes.'

She made me a cup of tea and talked about Stephen for a good half-hour while the three children played around us and joined in, both in Greek and English. Stephen was a mischievous boy who often went missing for hours on end but then, one night, he had simply never come home. I let Anastasia talk as much as she wanted; there comes a point when you've told everyone you know everything you can think of but you still need to talk and a stranger can come in very useful then. I saw pictures of Stephen from his birth to three months earlier and my heart broke at the knowledge that he would never be coming home; and yet I could say nothing.

Of course, if both the voice in my head and Lucie had been

lying, maybe he was still alive. But strange though it may seem, I knew I could trust the spirit voice even if Stephen were not lying underneath my rhododendrons.

Anastasia knew that the police had been looking in my garden but had found nothing. She was understandably curious as to why they had been searching there. I said they'd had a tip-off which was true enough.

It was only after I said goodbye and walked back to the car that I realised the significance of an hour of switching between Greek and English with a mother and three children. If Stephen had been fluent in Greek, was that the language in which he had spoken to me and I hadn't noticed? I tried to remember if he had actually said, 'Leaving now. You hearing me opened pathway' in English or in Greek.

So, that's how I came to be kneeling under the climbing standard rose tree in my front garden, grubbing around on the grass, because Rhododendron is Greek for 'rose tree.'

Chapter Eighteen

HIDDEN AT THE bottom of the tangled climbing rose, mostly hidden by overgrown grass, was a trap door leading to some kind of mini-cellar or ice box. I had no recollection of its existence which seemed strange as I'd recognised the rest of the house. Maybe I'd never found it before? Even the edges were disguised by the grass and leaves but if you looked carefully there was a rectangle about three feet long and eighteen inches wide. It had been opened recently. I took hold of the metal pull-ring in the middle and tugged.

It was the smell that told me; I didn't have to look. Gagging and with trembling fingers I re-laid the door, got to my feet and stood, rocking slightly and steadying myself with my good hand against the wall of the house.

I'm not proud of the fact that my second reaction, after the horror, was annoyance that my home would now definitely be a crime scene and I'd have to leave the house until the police had finished with it. I supposed I could move into the parish house and share with Lucie—assuming the police had let her go—but the very idea made my heart sink.

But shallowness aside, I knew I had to call the police at once. I had Sergeant Marks's business card so I rang her.

'You didn't look in the front garden,' was all I had to say.

'Where?' her voice was crisp.

'Under the rose tree.'

'Okay. Don't touch *a thing.*' The phone went dead.

I made my way rather shakily to the kitchen and put the kettle on. Stuff doing nothing; they'd already searched the whole of the inside of the house twice although I was sure they'd be checking again. While the tea was brewing, I went upstairs and clumsily pulled a small bag down from the top of the wardrobe so I could pack it with essentials for a couple of nights away. Interestingly, the first bag that came to hand already had some face cream, toothbrush and toothpaste and some clean (and pretty) underwear in it. More, there was an envelope containing a key. There was also a ring box tucked into one of the side pockets. Curious, I opened it to find a yellow gold engagement ring set with a rectangular ruby with square-cut diamonds either side.

I suppose I'd left it there for safety when I went to Worcester. Who knows if the police had found it and left it or missed it? If it were the latter they were pretty appalling at searching, a thought that registered a little niggle in my mind but there was no time to reflect further as they had arrived. Hastily, I packed some essentials and shoved key, box and ring into the pocket of my fleece before I went back downstairs.

Stephen's body lay twisted and grey in that tiny, unknown and previously disused cellar-room and, after the Detective Chief Inspector and Detective Sergeant had talked to me at length in the kitchen, I'd given a statement, had a DNA swab taken and given a set of fingerprints, as I expected, I was told to make myself scarce from the crime scene. The first thing to do, obviously, was to go back to Anastasia and Robert's with Sergeant Marks ('call me Eleanor') to tell them that a child's body wearing the same clothes as Stephen had been found. I wished and wished I could tell them that Stephen had spoken to me and that he had gone through safely but that kind of talk, sadly, is unacceptable in this secular world. All I could do, practically, was hold Anastasia as she wept and then distract the children a little until Robert's mother could get there to help.

When they wanted to know what had made me look in the front garden, that was easily answered. I just said that I hadn't realised that the police hadn't looked in the front until I got back home. Privately, I suspected someone might be looking at that omission in more detail later.

Once I had stayed for as long as I could be of at least some use as a comforter, and made some excruciatingly difficult phone calls on their behalf, I headed off. I could probably have gone to

Alessina's but I chose to drive to Exeter because I knew exactly where the key in my case would fit. It was nearly dusk and there were no lights on at the bishop's palace. I looked around for a side-door that would lead to Paul's own apartment and, when I found it, luckily there was no crime scene tape to prevent me from trying the key in my pocket. It opened the door easily and I slipped inside.

Yes, this place was familiar; from the kitchen where I was sure we had cooked together, to the living room—not the one where he had died; that was in the official part of the residence—and the bedroom where, presumably, we had been lovers.

I found no traces of me there; I suppose sleeping with one of your vicars isn't top of the list of recommended practices for a bishop, so we would have kept ourselves low profile even if we were planning to marry. However, this was somewhere that I could hide out; think and regroup a little even if only for one night.

There was some milk and two eggs in the fridge, canned and packaged food in the cupboards and plenty in the freezer, including a couple of Tupperware pots of leftovers with my handwriting on the top. I opened 'pheasant casserole' and was pleased to find that there was the perfect amount for one. Legally, it all probably belonged to Paul's mother now but I didn't care.

While it was defrosting in the microwave, I made my way through to the public part of the building and to the reception room where he had died. Nothing seemed out of place; even the chair that he must have stood on was standing neatly against a wall by the door to the hallway. There was no clue as to which light-fitting he had used and I was slightly concerned at how utterly *not* upset I still was about his death. Yes, it was tragic but there was very little sense of personal loss. I was far more affected by that sad little body in the cellar under my rose tree. After I had eaten my excellent casserole from a bowl on my lap in the private living room and flicked around the television for some passing entertainment, I got up and made a thorough search of the whole flat. Yes, I knew the police had already been here and no, I didn't know what I was looking for; it just seemed like the right thing to do.

I used the lights, of course, so anyone could have seen that somebody was resident. There was no intention of hiding but, even so, when I heard the sound of a knock at the side door at about nine o'clock, I jumped like a guilty burglar.

Before I answered, I took the ring box out of my pocket and slid the ruby onto the third finger of my left hand where it fitted perfectly and glittered in the electric light.

Something in my head said, 'Showtime!' and I opened the door.

A man and a woman stood there, silhouetted in the light from the hallway.

'Yes? Can I help you?' I said, as though this were my home.

'Oh! Reverend Amabel,' said the man. 'We didn't know you were here.'

'Not my usual night?' said the part of me that obviously didn't care.

'Er... no,' said the man. 'Um... May we come in?'

'Perhaps you'd be kind enough to introduce yourselves?' I said. 'You may have heard that I've lost part of my memory.'

'But you remembered how to get in here,' said the woman, crisply.

'Yes, it's very haphazard,' I said. 'But I'm afraid both of you are a complete blank.'

No one likes being told you don't know who they are. Both the man and the woman bristled slightly.

'I'm the Archdeacon,' said the woman. 'Josephine Malone. And this is the bishop's chaplain, Bill Prentiss.'

'How do you do,' I said, not moving.

'May we come in?' said the Archdeacon.

'It's quite late,' I said. 'Was there something particular that you wanted?'

'Yes,' said the Venerable Josephine, tartly. 'We wanted to know why you are here.'

'I'm here because I found the body of a child hidden in my cellar,' I said. 'The police are there now and, as a crime scene, my house has to be evacuated. This has been my second home for a while and I'm sure Paul would want me to make use of it.

'As you can see, I'm not at my best; my arm was broken by my new assistant yesterday—she attacked me with a church candlestick and she is currently helping the police with some separate enquiries. So, I'm feeling just a little bit fragile and suspicious at the moment and would rather not ask anyone in tonight.'

'But Bel, this is no longer a place where you have any right to be,' said Rev'd Bill. 'There will be a new bishop appointed very soon.'

'Very soon is not now,' I said, holding my ground. 'Was it you who found his body, Bill?'

'Yes, it was.'

'Then you can come in.' I stood back and opened the door.

They took that as a dual invitation, which it wasn't, and both walked in. I offered them tea which they declined and I sat down in the room's one armchair after inviting them both to sit, too.

'Really, I don't think you can be allowed to stay,' said the Archdeacon, perching on the sofa. 'Apart from the fact that you seem to be racking up disaster after disaster wherever you go, this is church property.'

'Wouldn't that be up to the Dean?' I asked, unperturbed. 'I don't really know why you are being quite such a stickler. These are very unusual and upsetting times.'

Even though she was being a queen bee, I realised that I rather liked her. Rev'd Bill, on the other hand, wasn't to my taste at all. Everything about him felt slightly creepy. Even so, I asked him to tell me everything he could about Paul's death.

He obliged, albeit reluctantly. As Paul's fiancée, I did have every right to ask. He said he had missed Paul after Matins when they were due to have a meeting and went to find him. He was already dead and had been for some time.

'And you found the note?'

'I did, I'm afraid.'

'And you noticed that it mentioned someone called Annabel?'

'It mentioned you, yes.'

'No, it mentioned *Annabel*. That's not me.'

'Now who's being a stickler?' he said but he was rattled, I could see. I could also see that there was some energy with him that was creating the creepiness; he was part of the problem.

'Paul would never misspell my name,' I said. 'The police are now treating his death as a murder enquiry. Murder made to look like suicide.'

That made them both sit up and take notice but it rather backfired on me.

'Murder?' said the Archdeacon. '*Murder?*'

'Then this is a crime scene,' said Bill. 'Even more reason for you not to be here. You could tamper with evidence.

'Frankly, I'm surprised the police aren't questioning you now if Stephen Rivers's body has been found where you live.'

'Bill's right, you can't be here,' said the Archdeacon. 'You can stay with me tonight and we'll work something out tomorrow.' That was kind of her but I had no intention of moving.

'I didn't say it was Stephen Rivers's body,' I said to Bill.

'Well obviously it is,' he said without hesitation. 'What other child is missing?'

'That's a good question. Do you know the answer?'

'No, of course I don't!' He was getting rattled again. Good.

'Look,' I said. 'I didn't want to have to say this but I am here with the permission of Sergeant Eleanor Marks who is a part of both investigations. Yes, it's unorthodox but as long as I stick in the private apartments, I'll not be adding a new set of fingerprints and, even though my memory is patchy, I am starting to remember things so she actually thinks it's a good idea that I'm here in case something relevant strikes me. So, I'm kind of here officially. You can call her and check if you like. I've got her number.' I waved the business card.

The bluff worked. Whether the shock of the news of Paul's murder helped, I don't know, but once I'd made it clear I wasn't leaving they couldn't get away fast enough.

I felt heart-achingly lonely after they had gone. This was such an empty space and so was I.

Jon arrived about half an hour after I'd gone to bed. I wasn't sleeping; there was too much running through my mind and I was hoping he'd come.

'No problems finding me, then,' I said as he sat down on the edge of the bed.

'None at all. Sorry I didn't show last night. Heard about your arm and thought you might appreciate a bit more rest.'

'How do you "hear about" stuff that happens on Earth?'

'Celestial universe-wide web,' he said with a grin. 'It is a bit like the Internet but without outages, continual re-starts and frozen screens.'

'Run by Apple, then.'

'Yeah, looks like they got the contract back after the resurrection.'

'It wasn't an apple, in Eden, you prune. More likely a fig.'

'Ah that's my girl; over-thinking a myth like a true theologian.'

'I don't know if it happened, and I don't know if it didn't happen, but I know that the *story* is true,' I quoted one of Jon's favourite sayings while I was growing up.

'Exactly. Right, are you ready?'

'Can I still come with a broken arm?'

'Good question. Let's see what happens to it, shall we?'

What happened was that the plaster stayed behind and the arm was healed. That made no sense whatsoever given that the clothes I wore on Earth travelled with me—as did chocolate. But it wasn't as though chronological time had any remit in the higher worlds and I was getting quite used to oddities and miracles by now.

As we drove through the solar system, I started telling Jon everything that had happened.

'How swift it is, the move between wonder and the norm,' he said and, rightly squashed, I realised how right he was. Less than a week ago I had been struck dumb by the view around me; now I was only interested in my own business.

'How about we stop for a while in the driveway and you can tell me then,' he suggested. 'I've been driving this route for twenty years now and I still want to gaze at it.'

So we did just that. And he did an extra circuit of Hyperion, the amazing, asymmetrical moon of Saturn, just to make the point.

'You know I can't really comment or advise,' said Jon as we sat, parked, by the road to the country house. 'Life isn't my business any more. But I love how the bees are involved. I'm sure you can trust them. And Alessina. And probably yourself. But until you find the root of this darkness, you're not going to be safe. I'm glad you've got Rus-el and Ariel. If you need bigger guns, they'll be able to send them.'

'What I don't understand is Paul's conviction that he brought most of the darkness across with him when he died. And yet I'm sure I saw it in Bill.'

'I expect you did. You haven't realised, yet, the truth in Jesus's parable of the man who cleaned out the space in his head where the demon lived. There were seven more demons only too willing to move in.'

'Oh my God. Then will it never end?'

'The Work is to make sure it does. I think you have a cluster of darkness—if it is an actual paedophile ring then all the participants may be affected. If it's any comfort, energy does clump together so every time you clear some out, then you're weakening the whole. In a movie, of course, the hero would draw them all together in some kind of final showdown and clear up the mess in one go.'

'But life isn't a movie, right?'

'Well, movies have to get their inspiration from somewhere and truth is stranger than fiction.'

'I suppose…' He had made me think but now it was time for this night's work and that was going to need all my attention.

We were working with Sam and Callista tonight, trying to reconnect souls with living people.

'What?' I couldn't get my head around that one at all.

'Psychopaths, mass murderers, all the people who seem to have no soul,' said Callista. 'Sometimes they don't. Or, at least, they have never accessed it so it virtually withers away for that lifetime. Everyone is still connected with the heavens when they are incarnate—that's what they call your "higher self." But if you never use it, your soul goes into a kind of suspended animation. Or, if you make a pact with the darkness, it is part-devoured.'

'Devoured? You mean forever?'

'No, we can always reclaim them because the source of all souls is here and they are immortal. Even if there is only one fragment left in a human, we can re-grow the soul from that.

'And if there is no fragment?'

'There is always a fragment.' Her colour changed as she spoke and I could see that wasn't totally true. 'Nearly always,' she amended.

'But those cases are above our pay grade,' I said.

'Something like that.' When Callista smiled the whole heavens lit up. 'There is always Grace. Radical Grace heals all things, even non-existent souls. You must never believe that there isn't always healing; it just sometimes takes a lot of time and effort.'

'And you wouldn't ever leave those cruel, soulless people to stew in their own juice?'

'No. Everyone is valuable to God.'

'Which could be why so many people don't like God!'

'Yes. Radical Grace could never be popular. Humans are too invested in retribution and judgement to be able to handle it. Hence all the stories of God's wrath that make it seem that you have to earn Grace.'

'But you don't?'

'Bless the girl! You can't! Haven't you read your St. Paul?'

'He's not *my* St. Paul,' I muttered. I'd always had the usual women or gay folk's problems with that saint, even though my academic research made it clear that he was only working within the social remit of his times and that much of the divisive stuff had actually been edited in.

'Okay, well tonight's job is to reacquaint a very bad human being with his soul to see if it will change him and solve a few problems around him. Are you up for that? Because *nothing* about it will seem fair.'

'The real question is whether the soul will manage to stay with him,' said Sam. 'We can reunite and reunite but the lower self can also reject and reject. But we have to keep trying.'

'Aren't we just dealing with drops in the ocean, here?' I asked. 'Even if we work together three hundred and sixty-five nights a year and I live another forty years and every mission succeeds, that's fewer than fifteen thousand people helped on one planet with more than six billion.'

'Yes, well, luckily it's not just you,' said Sam. 'There are thousands of souls like you working with us. If you're lucky, you may even get to know a few of them over the years. And every act of kindness of soul-retrieval impacts everyone else in that person's circle, dead or alive. So, it is incredibly worth it. And we aren't exactly short of time, up here.'

The soul I was carrying in my heart that night was like a little pool of silvery mercury; heavy and slow-moving. There didn't seem to be anyone in it to greet or communicate with me and although it slipped easily into my heart, all I felt was a small, cool weight. This time, there was no need for the Prozac-water as we were returning to Earth and soon I found myself walking in a modern office building with Callista by my side. We were dressed in business suits and wore lanyards with official ID.

'Are we ghosts?' I asked.

'I am; you're not, although you don't belong here,' said Callista. 'We are fully corporeal with a little bit of stardust to get us through the security barriers.'

She was right; we breezed through turnstiles and scanners with people only half-noticing us. I found that if I looked the security people in the eye, they turned their head away. One, however, did hold my gaze; a middle-aged woman with clear grey eyes who blinked twice as if doing a double-take and then reached out to touch me on the shoulder briefly.

Something made me hold the hand on my shoulder in return and smile, just for a moment. As we walked on Callista said, softly, 'You reminded her of her daughter who died when she was very young. That's Grace. She now has an image of what that child might have grown up to be. You blessed her, even though you didn't know it.'

'But how?'

'Through the powers above our pay grade!' she chuckled. 'Honestly, Bella, you can have no idea what can happen when a human being offers itself to the Work. You'll never know ninety-nine per cent of the good you do but you are do it all the time, nonetheless.'

'But do I actually look like her daughter?'

'I doubt it. She saw what she saw by arrangement of her soul and her daughter's soul. Have a look in your left pocket.'

I did and found a handful of tiny silver spheres. 'What are they?'

'Soul sparks. They come from the souls of the healthy dead that wanted to travel down to touch people they once loved. I know, I should have told you but I thought you'd be worried about hitch hikers after the last time. But these are all tiny instruments of Grace to help those down here.'

'Do they make me look like other people to do that?'

Callista laughed. 'I don't know, Bella. I don't know what they do; I just know that when a living human carries them, they can do more than if I carry them. I don't know how they do anything; I just know that they do.'

By the time we got to our destination, half of the tiny silver marbles had disappeared from my pocket. I tried to spot where they went but failed dismally. It simply wasn't my business.

Finally, we found ourselves outside a dark, panelled wall with one closed door. Three desks manned by personal assistants stood in the corridor leading to it and all three people working there studiously ignored us. I tried to remember if I had said 'Good grief' at any point.

The mercury-soul in my heart stirred and woke. I felt a wave of old and deep sorrow wash over me and then it was still and silent, waiting.

'Here goes,' said Callista, opening the big, wooden door.

Inside was a fully-panelled room decorated throughout with what looked like incredibly expensive modern art. All of it was discordant and dark. *Feral* was the word that came into my head for some reason.

Leaning back with his feet on the desk, waving a TV remote at a screen on the wall, was a man I recognised from the television news. No, I'm not going to name him; he is well-known enough without giving him any more visibility. Suffice it to say his power in the world has, in my opinion anyway, been incredibly destructive.

He turned towards us. I'm not actually sure what he could see;

but he picked up something. The little soul in my heart leapt but not with joy. I could tell it needed me to pick it up in my hands and carry it over to the man. And I could tell that it wasn't looking forward to going.

'Who are you?' he said as I walked over to the desk, his soul in my cupped hands. 'I don't have any appointments. How did you get in?'

I didn't reply, just held out my hands.

A look of greed passed over his face as he saw the offering. I got the distinct impression that this man actually *ate* souls. He reached out with one hand to grab hold of it and looked up at me.

'Yours?' he said. 'How dainty. Hardly used by the look of it.'

I let him pick up the fluid mercury and put it in his mouth.

For five long seconds, nothing happened. He chewed, thoughtfully, and then swallowed.

'Quite tasty,' he said. 'I've had better.'

Then his face changed, aging about fifty years and then reverting to that of a child. His mouth opened and shut but he couldn't articulate anything. I saw a vague silver sheen spread throughout his body.

And then he died. He simply closed his eyes and died, right in front of me, sliding out of his chair and landing in a kind of heap on the floor.

From him streamed a darkness but it was encased in silver and it rose swiftly up through the ceiling and vanished.

'Wait,' said Callista. We waited.

After five minutes, when nothing had happened, she sighed with relief. 'Got him,' she said. 'Well done.'

'I didn't do anything!'

'Oh, you did. You reminded him of one of his daughters. He was open to your soul so he received his own back without question.'

'And it was strong enough to take him through?'

'It was strong enough to take his life and save it, yes.'

'But his empire will live on.'

'It may; it may not. We have done our work and that's all we are meant to do. And many souls have been touched today inside this building. Who knows what may happen? It's no good speculating.'

'But what happens to him, now?'

'He wakes up. Literally. He sees the whole of his life and everything he has done in total clarity. He sees every single act of harm he has committed as exactly what it was. He goes through the hell of realisation. And then he makes reparation. He has all the time in the Universe to make reparation.'

'He's going to need it,' I said, slightly bitterly, aware that I carried the very human inclination of wanting that man to suffer for a very long time.

We left the office quietly, walking past the unaware assistants and back through all the security areas until we reached the front door. Jon had parked the blue Panda on the pavement outside and was enjoying a brief altercation with a traffic warden who was threatening to have it clamped.

'They can see him, then,' I said.

'Only because he wants them to,' said Callista. 'He's never got over winding up traffic wardens.'

'What happens if it does get clamped?'

'The clamp falls off somewhere near the Kuyper Belt and becomes another piece of space debris. No, I'm joking. I don't know what would happen. I don't think that car ever has been clamped.'

'Oh, it has!' I said from fond memory of the time Jon had cut off a real-life clamp with an oxyacetylene torch.

I noticed that the last-but-one silver marble in my pocket went to the traffic warden who, miraculously, began to laugh and told us all to clear off or she really *would* book us.

As we trundled off down the road before taking off into the sky, that final silver ball felt like a tiny prickle of fire against my hip.

'I've still got part of a soul with me,' I said. 'It feels quite strong. More than a spark.'

'Yes. There'll be reason for that,' said Callista. 'Don't worry about it.'

So I didn't.

188

Chapter Nineteen

JON DROPPED ME off, as usual, about ten minutes after he had picked me up. I would have loved to have had a bath and gone to bed but I had had one of those ideas that just won't wait. Whether it was a cunning or an utterly stupid plan only time would tell. Maybe if I'd stopped to consider—or maybe remembered that I had the option of checking in with Hero—I wouldn't have done what I did. And I *know* that when you aren't willing to stop and consider you are often doomed to be, at the very least, a prat.

But that's hindsight. Instead, I found Paul's key for the clergy door into the cathedral and walked across the precinct to let myself in.

The area around our cathedral green is criss-crossed with pathways and surrounded by houses dating back to the seventeenth century. Most of them have shop fronts nowadays but it is still a pleasant, open place with cafés and artisan products. At Christmas time we have a wonderful market on the green where you can buy goods from talented people from all over the world and stuff yourself silly on street food at the same time.

Tonight, the green was empty apart from one presumably homeless man, his face hidden by a hoodie, sitting motionless with his arms around his legs, in the doorway to the Edinburgh Woollen Mill. I felt a slight vibration in my pocket as I passed him, paused and drew out the last silver soul-marble. It slid into him gently and he made a mumbling noise. I sent a prayer with it, that he might find a life that he loved and that suited him and, turning back to look again, I'm sure I saw a flash of golden-silver light enfold him. Oh God, had I killed him too? But he sat up straighter while I was watching so, phew, not this time.

The key to the clergy door turned easily and I slipped inside into cool, still darkness. I'd never been in the cathedral alone at night and it was strangely eerie as though all its ghosts were watching. Maybe they were. I would have to find some light switches but, for the moment, there was enough radiance through the stained-glass windows for me to see my way around.

I went to the vestry first to find myself a white alb. The only one there was far too big for me and I had to hold the skirt up to avoid tripping over it but, if what I thought might happen, happened, I would want to look the part. Luckily, the sleeves of albs are wide so it was no trouble getting it on over the cast that had magically reattached itself to my arm when we landed back on Earth. Next, I switched on all the cathedral's microphones. If there was going to be someone else inside at any point, I wanted to be able to hear them. Then I went to the high altar, looking for the angel. It wasn't there or, at least, it wasn't showing herself to me, so I knelt on the chancel steps and began to pray.

I prayed St. Patrick's *Lorica*, the Lord's Prayer and the 23rd Psalm which should easily alert any Divine presences as to the nature of my visit and then I gently asked the angel to show itself to me.

She was in the chapel of St. Gabriel. Not many churches have such a chapel, let alone cathedrals, but it had always been my favourite place in our cathedral. I knew she was there because she called to me the moment I spoke to her but seeing her was difficult; she was virtually transparent.

'Do you have a name?' I asked out loud. It just seemed friendlier, somehow.

Of Gabriel.

'Can you act for me?'

?

'Can you call help for me, should I need it?'

Yes.

'You are very faint. Why?'

Few believe.

'But communion is offered every day here!'

No answer but then it wasn't a question.

'Would it make you stronger if I gave you a name?'

Yes. For a while.

I thought. Gabriel was one of the rank of Cherubim. No, that didn't help. The name meant 'the strong one of God' so what was 'strong' in Hebrew and could I add 'el'?

'Chazakel' I said. I was never very good at pronouncing the 'ch' which was a combination of 'k' and 'h' but it would do.

Chazakel! it replied and appeared to be pleased. The glow increased.

Next, I took a tiny phial of holy water I'd brought with me and poured it into the font. That elevated all the water, should I need it. I refilled the phial, too, and put it in the pocket of the alb.

Just before I turned the great cathedral's lights on, I remembered the all-important question.

'Chazakel, read my thoughts.' For less than a quarter of a second, I thought, '*Demon. Where?*'

High altar.

So, it wasn't in the communion altar in the Nave but in the high altar. That was interesting. But then, the high altar isn't used much nowadays anywhere, more's the pity, which is probably why Chazakel wasn't there.

There wasn't anything else I could think of to do apart from pick up a small wooden cross from the vestry, turn on the lights and begin. This was a big, big gamble and my teeth were beginning to chatter both from cold and from fear.

I went up to the high altar and addressed it.

'I am the Reverend Amabel Ransom, priest of this parish. Show yourself.'

And absolutely nothing happened.

Bugger.

Plan No. 1 was to try an exorcism. But then, that was always a stupid idea. No one is supposed to do an exorcism on their own. You are required to have back-up in case you are compromised and, if you are compromised, you are in big, big trouble—as one dead bishop demonstrated quite clearly.

Yes, I could have taken Robbie or Alessina with me to the cathedral but Robbie had already shown that he could be compromised and, if this place was the heart of the problem, then

I couldn't risk Alessina too. It was possible that the energy was enough to take both of us down.

And anyway, this was personal. Attacks on my life, a dead fiancé and now a dead child in my cellar. This was very, very personal. I had to face this alone.

'Show yourself!' I commanded.

Nothing from the altar but the very air shimmered around me.

Chazakel stood to my right, radiating light.

You are not alone.

Rus-el stood to my left, glowing scarlet.

You are not alone.

Behind me, I sensed other presences: benign, helpful presences. One of them was Ariel.

Angels from living churches, she said.

I had back-up. I suppose that should have reassured me but, in fact, it made me even more afraid. It showed how wide the corruption was and how big the fight might be. For a moment I wondered if nearly all the churches in the country, or even the world, were compromised. That alone would explain a lot...

Yes. Many.

'Why?'

Law over love.

Yes, that made sense. Any time a religion focused on law over love, it turned its heart from its founder. Christ, after all, used love to define the law, not the other way around.

I sighed. I'm getting good at sighing. All the angels sighed too, in unison, which was odd as angels don't breathe. It was as if they were mimicking my actions. But then they began to sing.

It was a song of bone-melting sorrow and beauty and love and it was glorious. If you had to die, you would want to die hearing this music.

Which was probably exactly what was going to happen.

I did at least have the huge luxury of knowing that there *is* life after death and, with any luck, I would take another significant part of the darkness with me, but knowing that didn't stop the fear.

I felt, rather than heard, the sound of people entering the cathedral and turned around to see them.

Yes, as I rather suspected, it was the bishop's chaplain and the Detective Chief Inspector together with two other men whom I didn't recognise (but of course that didn't mean I didn't know them). There had *better* be some cosmic help around because four men and one demon against one rather short, middle-aged woman, with a broken arm, was not going to be fun.

'I hope you've got reinforcements,' I said, the cathedral microphone picking up my voice and echoing it. 'You are seriously outnumbered.'

Nobody smiled.

'This isn't a movie, Miss Ransom,' said Chief Inspector Johnson. 'You're not one of Marvel's Avengers or a shaven-headed man in a dirty vest. I expect you know why we are here.'

'Because you are demon-infested,' I said. 'You were probably quite nice before that happened; just that one fatal flaw of liking little boys let all the darkness in.'

'Yes, yes, the modern view,' said the Chief Inspector. 'In Jesus' day, it was quite acceptable for children to be bought and sold for sex. You never mention *that* in your sermons, do you?'

'As a matter of fact, I do,' I said. 'But as you've never heard one of my sermons you naturally wouldn't know. And the First Temple may have had child sacrifice, too. But just because it always has happened and maybe always will happen, doesn't make it right. It's against the law *now* and I support that law.

'My question is, why try and make it public by blaming us when you'd be so much better off underground—in more ways than one.'

'Ah, yes, very witty,' said the Chief Inspector. 'I'm afraid your annoying little practices were starting to affect our sponsors.'

'Your *sponsors!*'

'It's as good a word as any.'

'Yes, it is. Demons are probably in the marketing world too.'

'Oh, everywhere,' said the Chief Inspector, cheerfully. 'And, of course, this is the part where you expect me to invite you to join us.'

'I'd rather...'

'Yes, quite.' He interrupted. 'You'd rather die. Which is

fortunate because we aren't interested in inviting you to join us and you *are* going to die.'

'And I'll be more powerful dead.'

'Oh, I don't think so. We didn't handle the bishop's passing quite as well as we might have done but everyone has to begin somewhere, eh? We've closed that loophole, so you won't be going anywhere nice.'

'Why did you kill Stephen? Was that an accident? Is that why you've had to attack us?'

'No, Ms. Ransom, it wasn't an accident at all. It was necessary for our plans.'

Now, I felt searing anger trying to replace the fear. It was tempting to allow it but I suspected that would be unwise and I was still capable of being wise.

'And your plans for me are?'

'Oh, pretty much the same as for the bishop. Suicide. A somewhat more explicit note. Discredit for the cathedral and all the parish; another nail in the coffin of a dying and increasingly irrelevant church.'

'Yes, a church that you have to attack because it *is* relevant. A church that is going after evil and offering light.'

'In your dreams. You are such a stupid minority.'

'A drop in the ocean, in fact.'

'Exactly.'

'A drop of love in an ocean is more powerful than a drop of poison.'

'Oh, I don't think so.'

Now all four of them were standing within a couple of metres of me. My heart was pounding and it was hard to breathe.

To my relief Rus-el moved in front of me as a barrier of red light. At once, Bill, the chaplain, stepped to one side and made a circular movement with one hand. *Something* shot from that hand to the altar behind me which erupted in a blaze of scorching black light. I sensed, rather than saw, Rus-el fight for a moment and then dissolve into the ether.

'Rus-el!' I said under my breath to call him back but he didn't come.

'He's not coming,' said Bill with a nasty smile. 'Your pathetic little protective angel is destroyed. Our power is much greater than any *you* can summon.'

'Good grief,' I said, to buy myself some time at least. No one reacted to my vanishing because I didn't. Without Rus-el, there was no power to make me invisible.

Bugger.

Yes, I was still surrounded by angels but the thing about angels is that each has *one* job. They can't multi-task and the angels around me were angels of praise and healing. They weren't going to be able to weigh in with any mallets any time soon. Hero was surprisingly absent.

'Okay then,' I said. 'Do your worst.'

To my surprise they all stood back, creating a space between Bill and the Chief Inspector. In that gap, a kind of greasy golden smoke began to form, whirling and flowing. It drew energy from the high altar and, as the stone emptied, it sagged. The cross and candlesticks fell onto the floor with a sickening series of clunks and the energy laughed as it tickled my hair in passing and morphed into the form that was still developing. It changed shape several times and then grew upwards until it was about nine feet tall. After about thirty seconds it took on an almost human form, that of the most incredibly beautiful young androgynous boy. Michelangelo's David and Leonardo da Vinci's St. John were complete mingers compared with this chap.

He looked at me with dead, golden eyes and cocked his head on one side, assessing.

'Oh, you are disconnected, aren't you?' he said. 'No wonder we couldn't get in. No pain to bore into. But we can fix that.'

'Lucifer?'

'Wouldn't you just like to be that important? No, just a minion. But I'll do very well.'

I noticed that this dark angel was actually speaking rather than transferring communication and that it was capable of chat. And it could laugh. That meant it was at the level of an archangel. This was dangerous but it also meant that perhaps it could be bamboozled. Its eyes were the eyes of a shark. I know a lot about sharks...

I think I went crazy. It seemed like the only sensible thing to do.

'Of course, not Lucifer. Silly me. What was I thinking? I've met Lucifer himself and I survived. You're a minion. You're actually a minion! Well, you are yellow...'

He didn't like that.

'BA-NA-NA!' I said waving my hands in the air. I'm sorry, but I couldn't resist it. It made me laugh at least but it turned out that none of the four, nor the dark angel, happened to have watched *Despicable Me*. They just stared at me, momentarily mystified. That made me laugh all the more and, the strangest thing happened, just as it had when I was dead. They lost power. Laughter weakened them. However, it strengthened the good angels and I felt them cluster around me.

'What is her name,' the dark angel asked the Chief Inspector.

'Annabel Ransom.'

'It's *Am*abel,' corrected Bill.

Damn. I should have kept my mouth shut at the Bishop's Palace.

'Better. But there is more. I need her full name to destroy her.'

I made my mind fill itself with other names to prevent any probing intelligence. 'Alessina, Robbie, Jon, Callista, Mrs. Tiggy, Odysseus (where did he come from?), Hector, Paris, Helen, Agamemnon, Menelaus...'

The dark angel reached out with one golden hand, pointing to my forehead.

'This will hurt,' he said, with a very happy smile.

It did. With that one gesture, he re-wired part of my brain, restoring my memory of Paul; of the man I loved with all my heart and soul; the man who had held me in his arms and turned darkness into light; the man who had shared so many jokes with me; the man I trusted most in the world; the man with whom I had wanted to spend the whole of the rest of my life.

The emotional surge was like drowning and I went down on my knees with the shock of it. There was nothing I could do to control that wave of anguish; grief is a living thing; when it has you, it will have its way with you. And this grief was savage; it was filled with anger and loss and regret.

As it washed over and through me, the angels began to sing again, softly to start with, like cool water trickling into the broken, aching cracks in my mind, instantly soothing and reassuring. Time seemed to stop. Gradually, their voices lifted, swelled and soared in harmony, singing of love and healing in some ancient, spine-tingling language. In the glorious crescendo I felt Hero, too, wrap her wings around me and in the midst of the terrifying grief came the knowledge that I had loved and been loved; that grief was the agreed price of love, no matter how short the time of loving, and that grief was proof of love. Love, love, love!

The angels' song transformed my grief and anger into sorrow which is softer but just as deep. Somehow, I knew that sorrow held the love safe. Grief with anger and resentment was what the dark angel wanted—no, *needed*—from me. Sorrow was no use.

Strengthened, I stood up again and, from that moment it was almost as though there were two of me: one observing, the other reacting. My guardian was with me; I was surrounded by angels. I might still be going to die but, my God, was I in marvellous company…

I observed myself crying beautifully and standing with some strange kind of dignity before the four men who were completely still, as if paralysed, by the golden darkness that now engulfed them.

Time began again.

'What is your name?' said the dark angel.

'What is yours?' I replied. 'Do you even have a name? Would you like one?'

For one fraction of a second, he hesitated. A demon would have vanity and, if an angel of light liked having its own name, how much would an angel of darkness?

Then each of the four men raised an arm and began shooting what seemed like lead pellets at the angel host around me. I'd never realised that angels could be killed but they can. They simply dissolve. And as each one vanished, I felt my ridiculous-seeming confidence fade. Hero remained. She whispered into me, faith and what seemed, at that moment, the incredibly unhelpful knowledge that faith and certainty were opposites took centre stage in my brain.

And then even seemed to be gone. I knew she couldn't be; she was a part of me and as long as I existed, so would she, but I could no longer feel her. Chazakel was gone too. I was as alone as a woman who didn't even believe in angels might be.

'Now. What is your name?' hissed the dark angel.

'The same as yours,' I said.

'?'

'Your name is Faydra. I give you that name now. That means that your name and my name are the same. The name of someone who lies and betrays. I am Faydra Amabel. You are simply Faydra. It means 'bright' and you are bright.'

'Faydra.'

I swear I saw the dark angel preen for a moment. But just for a moment.

'Faydra Amabel Ransom. Prepare to die.'

Hero whispered softly to me, Here. Always and she dropped a memory into my mind. Despite myself I giggled. This time it was a quotation from *The Princess Bride*. Well, why not? I knew already that laughter was my friend.

Dark-Faydra was already slightly perplexed at the giggle so when I spouted, *'My name is Inigo Montoya. You killed my father. Prepare to die!'* I really thought he/she (astonishing how you ascribe gender according to names; I now thought of him as a her) would be on a back foot as I laughed out loud at the quotation. But it kind of backfired.

'I did indeed kill your father,' she said and, with a sweep of one hand, catapulted me back in time to the car crash where both my parents died.

But I was still *me*. Yes, I was also, suddenly, a child in a car crash but this was a child who was also an adult standing in a cathedral who knew that more than thirty years had passed; who travelled in the upper worlds where the dead lived and whose abiding memory of the crash was not of death and loss (that realisation came later) but of Jon pulling her out of the car and holding her tightly and then of medics taking care of her. The memory was of shock and some pain but, primarily, of love.

If the demon had kicked me back to the moment in hospital when Jon told me that our parents were dead, that might have been a completely different matter. I was beginning to wonder if this angel was really quite as smart as it thought it was.

It took a moment to pull myself back into the present.

'You misunderstand,' I said, purposely patronising. 'The quotation acknowledges that you killed my father and says that, in return, I am going to kill you.'

'You cannot kill me.'

'Why not?'

'Humans cannot kill angels.'

'Is that true, Chief Inspector?' I said to one of the four men who was standing, as if paralysed, in the shadows. They were beginning to give me the creeps.

'They cannot speak or move without my permission,' said Dark-Faydra.

'Ooh, get you!' said Hopefully-Light Phaedra.

'You shall die now,' said the angel. 'Die and become a part of my power. There is no escape.'

So, this was it: the time when I would know if the gamble had paid off. The dark angel billowed, its greasy gold expanding to reach me and surround me. There was no point in running; this simply had to be endured.

It was like being eaten by dust. The same dust that was in the taste of the fig in the world between worlds. A horrible, heavy, metallic taste of evil that insinuated itself through my pores and into my body, bringing a level of dull pain that was panic-inducingly claustrophobic and suffocating.

'Submit and die, Inigo Montoya Faydra Amabel Ransom,' began as a whisper in my mind, growing in crescendo until it was an agony of pounding nails. I wanted to hate it, to fight it, to resist it. I did *not* want to love it but that was what I had to do. Love it, and be smart.

'This is for Faydra?' I said.

'Yessss.'

The pressure forced me down on my knees, arms over my head, gasping with pain and aware of a primal force inserting itself into every orifice. This was a rape of hatred, spite, fear and loathing, every one of which sought a place in me where it could dwell forever. What the hell it would have been like without the added, inaccurate, names was anybody's guess.

'For Faydra,' I repeated. 'Faydra.'

Then, grimacing and whining like a hurt puppy, I forced my hand into my pocket for the phial of holy water, pulled out the cork and put it to my lips and shouted as clearly as I could, 'then die, Faydra. *My name is Phaedra Amabel Velvet!*'

The world went black.

Chapter Twenty

DOWN, DOWN, DOWN I spiralled, screaming, into the void. Hero held me in her arms, cradling me like a baby, comforting, calming ... and slowly, steadily, lifting me back into the light. We fought, my guardian and I, because I wasn't sane at that point. It wasn't fun. I am delighted to say that she won.

I was back in the cathedral, huddled on the stone floor and aching in every molecule.

Shakily, I pulled myself upright.

The gamble had done the demon a lot of harm but hadn't killed it. But, then, I wasn't dead either so that seemed fair. It needed my correct name to kill me and it turns out that spelling *is* important after all, just as I had spent nearly forty years explaining. Naming the dark angel Faydra meant that its power short-circuited, backfiring into its own being, and that didn't do it any good at all.

By the time my head had cleared enough for me to be able to see again, there was only a three-foot, dark golden smudge, reeling in the air before me. The four men were still stationary, like waxworks.

I grabbed the small crucifix I had brought from the vestry but dropped—how long ago?—and began shouting the words of the greater exorcism. I was out of holy water and too far from the font to get more but I had drunk some so I spat at the darkness instead.

It screamed. And screamed and screamed. Then it exploded into a mass of sticky goo which hissed and sizzled before evaporating.

Right. So you can kill them, after all. You just have to do it in stages.

Behind me, the already-sagging high alter seemed to sigh and then crumbled completely in on itself.

All four men woke simultaneously. They surrounded me and

began to move towards me so I clubbed the nearest one, the Chief Inspector, over the head with the crucifix. I thought Christ would forgive that; it wasn't so very different from going after the money changers in the temple with a knotted whip.

Chief Inspector Johnson went down like a stone.

But that was the end of the good times. We were now out of the realms of the intangible and back in the land of brute force. One middle-aged woman versus three men is not good odds and within seconds Bill had caught and twisted my broken arm in a way that hurt so very much that I fell down and then I was trapped. This was that point, half an hour before the end of the movie, when everything suddenly goes horribly wrong.

They seemed quite cheerful about it all; there were no concerns about any great, evil dark angel that might have been around or not. When I had time to think about it, I wondered if they had ever, consciously, known it was there at all. Perhaps they thought it was just one of them.

Their plan was quite simple; hurt me sufficiently to force me to write a suicide note and then hang me, just as they had hanged Paul.

Considerately, they had even brought paper and pen.

I can't say I've always wondered whether I'd be able to stand up to torture but it's a fact that I can't. There's a level of pain that cracks you open and you would do *anything* to make it stop even if you know you are still going to die if you obey. They were very clever; they only hurt the already broken arm so it wouldn't show that much. After all, I could easily have pulled a fingernail off while hanging myself, couldn't I?

I wrote the note, at Bill's dictation. Just as Paul had, I changed some spellings and signed it *Annabel Ransom* in the hope that Bill wouldn't notice and Eleanor Marks would—should she get the chance to see it.

Bill did notice and that was another ocean of pain and a second note to be written.

In it I confessed to aiding and abetting a paedophile ring headed by Bishop Paul Joans and apologised for my actions which, apparently, I couldn't live with any more, since the death of little

Stephen. I couldn't even spell Paul's surname wrong because his secretary and his chaplain knew it well.

Even in the torrent of pain and fear (humans are *so* much more evil than demons) I was pathetically grateful that, if I was to be a suicide, they couldn't rape me. They discussed it and they wanted to. Not for pleasure, obviously, their being paedophiles and all that, but then rape was never about sexual pleasure. It's about hatred and power.

Eventually, Bill and the chaplain left me, albeit briefly, on the floor of the cathedral with the remaining unknown-to-me man, as they set up the rope in the vestry.

I sat crookedly on the floor, nursing my broken and bloody arm and hand, next to the still-unconscious Chief Inspector, and trying to break through the pain enough to think; trying to reason. But there was nothing to be done. Nothing but prayer to have enough courage to cope with what was happening and what was about to happen. Even Hero was silent. Was she gone, destroyed by the effort of bringing me back?

Christ be with me.
Christ within me.
Christ behind me.
Christ before me.
Christ beside me.
Christ to win me.
Christ to comfort and restore me.
Christ above me.
Christ below me.
Christ in quiet.
Christ in danger.
Christ in the hearts of all who love me.
Christ in the mouth of friend and stranger.

I managed the whole *Lorica* just once and then repeated *Christ be with me, Christ within me,* over and over again.

He came.

Not in any familiar form; not in a blaze of light or healing but in the persona of one rather scruffy, homeless man in a hoodie who had seen lights in the cathedral and tried the clergy door to investigate. He said later that he was only looking for somewhere to sleep but then, you can't go around saying, 'She brought my soul back and then her guardian angel came to find me. Of course I had to help her.'

The door went right into the area next to the vestry and he was sharp-witted enough to realise that two men setting up a noose were probably up to no good. A second look indicated that the woman in a white robe, who was crouched and praying on the floor of the cathedral Nave while a man stood over her, was probably in some kind of trouble.

He said later that he wasn't a fighter; he wasn't a hero; he didn't dare take them on. Instead, he noticed the key which I had left in the vestry door, pulled it shut and locked it. So simple, so sensible and so effective. Bill and his companion were trapped. They realised at once and began to shout, alerting my guard. He turned away from me and adrenaline allowed me to move almost as fast. With my good hand I reached for the crucifix that was still lying on the floor and, with my last ounce of energy, hooked his legs out from under him just as he began to move. The man went down like a one-sided seesaw, his head making a satisfying crack on the stone floor.

So, that was two men unconscious, two locked in a vestry, a vicar with one hand dangling at an odd angle and the other clutching a now-broken crucifix and a scruffy, perplexed bloke wondering what on Earth he had got himself into. I was so confused that I nearly hit him with the crucifix, too, but he held his hands out in the age old 'I'm unarmed; I'm a friend' gesture, knelt beside me and asked, kindly, if I was all right.

'No,' I said.

'Can you walk?' he asked. 'We've got to get out of here.'

Five minutes later we were outside the cathedral and had locked the door behind us. Of course, neither of us had a phone to call for help and, anyway, the card with Eleanor Marks's phone number on it was in the vestry with my clothes.

'You need to get to hospital,' my saviour said, sensibly. I was about to protest when the world started swimming and waves of nausea overwhelmed me. My last memory was of throwing up over both of us.

*

I was back in the wood, that silent wood without birdsong. Which meant I was dead again. At least it wasn't dark this time.

The light was confusing; clearer than it should have been, given the density of the leaf-cover overhead, and the grass was a darker green than I was used to, too. I was sitting with my back to a tree and my left arm was whole, without pain. The trees around me were all fruit trees as far as I could work out and, here and there, they were divided by the same pools of still, clear water.

'You did love *The Magician's Nephew.*' The voice came from behind me and a youngish, dark-skinned man with black, curly hair appeared from behind one of the larger olives. I recognised him from the hospital but this time he was dressed in a short tunic. He still had strong, workman's arms.

'You probably want to know where you are,' he said, sitting down next to me on the grass. His scent was pine-like, fresh and uplifting.

'No, I don't think I do,' I said. 'I'm quite happy just to sit and allow the place to show itself to me in its own time. I rather like the not knowing.'

'Because you're safe,' he said.

'Yes. I do feel safe.'

'Well, you know, you're always safe,' he said. 'The pain, the upset and the fear are the passing show. Humans nowadays pay far too much attention to the passing show.'

I didn't answer. There was no need. And whopping him over the head for being a smart-arse was probably inappropriate.

He held one hand out, palm up, and I placed my left hand in it. It was warm and strong and not a little calloused and it felt wonderful. The scar was still there on his wrist.

'That was quite a passing show you got yourself involved in,' he said, after a while.

'Yes.'

'You were willing to give your life.'

'I didn't have much choice.'

'Yes, you did. You could have locked yourself into the bishop's rooms. You didn't have to go to the cathedral. You didn't have to broadcast your presence there.'

'I suppose, if I had to die, I wanted to do what Paul did and take the darkness with me but it didn't work.'

'Bella,' he said, squeezing my hand. 'It did work. Between you, you've cleared that patch of the darkness. That's what I'm here to tell you. Otherwise, you'll not believe it. However, it's not the only patch of darkness on Earth and you will encounter more.'

'I'm not dead, then?'

He laughed. His laugh was like a cascade of cool water on a hot day.

'No, not dead. Not dead *again*,' he said. 'Virtually indestructible.'

'So, I'm going back. To face more darkness?'

'And more light. There will be a respite and time to enjoy the beauty of Earth and the magic of Grace. But then, yes, there will be more darkness.'

'Did I really sign up for this?' I asked, perplexed. 'There I was, an archaeologist specialising in languages who rarely gave God a passing thought and...'

'Yes, you most certainly did sign up,' he said. 'Maybe it's just as well that you don't remember. But you didn't want to live a quiet life as a rural vicar. You wanted to do The Work.'

'Will I ever remember that?'

'I don't know.' He smiled. 'See, not even I know everything! 'But why don't we walk and enjoy ourselves, while we're here?'

He stood up, and pulled me to my feet, too. We walked through the trees hand in hand, our other fingers tracing the beauty of the bark on the trunks of the trees and playing with the leaves as we wandered past. We paddled in the shallower pools, laughing and splashing each other like children. When I commented that there was no birdsong, he asked, 'would you like some?' and the moment I nodded, my ears were filled with lilting, chirping music and that tight, whirring sound of wings that you only hear when the birds trust you enough to come close. The birds themselves followed; from wren to bird of paradise, swooping, hopping, carolling, chirruping and peeking at us through the leaves.

A green Amazon parrot sidled up to my shoulder and I laughed with pleasure. I'd always thought I'd love a parrot. It let me stroke it before taking off in a haze of soft, green feathers, only to be replaced by a tiny hedge sparrow that hopped onto my shoulder and nuzzled up to my neck.

'Not a sparrow falls…' I said, inconsequentially.

He let go of my hand but only to put an arm around my waist. Now we had come to a part of the wood which was more open. The sparrow chirped and flew away because it saw a child peering into one of the pools. It was Stephen. His guardian angel sat beside him, looking at him with love and Hero—my Hero—sat the other side. She looked astonishingly like me.

'Hello,' Stephen said, looking up as we approached. 'I'm watching Mummy. She can feel me. Look!' He leant down and reached down into the water to touch his mother's hair from above. I could see her through the water, too. At once, she raised her hand to smooth her hair down.

'Thing is, she doesn't seem to know it's me,' he said, perplexed. 'I keep trying to talk to all of them but they won't listen.'

'You have a different resonance now,' said my companion. 'She would know if she had been taught how to feel you but she hasn't. Let's see if I can help.'

He leant down too and blew into the water. It parted and Stephen's mother looked up, feeling some kind of movement in the air. As she did, a white feather floated down past her nose and straight into her hand.

'Stephen!' she whispered, and looked up.

'Mum!' he said. 'I'm all right. I'm fine. It's lovely here. It's okay.'

She didn't hear him, of course, but a look of peace settled into her eyes for the moment, at least. My companion sat back on his heels and held his arms out for the boy. Stephen looked at him for a moment and then beamed and hurled himself into the embrace.

The two of them played rough and tumble on the grass while the guardians and I watched, smiling. And then a group of human souls approached and Stephen greeted them with delight. He knew them all and the mutual love was palpable. They drew him away and, as I watched him go, I saw him grow until he was as tall as they were.

'Souls are always complete,' said my companion. 'Even if you die a child, you are fully mature when you live here.'

'Why?'

'Because you were complete before you descended into the physical. It is hard for a soul to compact itself into a baby but it must be done to learn the rules and the practices of the times.'

'So, when someone dies as a child, they grow up here?'

'Sort of. Of course, it's more complicated than that but everyone's story is different; everyone grows according to their story.'

'*And no one is told any story but their own,*' I said, quoting Aslan.

'They are good books, aren't they?' he said.

'I loved them. I always wanted to meet Aslan.'

'And you shall, dear one,' he said. 'One day, you shall.'

We walked on. And on. We walked through woodlands and out onto moorland. We walked by streams and rivers and seas. We saw a great ship coming into harbour and docking with its cargo of people, newly dead. Most of them looked old and tired but soon all of them were exclaiming with joy at the beauty of this new Earth and the ease with which they could move again. We saw as their eyes opened with wonder as they saw and recognised their guardian angel. We saw friends and families (and their angels) reunited after decades; we saw pets come racing through the greenwood to greet their old companions. A big bay horse cantered past me to greet and lay its head against an elderly lady who was transformed back into her youth again the moment she recognised him and spoke his name. A hundred dogs raced into their owners' arms squeaking and barking with joy; even a few cats showed up because they just happened to be passing...

It was an afternoon in paradise. Just being; hanging out; relaxing and watching the passing show. My companion pointed out another ship, ready to sail with souls boarding it. Many of them seemed nervous and some sad at leaving companions here.

'I don't want to have to forget you.'

'I'll see you again in twenty years.'

'I don't know how I'm going to cope, being a girl.'

'Make sure you don't marry anyone else!'

'Remember to focus on the arts this time.'

'Watch out for redheads. They're feisty!'

'God, I hope I'm good at maths this time. Or sport. Either would do.'

'I hope they still have lemon meringue pie. I could murder a lemon meringue pie.'

It was fascinating that it all seemed so run-of-the-mill, so everyday, so ordinary here. Souls going out; souls coming in.

'Is this how it happens everywhere?' I asked.

'No. There are all sorts of ways. The traditional dark tunnel—though that's most often for people who aren't staying here—boats, waking up in a different hospital, deserts to walk across, car and coach rides to country houses, the feeling of being born again. All sorts. This place is only for the souls who die integrated. The others can be a bit of a mess, as you well know. They take a bit more time and effort. But everyone gets through in the end.'

'Radical Grace.'

'Yes.'

'What about those who can't handle that?'

'They receive radical Grace too. Until they can. They can take as long as they want. There's no linear time once you go further up and further in.'

'So, why are you walking with me? Why aren't you in at the sharp end of this, sorting things out?'

'I am. You are with one personification of me—the icon you are used to. But I am everywhere. No linear time, remember? I am the chaplain visiting a stranger in hospital; I am the atheist who says a kind word; the dog who puts a welcoming paw on someone's lap. I am the whisper that encourages a child to try again. I am the silence and stillness of death. I am the white feather that falls into a grieving mother's hand; I am the butterfly that shows the hope in the death of the caterpillar; I am the blueprint.'

'The Logos.'

'Yes. Don't you think 'the Love' is a much better translation than Word?'

'I do.'

'And because you do, they try to string you up in a cathedral.

Ah, it's a hard existence!' He was laughing at me. 'But it does have chocolate! Don't forget, I never got to eat an Easter egg or a Lindt chocolate Santa.'

'No, I know. You lived in a cardboard box in t' middle o't' road,' I said.

'Ooh, a cardboard box? Luxury!' We both roared with laughter.

And then I woke up.

In hospital.

I'm really quite good at that.

Robbie was sitting beside me and standing behind him was Sergeant Eleanor Marks. And standing behind both of them were their guardian angels.

'Hero?' I said, woozily. They misunderstood me.

'Yes, Bel, dear,' said Robbie. 'You are an *absolute* hero!'

'Welcome back, Rev'd Amabel,' said Eleanor Marks. 'You've had surgery on that arm. It's going to be okay.'

I looked at my left arm which was encased in a blue strappy thing. It didn't hurt but I suspected it soon would.

'Do you know who saved me? Did you get the men?'

'I do and we did, thanks to his quick thinking and your extraordinary antics.'

'Oh, thank God.'

'Don't thank him too soon,' she added. 'I'm afraid you are under arrest for attempted murder of a police officer, causing grievous bodily harm with a crucifix *and* for criminal damage to a cathedral.'

'What?' said Robbie.

'Ah. Yes, I suppose I might have expected that,' I said. 'Your Chief Inspector is *not* under arrest then?'

'Would you give us a moment, please?' Eleanor said to Robbie. He got up, rather huffily, and moved away.

'Don't you dare arrest her. She's a complete heroine,' he called back as he left the room. This time I was, at least, in a private area. Probably all the better for a police interrogation, I thought, glumly.

'Yes, well…' said Eleanor and sat down in the vacated chair. 'Right. How *compos mentis* are you, really?'

'I have no idea,' I said.
'Fair do's. Well, here's the deal.'
And she told me.

Chapter Twenty-One

OUTSIDE THE CROWN Court, reporters were waiting for us. Eleanor and I checked each other over for sagging hems, smudged mascara and broccoli in the teeth (I swear that stuff can turn up days later out of the blue, flossed or not). I was still feeling quite shaky and exhausted from nearly two days in the witness box, carefully saying only the things that were verifiably true. The *whole truth* would have got me committed to a mental institution. That was the first night I had ever said 'no' to the Work. I didn't think I would sleep but I simply didn't have the mental energy for such a double life. Let's face it, I'm living almost twice as many hours as the average person on the usual amount of sleep. Instead, Jon took me and a pot of Ben & Jerry's with two spoons to orbit around Alpha Centauri.

We had to get to Alpha Centauri via New York as Ben & Jerry's had stopped making my favourite flavour in the UK but that wasn't a problem for the blue Panda.

'It's fuelled on cow farts,' said Jon. 'Just clearing up the atmosphere while we're saving souls.'

'Really?'

'Oh Bel, you were always so gullible!'

'Could be true. Stranger things have happened. Stranger things are happening right now,' I said, taking another spoonful while we observed a previously unknown planet, that definitely would not be the next potential home for humanity, attempt to blow itself up three times with varying levels of success.

Back on Earth and outside the court, Eleanor and I joined our solicitor who had already announced the judge's direction to the jury to find me not guilty and the arrest and remand in custody of the four men with more to follow. They had been ashen-faced;

proved by their own words to be guilty as hell. Two of them still had something staring out of their eyes that didn't belong in there and I shuddered to think what effect that darkness would have in a possibly already-infested prison.

It is like infestation; internal fleas that bite and nip and poison the blood. They get in through our cracks of resentment, rage, jealousy, self-pity and spite, feed on them and excrete more until we are so addicted to the process we come to believe that our beliefs and negative emotions are the truth, the whole truth and nothing but the truth, to the extent that everyone *but* ourselves is responsible for our wellbeing and that anyone who disagrees with our views is either (ironically) evil or deranged. The only reason they didn't infest me was because, without much of a memory, I didn't have many holes they could get through.

Barney, the solicitor, was citing *Singh v Singh*, EWHC 1432, as the justification for the judge allowing the recordings of my time in the cathedral as evidence. What had saved me and the whole situation was that, in turning on the cathedral's microphones and not knowing the equipment, I had accidentally set every single one to "record."

Eleanor, bless her, had sussed that out while the Chief Inspector was still in surgery for his cracked skull. Without the recordings I would certainly have been jailed because no one was going to believe me over a Chief Inspector, a bishop's secretary and chaplain and another other white, male pillar of the community. I only mention their colour because they mentioned mine in court, accusing me of being an unsuitable fiancée for a bishop, part-Pagan, part-Hindu and 'not a proper vicar.'

We let them get away with it to start with; let everyone believe for several painful months that I was the one facing charges while Eleanor got the tapes to a solicitor to ensure they would be admissible evidence. He managed to wipe them, claiming they were blank in the first place, so that told us how wide the corruption had spread. But she was canny; she had only given him a copy.

I stayed with Alessina much of the time; At least I had bail... but I was suspended from my job, facing being unfrocked and a locum was called in to paper over the cracks. They were not terribly good times and I spent a lot of them in bed. Or in the afterlife. I drank a bit too much in the latter… but you don't get hangovers there which helped.

Finally, the trial began and I had to sit for days in the dock listening to horrible, horrible accusations and bite my lip. My time would come. And it did.

Only one member of the press was interested in the long extracts of the tape where I appeared to have gone mad and was talking to myself. The whole truth there would not have gone down well so, when questioned about what was happening then, I said I was almost mad with pain from my arm and half the time I didn't know who I was talking to.

The recording was deemed valid even though it had not been previously declared (thank you *so* much *Singh v Singh*, EWHC 1432) and, duly exposed by their own voices, the men coughed up the names of the others in the ring as a plea bargain to try and earn more lenient sentences. They hadn't meant to kill Stephen; it was an accident. They had buried him in my cellar to implicate me. They had to kill the bishop and plant evidence on our *WhatsApp* group to defend themselves.

Now they've explained it, it all makes perfect sense, doesn't it? That's how evil starts, with ridiculous half-truths and, all too often throughout history, we have let the perpetrators get away with it.

The reporters wrapped the whole story of the paedophile ring in a catalogue of romantic angst, with Paul and me up against the world because we had found out about it and were going to expose the participants. For a good fifty per cent of the media we were the obvious good guys because of our forward thinking, inter-racial policies and our personal relationship. We could almost be forgiven our archaic Christian religious beliefs.

'What made you believe that Mr. Joans had *not* hanged himself?' the right honourable Timothy Raglan QC (prosecuting) had asked me.

'Because the note he wrote spelled my name incorrectly,' I said.

'Oh! And is spelling your name correctly so very important?' he asked with a sneer.

'All names are important,' I said. 'The ability to name things is one of the things makes us human. Names have meanings. I know that; Paul knew that. "Annabel" means "grace and beauty." "Amabel" means "loveable." We had an ongoing joke that I was neither graceful nor beautiful but he found me intensely lovable. Deliberately spelling my name incorrectly was a very clear sign to alert me that something was wrong with the whole situation.'

'He thought you neither graceful nor beautiful? I see.' said the Rt. Hon. QC, purely for the purposes of being unpleasant.

'You don't need to be graceful nor beautiful to be lovable,' I said, purely for the purposes of making a very important point. I'm glad I did, even though it made me a favourite daytime TV morning guest for far too long afterwards.

I know I'll have to watch my obsession with spelling; it could become one of those holes that evil can access. But, for the moment, it had saved my life and destroyed a demon. Thank God it turned out that getting a demon to name you incorrectly is like trapping a bullet in the barrel of a gun. I owed that demon a small vote of thanks, both for that useful piece of knowledge and for its desire to hurt. Had it not intended to cause pain by restoring my memory, I would never have remembered that lovers' joke.

So, here I am, Phaedra Amabel Velvet Ransom, re-established Rector of this parish, exorcist and retriever of souls, walking on the moor behind my house above this great panorama of Devon fields, white cottages, spires of churches and the castle nestling in trees on the hill opposite. I raise my face to the afternoon rays from the yellow star I know so well with its pale aureole. I'm relishing the last of this day's sunshine and celebrating the release of my battered arm from its final bandage.

All around me the bracken is dark rose-gold, dying back to reveal the ancient pathways and the roots of Bronze Age stone huts that it has hidden all summer. Beneath my bare feet blossom the last of the tiny, elegant and bright yellow *Tormentil*; a flowering herb that helps those suffering from the ills of its name—if you know how to harvest it which Alessina, of course, does.

It's hunting weather and the scent is high so all the passing

hounds enjoying this last trace of the Indian Summer have
twitching noses and waving tails. I exchange greetings with them
and their owners and with the regular horse-riders on their glossy-
coated bays and greys and the one palomino, glad to share the
glorious beauty of the majestic moor. Very rarely do they ever
notice that I walk barefoot here, relishing the feel of peat, grass,
rock and even prickles on my soles.

The sheep-cropped grass is fading to a soft yellow gold; there
are pools of clear water in peat-lined dips; the wild ponies are
getting shaggier by the minute and the silence when, finally alone,
I stop to look and listen, is profound.

Today I have brought the sacrament to the ancient stone circle
that lies between the two hills behind our village and I offer it in
humility to the Christ that always was, is and always will be. The
Christ that was always Plan A, not any rethink, the Christ that is
the Logos—the Love that binds the moon and the stars together;
the Love of the presence of God in the world; the Love that is the
purpose of all creation; the Christ that manifested as a human
being to show us all the face of a God who willingly joins us in
all our suffering.

'I offer what Earth has given and human hands have made,' I
say, laying a wafer at the foot of each stone, leaving it to find its
way into the eco-system in whatever way the land should choose.

On my way back, my mind is distracted by the details of
the not-so-everyday vicar's life. On how my still breathtakingly
beautiful assistant is in need of a better spiritual director than I
who will be able to help her heal what she has been through and
her understandable fear that it might happen again. Robbie needs
more help, too. We talk for hours, Robbie, Lucie and I. This was
their shark bite and both are terrified of what else might be in
the water. Touching the scars on my thigh through my jeans and
pushing up my sleeve to see the operation scar from the plate that
holds the arm together, I ponder how much easier it is to cope
when there is a physical scar rather than an emotional space that
must always be filled with Grace in case it falls for temptation
again.

'I wanted to feel special,' Lucie said. 'I've always been discounted because of my looks. People assume I'm stupid—and sometimes I am. I was so excited to be posted here that I prayed to be visible; to be admired; to be recognised.'

'I wanted to be more important,' said Robbie. 'I've been an assistant too long and never been selected for my own living. I wanted that so much…'

I'm teaching them both exorcism. Together the three of us went back to Worcester to clear that little hornet's nest that started the whole shebang. We visited Celeste's grave, too, and they trusted me when I told them that her soul was free and safe (I knew it was; Sam had made sure of that).

In these intervening months, I have spent my time re-learning my job, my friendships and my life. It is a time to grieve for a love that, briefly, made my world shine so brightly, to laugh over the unspoken astonishment of all Galel's relatives that his ex would Christen his daughter by another woman, to celebrate the beauty and sanctity of life—and to realise that much of my memory may never return. I truly am born anew.

It's a simple enough life once you can rise above the squabbles, the parish council (see? I've managed to get them into lower case letters) and the constant challenge of creating new and engaging sermons that make the congregation think without rocking the boat too savagely.

We still have a lot of healing to do in a diocese that has been torn apart by abuse and cruelty, not just in the children and their families but in the horror of the revelations experienced by the unaware families of the men now awaiting trial. I think we will be Therapy City for some time to come. I see a counsellor regularly, myself, on the judge's orders; he thought I was likely to be "exceptionally fragile" after my experiences in the cathedral and the murder of my love.

'You? Fragile?' said Jon and didn't stop laughing for half an hour.

Obviously, I can't tell the counsellor everything but shark bites are useful analogies for all of us, I guess. Ironically, I seem to owe those physical sharks as well as the cathedral demon, both for the scars that taught me I could survive pain and for the emotional strength of someone who has survived two shark attacks and is so pig-headed she'd be willing to face another. Much as I still have much to do with my relationship with St. Paul, I have to agree that 'all things work together for good to those who love God.'

As I walk slowly back down the hill I can see Alessina checking the bee hives. This is the time of year that desperate, dying wasps may try to invade for the sugar-kick of honey. We wave and she signals that all is well. I'm going over for supper later and we'll be able to talk in depth as she teaches me more about the magic of the Great Mother and I tell her more of the great patterns within my own faith. Never once have we failed to find a mutual point of reference and understanding. She is my sister in faith, my rock and my greatest living friend.

And every night, I journey into the stars with Jon to seek out another disconnected soul and bring her home. These last months have been amazing; visiting lands and times I'd never heard of or only ever read about; seeing the wrecks of what were once people restored and revitalised. We have failed many times but we try again.

As I get closer to home, I can see a rather battered blue Fiat Panda parked outside the house. I sigh. That's early. There must be some kind of crisis.

In the kitchen, Jon is trying and failing to open a packet of Jaffa Cakes. We have no need to greet each other now; we are virtually twin souls. Instead I reach out my hand for the packet, open it and hand him two cakes. He knows perfectly well that he can't handle physical things without me there but still, he tries.

'Tea?' I say and he nods.

As we sit at the kitchen table, he tells me of yet another hospice where they have de-sanctified the chapel, effectively closing off a portal to the afterlife that had been open for decades. The sleeping dead can't get out and they are turning destructive on the awakened dead who are being damaged as they try to find their own route to leave.

To sort it, we have to find a group of souls who left via the old chapel so that they can help us re-instigate the portal. Two souls in a billion, billion, billion. Should be a piece of cake.

So, off we go. I'll leave a note on the front door out of habit, saying that I'll be back in a couple of hours, when I'll probably be gone no longer than ten minutes. At this rate I'll have lived to more than a hundred even if I drop dead by the age of fifty.

'We'll have to go through the Earth again today; it's still light and we don't want to be seen taking off,' said Jon.

'Right,' I say, as if I actually understood any of the reasons behind that. I'm sure I'll get it some day.

As we float down through the rock strata, I remember something that's been nagging at me.

'Jon?'

'What?'

'Since you handle food and you can't eat unless you're with an incarnate human, how come you were able to get me chocolate from the vending machine on that first night?'

'I lied. It had been in the glove compartment since the days of your predecessor.'

'I had a predecessor?'

'Well I'm not a soul retriever chauffeur virgin, you know!'

'All I do know is that every day I know less. I get less certain and more amazed.'

'Oh, I forgot, there's something you need to do,' he said, feeling in the pocket of his jeans and pulling out a pad of Post It notes. 'For the timeline. You have to write that note you read in Eilat.'

'The one that vanished?'

'Yes, it vanished because you forgot to write it.'

'*What?*'

'Never mind. It's ineffable. I just need you to write it now and I can place it where you saw it.'

'Okay.'

So, I took out a pen from the glove compartment and wrote:

You are Bella Ransom.
You are currently 43 years old and single.
You live at the Old Rectory, Tayford, Devon.
You work in between worlds in soul retrieval.
You are protected.

Jon will come to fetch you in the blue Panda.
You went night riding with Josie in Rador when you were
16. The pony was dun with two white socks. There were
five stones, not four.
Bel x

We drove through the Earth's magnetic core and its terrible beauty silenced us completely for a few minutes. Emerging into the depths of the Pacific Ocean and swimming up to the light while confusing the hell out of a couple of stingrays, some giant jellyfish and a Right Whale was pretty breathtaking too. Then we were flying out into the atmosphere a few hundred miles south of New Zealand.

'So, are you going to tell me about this new man in your life then? The former hobo who saved you in the cathedral and turned out to be quite respectable after all?'

'He's *not* the new man in my life! It's *far* too soon.'

Jon laughed. 'Is he going to be?'

A silver waning gibbous moon beckoned and, beyond her, the solar system and beyond her... well, who knew?'

I am Bella Ransom and I retrieve souls.

Acknowledgements.

Douglas Adams for the whole of *The Hitchhiker's Guide to the Galaxy* in all forms.

C. S. Lewis for the *Chronicles of Narnia,* particularly *The Magician's Nephew.*

Lightning Source UK Ltd.
Milton Keynes UK
UKHW041054171120
373552UK00001B/252